THE REVOLUTION II

SEER, SPY, HEROINE

THE REVOLUTION II

SEER, SPY, HEROINE

Written by
Debra Ann Pawlak
and Cheryl Bartlam du Bois

A Place In Time.Press • Beverly Hills, CA

A Place In Time.Press
8594 Wilshire Blvd., Suite 1020, Beverly Hills, Ca 90211
310 428-1090 or info@aplaceintime.press

A Place in Time.Press
8549 Wilshire Blvd. Ste. 1020,
Beverly Hills, CA 90211
310 613-8872
e-mail:info@aplaceintime.press
Website: aplaceintime.press

Cover Design & Layout:
Christopher Staser, brandweaver.tv
Map Design & Illustration: Steve Luchsinger

Library of Congress Cataloging-in-Publication Data is available on file.
Print ISBN: 979-8-9893814-0-1
Ebook: ISBN: 979-8-9893814-1-8

HISTORICAL FICTION
Printed in the United States of America
Our books may be purchased in bulk for promotional, educational, or business use. Please contact your local bookseller or the publisher: aplaceintime.press

First U.S. Edition 2023
Copyrighted Material © 2023

This book is dedicated to all the brave patriots who fought for their freedom and, in the process, created a great nation. Had the statesmen, soldiers, sailors, spies, and civilians, who sacrificed so much to form a new and democratic union, not given their all to the cause, we would surely be a continent comprised of English and French colonies today.

DEBRA ANN PAWLAK

History has long been a fascinating subject for me. The men and women who came before us are often forgotten from one generation to the next and that is a sad state of affairs. Everything has a beginning and a brave soul who dared to take that first step. As a writer, I like bringing these historical people to life and putting them front and center for my readers. While I feel a book should entertain, I also think it should teach you something. I sincerely hope that I have reached that goal whether it be a book, short story, or magazine article.

The research can be daunting, and somewhat overwhelming but in the end, when I find that 'lost' piece of information, I can't wait to share it. We should never stop learning and we should always shine a light on those who came before us whether they be explorers, inventors, or rabble rousers. Most surprising are the individuals whose lives you delve into who turn out to be the most colorful characters. For me, while writing this book, I discovered Brigadier General John Glover—a true hero of the Revolution who is little known today. Without him and his integrated troop of Marbleheaders, the war would have surely been lost. I am happy that we had the chance to let his light shine again. He deserves it. Maybe some of our readers will be inspired to do a little research of their own. A writer couldn't ask for more!

On a personal note, I would like to thank my writing partner, Cheryl Bartlam du Bois, for being, not only someone easy to work with, but also a dear friend. I can always count on a good time when we get together—even when we are surrounded by piles and piles of paper. Our research trips have been energizing—especially when emus give chase. Another thank you goes to Leigh Carter who always gets it and makes it better with her editing skills! Then there is my personal support squad: my BFF, Linda Wells, who listens to it all with a patient ear and, my cheerleader, Alberta Asmar, who always tells me that I can do it. I must also thank my husband, Michael, for putting up with the many hours I spend writing and researching. I also owe a very loud shout-out to my grown children, Rachel, her husband Jon, along with my son, Jonathan, and his wife, Stacey! No ship has a better crew. Last, but not least, I must thank my little people for always making me smile—Madeline, Olivia, Michael, and Lucas. I love you all to the moon and back!

CHERYL BARTLAM DU BOIS

In 1979, just after I graduated college, I moved to Florida to start a sailing charter company with my boyfriend. I had been on the water for years with my family and had enough experience to study for and take the United States Coast Guard Merchant Marine test for my six-pack Captain's license. I went to Jacksonville and took the written test, acing it and completing all qualifications to obtain my license. When it came time for my oral interview with the Commander, Lieutenant Lewis, in charge of licensing that day, I suddenly realized the mistake I'd made. Trying to look nice, I'd worn my best dress making me look quite feminine and young —I was all of 105 pounds. It seemed he took one look at me and made the determination that I wasn't qualified to drive a boat for hire. It also seemed that the only woman to precede me on the east coast had been involved in a terrible accident, through no fault of her own, in which a passenger was killed. So, it seemed I was to potentially be the second woman to ever receive my license on the east coast of the U.S.

I looked at him and demanded he name the deficit in my qualifications which would prevent me from receiving my license. All he could come up with was that I was a woman. My response,

"Well since I don't plan to have a sex change anytime soon it seems to me that you are being very prejudiced and chauvinistic and I don't think that will look very good for the Coast Guard." He mulled that over for a bit, I'm sure considering how sexist that would look, and he finally whipped out the certificate to fill in my name. However, when he got to the part where it read, *"This is to clarify that Cheryl Winifred Bartlam has given satisfactory evidence to the undersigned that 'he' can safely be entrusted with the duties and responsibilities of operator of..."* He looked up at me quite dumbfounded, uncertain what to do with the word 'he.' I just said stick it in the typewriter, XX out 'he' and type in 'she.' Without another word he did just that and signed it, shrugged his shoulders and shoved it at me. "Here you go," was his only comment. I thanked him and went on my way.

Now forty-four years later I hold my USCG Merchant Marine Master's Document for driving one hundred-ton vessels with sail auxiliary and I have no intention of ever letting it go. In fact, I am in the process of upgrading my license to two hundred-ton after many months of crewing on and driving a three hundred-foot casino ship out of Port Canaveral. I fought for my right as a female to do a man's job as I have done throughout my entire life in sailing, architecture, and film and I'm proud to have accomplished what I have as a woman, against all odds. When I look back on women such as Fanny Campbell and Sarah Emma Edmonds who found it necessary to disguise themselves as men in order to pursue their destiny, I can fully appreciate their reasoning and their struggle to accomplish more than most men can boast, as well as having more courage than any man I have ever known. Although Moll Pitcher did not don a masculine disguise, she did use her gifts of intuition and clever subterfuge to spy for our new burgeoning nation at great peril to herself and her family, for a cause she truly believed in and saw in the clouds to be our future nation.

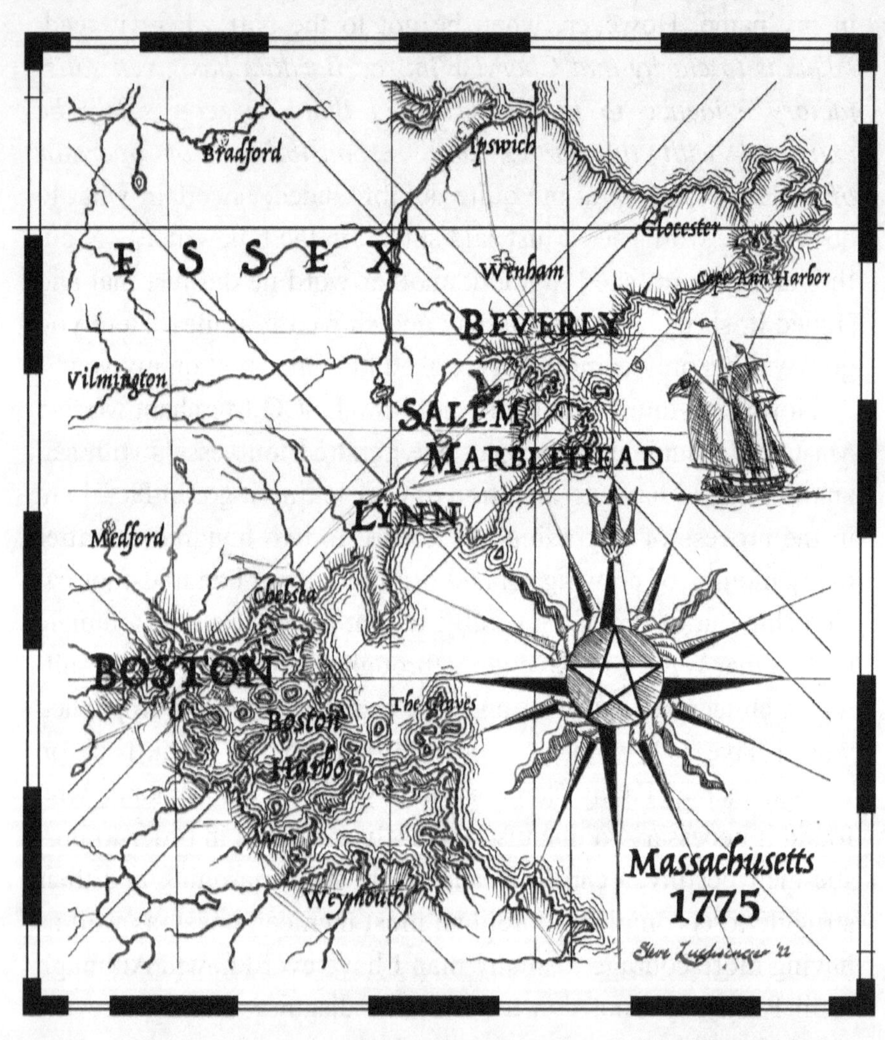

Bradford
Ipswich
Glocester
ESSEX
Wenham
Cape Ann Harbor
BEVERLY
Vilmington
SALEM
MARBLEHEAD
LYNN
Medford
Chelsea
BOSTON
The Graves
Boston
Harbo
Massachusetts
1775
Weymouth
Steve Luffsinger '22

CONTENTS

"The New Englanders are fitting out light vessels of war, by which it is hoped we shall not only clear the seas and bays here of everything below the size of a ship of war, but that they will visit the coasts of Europe and distress the British trade in every part of the world. The adventurous genius and intrepidity of those people is amazing."

--Thomas Jefferson, July 1775

The Wizard

(1 6 7 5 – MARBLEHEAD, MASSACHUSETTS)

In early September of 1675, the wicked winds of a deadly hurricane wreaked havoc along the Atlantic coast and on Marblehead's once-sturdy trees, their massive branches snapping and blowing away like fragile twigs. The torrential rains soaked the ground and beat upon the windows, daring anyone foolish enough to come outside. Edward Dimond, affectionately known by locals as 'the Wizard,' did his best to shut out the din of the storm, but he couldn't ignore the faraway fishermen's cries for help. Their shouts surged through his head as they battled raging seas. He also heard those sailors sitting nearby on anchor in the harbor—hammered by twenty-foot waves. Their frantic pleas rang inside his head.

"Help us, Wizard! We'll surely die in this tempest without your help!"

"Please, if you can hear us, guide us back home to safety!"

"Don't abandon us, Wizard! You are our only hope now!"

When he could take no more, the Wizard of Marblehead donned his long black oilskin cape, careful to cover his head, and stepped outside, tightly clutching his curlew-peewit whistle against his chest. The powerful storm seemed to grow even more furious as he made his way uphill to the old burial ground behind his home. Stepping over downed branches and dodging flying debris, he pushed the rickety gate aside, surprised it was still standing, and entered the cemetery disoriented from the dizzying storm. He stopped a moment to catch his breath and steady himself as he stared upward at the darkened sky. He had seen many storms before—even sailed in a few himself, but this was one of the worst he could recall. A chill passed through him as he put the black whistle to his lips and blew hard. Its shrill sound blasted through the darkness.

"Can you hear me, boys?" The Wizard shouted as loud as he could, calling upon the ancient mariners for council, then paused to listen as the rain hammered down without mercy. "Red Cap? Blue Cap?" he hollered again. "We need your help!"

"Aye we're here!" A lone voice rang out from a great distance.

"We're ready to help bring the boys home!" A second voice answered even fainter than the first.

"Let them hear me!" the Wizard ordered and then listened as the wind howled in defiance.

"Help!" Their anxious cries continued, distant at first. "Help us, Wizard! We're being pummeled by the storm! Please, save us! You're our only hope!"

"Listen to me!" The Wizard paced back and forth in between the gravestones, totally unaware that his long cape was being whipped to tatters by the wind and that his skin stung from the pelting rain.

"Tell us what to do!" The panic in their voices echoed their fear.

"Pull up your anchors, mates!" the Wizard commanded as he strode through the boneyard. "Pull up your anchors and sail east!"

"But the swells are too high!"

"If you want to survive this night, do as I say!" his voice boomed. "Sail away from the storm! When you reach calmer seas, wait there for two nights before you return home. The storm will be gone by then and you will be safe."

"But Wizard—"

The Wizard blew his whistle in angry response. How dare they doubt him when he had protected them so many times before? Now would be no different if they would only listen. "Sail to the east, I say!" he screamed above the din. "Do it quickly before the seas crush you on the shore or send you down to meet Davey Jones!"

"We'll do our best, Wizard…say a prayer for us!"

"Godspeed!" the Wizard whispered once again, cradling his whistle over his heart. He fell to his knees in the middle of the burial ground and murmured a prayer to St. Elmo for the sailors who were at his mercy. He had done what he could to help them, but their lives were in God's hands now.

By the next morning, the rainfall had significantly diminished, but a forceful wind still blew, making it difficult for Catherine Biddlestone to walk along the road that led to the Old Brig. Climbing across fallen trees and stepping over large branches, she frowned at the mud that was caked on her black shoes and coated the hem of her long gray cape. Her blonde hair blew freely about her head and shoulders since she hadn't taken the time to comb it that morning. After donning her wrap, she had left her small home in Marblehead in a hurry to consult with the man whom everyone knew could work miracles. She was worried about her husband and only the Wizard could ease her mind.

Before long, Catherine could see the Old Brig that stood at the junction of Pond and Orne Streets, directly downhill of Old Burial Hill. A large willow tree graced the front yard and the woman was relieved to see that no damage had been done to it by the terrible storm. She took it as a positive sign. Catherine let out a loud sigh as she stepped up to the front door, crossed herself to keep away demons, and then knocked.

Dark-haired Rebecca Dimond answered the door with an infant girl on her hip. "Catherine!" she said, smiling. "What brings you out after such a terrible night?"

"I need to see the Wizard," Catherine said, wringing her hands. "I need to know about Daniel."

"Did Daniel not come home before the storm?" Rebecca asked as the little girl began to squirm in her arms.

"No…he didn't." Catherine's eyes welled up. "I'm worried sick and I was hoping that the Wizard might know if he's safe."

"Come in. Come in." Rebecca stepped aside and let the trembling woman enter. "Edward! Edward! Catherine Biddlestone is here to see you."

The tall, reedy man with rumpled salt-and-pepper hair emerged from the back of the house looking as if he hadn't slept all night. "Are you here about Daniel?" he asked his frightened visitor as the baby in Rebecca's arms reached for him.

"Yes, Wizard." Catherine gave a little curtsy. "I was hoping you'd know if he is safe."

Edward Dimond took the wriggling infant from his wife and nestled her in his arms. "Your husband is alive and in two days' time, he will sail into the harbor at Marblehead. His vessel will be damaged, but the men aboard will all come home."

"Oh, thank you, Wizard! Thank you!" Catherine burst into tears. "I am so relieved. I don't know what I would do if I was widowed…especially now with a baby coming next year."

"It's all right, Catherine." Rebecca touched the woman's arm. "If Edward says that Daniel will come home, then he will. I am sure of it."

"Thank you for giving me some peace of mind." Catherine drew her cloak around her. "I'll be going now. I won't bother you any further."

Just as she pulled open the front door, Edward Dimond's voice caused her to turn back. "Catherine!"

"Yes, Wizard?"

"Take care of yourself so the boys aren't born too early."

"I will try, sir." She managed a smile, but as she stepped outside, she paused a moment. "Boys?!" she whispered out loud, but then shrugged. "I must have misunderstood."

⚓

Two days later, the Wizard rose early and walked towards the harbor in Marblehead. He squinted in the bright sunlight as he surveyed the destruction caused by the storm. Crops were damaged and strewn across the fields; many large trees had fallen and any that were left standing were missing hefty limbs. Several homes were all but destroyed, their unlucky residents picking through the rubble hoping to rescue anything of value. The New England coastline had taken a beating by one of the worst hurricanes to make landfall in recent memory. The Wizard wondered how the city of Boston and its harbor had fared. So many small towns like Marblehead had been hit hard by what later came to be known as The New England Hurricane of 1675, but people would rebuild and go on because that is what they did.

When he arrived at Marblehead harbor, workers were already carting away debris and trying to salvage what they could. The sea itself was calm and gave no hint of the recent tempest, but an unusually large number of women gathered at the docks that morning waiting for their husbands, fathers, brothers, and sons to come home. Catherine Biddlestone was among them, her blond hair now swept up in a neat bun atop her head. Edward waved to her and she nodded in response, but the two did not have time to speak for in the distance a fishing vessel, listing to starboard, could be seen making its way toward them, its pace slow but steady. The noise in the harbor suddenly came to a halt as everyone waited and watched in revered silence.

When the wooden ship grew closer, it became obvious that its rigging was badly damaged, but the men aboard waved and shouted, excited to make landfall safe at home. Once the boat was secured to what was left of one of the damaged docks, the ladies rushed to greet their men with tears and shouts of relief. Daniel Biddlestone, a handsome, strapping fellow, disembarked. He had a long gash on his forehead but was otherwise unharmed. The Wizard watched with a smile as Daniel picked Catherine up and swung her around and around.

"Stop, Daniel!" she said, laughing. "Put me down! You know I must be careful now."

"I know," he winked, his blue eyes filled with mischief. "We are soon to be three."

"Four," said the Wizard as he walked by with a quick nod of his head.

"What did he say?" Daniel blinked.

"I don't know," Catherine smiled. "The only thing I care about today is that you have come back to me."

"It was the Wizard," Daniel told her. "He and his whistle brought us home safe and sound."

"Do you think he works for the devil?" Catherine looked up at her husband as this new thought struck her.

"No, my girl," Daniel sighed. "The devil would have had us at the bottom of the sea and I wouldn't be here to tell the tale."

"Then God bless Wizard Dimond." Catherine snuggled against Daniel. "He truly has a gift and I will be forever grateful for his magical powers."

"I believe you are just one of many who owes the Wizard a debt of thanks." Daniel held her tightly. "He has saved many a man from the drink and we are lucky to call him our neighbor. One day soon, I must find a way to properly thank him."

⚓

The following March, after a long and bitter winter, Catherine

Biddlestone went into labor. Despite the piercing pains, her delivery was uneventful—except for the fact that she brought into the world not one, but two fine sons. She named them Daniel and Edward. The Wizard sent a basket of dried fruit, a bottle of ale, and two small curlew-peewit whistles that he had fashioned himself.

One Hundred Years Later

CHAPTER ONE

A Psychic Inheritance

(1 7 7 5 – LYNN, MASSACHUSETTS)

*I*t had been a long, unforgiving summer for the people of Boston and its surrounding areas. The British siege began that spring and redcoats dominated the streets. Residents were forced to give up their arms and many patriots fled the city in fear. Loyalists then moved in, with some even enlisting in the king's army. The isolation of the city and the blockade of the harbor caused a food shortage for the populace and a lack of hay for the horses. Businesses were shuttered and the colonists lived in constant fear for their very lives as the British soldiers plundered their homes and shops, helping themselves to whatever they wanted.

In early June of 1775, a group of colonists stormed the British-held Little Brewster Island, where a strategic lighthouse overlooked Boston's outer harbor. They removed the lamps and oil before setting the structure on fire to render the lighthouse useless to English ships. Caught off-guard, the redcoats immediately went to work repairing the damage.

On July 31, 1775, General George Washington sent Major Benjamin Tupper and about three hundred defiant Americans to Little Brewster Island with orders to attack and stop the lighthouse repairs. The raid was successful with only one casualty suffered under Tupper. Several lobsterbacks, however, were killed and many others taken prisoner, unnerving those still faithful to the king. Patriot or loyalist, everyone was on edge and wondering what would come next.

⚓

Moll Pitcher was a patriot known as the psychic or fortune teller of Lynn, Massachusetts. She came by her intuitive abilities and world-renowned reputation through her lineage as the grand-daughter of Edward Dimond, the great Wizard of Marblehead. Thanks to the respect he had garnered due to his accurate predictions, the psychic of Lynn became a trusted source for even the British military, who sought her out hoping to learn about their future fate in battle, as well as their place in history.

As such, Moll was fully aware of the struggles and hardships to come. She was also mindful of Fanny Campbell's every step, or perhaps it's better to say, of Captain Bartholomew Channing's every conquest. Moll felt responsible for Fanny's situation as she was the one who had sent Fanny to the West Indies disguised as the male Barbadian sailor named Channing. Moll's visions of Fanny had started when the girl was just a child. When the time came to save William Lovell, Fanny's fiancé, from certain death, Moll found Fanny to be a willing and dedicated student, able to step up to the most dangerous tasks at hand.

Although Fanny had been gone for months, Moll knew exactly when she had overthrown the *Constance*, a British vessel, and as Captain, made it an American brig bound for Cuba. She also knew when Fanny won her second British ship, the *George*. In addition, Moll had seen Fanny's daring rescue of William Lovell and Samuel Breed from Cuba's notorious La Cabana prison, as well as the taking of Fanny's last prize, the *Wellington*. She also saw the sinking of the *Crimson Blade*, a notorious pirate ship. Her visions appeared both in her dreams and in her tea leaves, giving her unwavering confidence that Fanny, as Captain Channing, would soon return to Lynn triumphant.

Just before midnight on the eve of September 3, 1775, Moll's thoughts of Fanny were replaced by a more immediate danger—a terrible storm that would be remembered as one of the worst ever to hit the East Coast. It first hit Martinique, which was very low in the West Indies and an unusual place for such a violent tropical storm. Two days after leaving Martinique, the hurricane hit Santo Domingo, causing major damage.

From there it had plenty of ocean over which to strengthen, but no one in America realized that they were in the path of such a formidable storm until it slammed into the North Carolina coast at New Bern. Residents of the Outer Banks were totally unprepared for the danger they faced when the rains started shortly after midnight. By the next afternoon, the storm had grown to hurricane proportion. More than two hundred people were killed, trees were uprooted, corn and tobacco fields were laid flat, and warehouses were filled with goods destroyed as angry waves crashed upon the shore and rivers overflowed their banks. A thirty-foot storm surge sunk ships as they lay at anchor in the many coastal harbors, while huge swells at sea forced vessels to the bottom of the Atlantic. The mountainous surfs and fierce winds continued northward to Norfolk and by that night, Virginia and Maryland also felt the brunt of the hurricane. When the tempest reached Boston, the seas still rampaged like a herd of mad stallions, pummeling the coastline and wreaking havoc not only with the ships at sea, but also with those unlucky enough to be caught in the unprotected harbors that dotted the coastline.

Moll knew that the *Constance*, the *George*, and the *Wellington*, along with every other ship out there, were all in trouble. Like her grandfather before her, she felt duty-bound to try to save them. Taking her warmest cloak, she covered her head and stepped outside looking skyward as the rain beat down around her. No one in their right mind was out on such a night, but lives were at stake. The powerful storm grew even more furious as she slowly made her way up the hill to the cliff at High Rock, dodging blowing branches and debris with every step. The small-framed woman was barely able to stand in the relentless winds as she clung to the outcropping of rock, clutching her grandfather's curlew-peewit whistle against her chest. When she finally reached the top, she called on the Wizard's powers, then put the black whistle to her lips and blew as hard as she could, but the screeching winds drowned out the sound. With everything she had, she blew it again. "Do you hear me, Fanny?! Run with the wind…stay offshore and you will be safe!"

Moll sheltered behind the rock, waiting for an answer. She must reach not only Fanny, but the other seamen whose lives now lay in the hands of Mother Ocean. She blew the whistle again and again. Suddenly, the howling winds grew silent, the pelting rain slowed and the cloud-filled sky started to clear. It was the sign she had been waiting for. Moll put the whistle to her lips and blew as long and hard as she could one more time. She knew the tranquil moment wouldn't last as it was only the eye of the storm. Moll closed her eyes and listened.

"I hear you, Moll," came Fanny's answer, faint at first. "We will run for our lives as you said."

"Beware of a friend turned foe!" Moll called back as loudly as she could. "And remember, he has given you the very tools you will need to outwit him at his own game!"

"Yes, Moll, and I promise you he will not win." Fanny's voice was now strong and self-assured. "I will be ready for him!"

Relieved, Moll looked up just as the first quarter moon broke through an eagle-shaped cloud. It was a message from the heavens telling her that her friends would be safe from the storm, as well from as their enemies. She then closed her eyes, remembering the other sailors unlucky enough to be at sea on such a terrible night, and quickly whispered a prayer to St. Elmo asking for their safe return. Moll knew in her heart that was exactly what the Wizard would have done.

The damp night air sent a shiver right through her despite her heavy cloak, which was now soaked through from the rain. There was nothing more she could do, but just as she began her descent down High Rock, a disturbance over in Lynn Harbor caught her eye. A large waterspout had formed just offshore, churning near the docks. She watched as it tossed aside everything in its path like matchsticks.

"Amen and Godspeed," Moll gasped with a shudder before returning to the safety of her cottage. Once inside, she bolted the door, struggling against the increasingly powerful wind as the storm's eye passed. Her worried husband, Robert, waited inside, pacing in front of the hearth.

"HAVE YOU LOST YOUR MIND WOMAN?!" he bellowed as fear and relief intermingled inside him.

"How long have you known me, Mr. Pitcher?" Moll scolded him with a smile as she removed her dripping cloak.

"Too long, I think." He frowned, taking the wet garment from his wife.

"Then by now you should know that I had to guide the sailors to safety and ask St. Elmo to save them."

"And did St. Elmo hear you?" He hung her wrap on a hook near the fire.

"I did what I could, but I left them all in the divine hands of our saint, although even he may need to call upon his holy helpers tonight."

"You're a funny girl, Moll Pitcher." Robert pulled her in front of the fire.

"But you married me anyway," she said with a grin.

"That I did," Robert sighed. "And by now, I should know better than to argue with the famed psychic of Lynn."

⚓

As the next morning dawned, much of the wind subsided, but a drizzle of rain endured, and the angry waves still crashed against the rocks near the harbor. It wasn't often that Moll was surprised by events, but when she answered a knock at her door, shortly after sunrise, the unexpected visitor shocked her. There on her doorstep stood Fanny Campbell's mother, Agnes, wet to the bone, bedraggled, and nervously wringing her hands.

"Agnes, what on earth are you doing out in this weather?" Moll reached for the woman's arm and tried to pull her inside. Despite the rain and her disheveled condition, Agnes resisted as if she were entering a witch's lair.

"Please, come in," Moll tried again. "And tell me what's brought you out here on such a terrible day. Is it our Fanny?"

"MY Fanny," Agnes corrected as she reluctantly stepped inside. "She's MY Fanny and I need to know if she's safe!"

"Come and warm yourself by the fire." Moll led Agnes toward the hearth, where the gaunt woman broke down, distraught and sobbing.

"I can't take any more! Not knowing where she is and if I'll ever see her again! Day after day, month after month! Mrs. Pitcher, can you please help a poor mother who is worried sick about her only child?"

Moll was stunned. Before today, this trembling woman had never once entered her cottage at High Rock. Agnes had always made it quite clear that she didn't believe in Moll's prophesies even if she did occasionally buy an herbal potion or two from Lynn's well-known mystic. Agnes fell just short of thinking that Moll consorted with the devil himself.

Moll winked at Agnes. "By the grace of God! I never expected you to come here and seek council from me, a real witch!"

"Oh please, Mrs. Pitcher! I am at my wit's end with worry. It's bad enough that my Fanny is gone, but knowing she is out there somewhere in this storm is more than I can bear."

"I know, my dear." Moll took Agnes's hand in a sympathetic gesture. "I'm a mother, too, and I'm very fond of Fanny. So, from one mother to another, please call me Moll."

"Can you ever forgive me for having such evil thoughts about you?" Agnes shivered and her voice shook. "I know you have done many good things for others and that you're a God-fearing woman."

"That I am, Agnes." Moll put an arm around her and offered her a seat at the small Queen Anne table she used for her readings. "Sit down and join me in a hot cup of tea. We can talk and I will try to put your mind at ease."

Agnes took a seat, watching as Moll opened the top drawer of a large wooden chest and retrieved a thick blue shawl.

"Becky, come here with some tea," she called as she carefully placed the woolen wrap around the anguished woman before sitting directly across from her.

Moll's daughter, Becky, appeared and took two small blue-rimmed cups from over the fireplace and placed them on the table.

"You remember my girl, Becky?"

The young, dark-haired girl smiled shyly at Agnes as she set out the cups and prepared the tea.

"Yes, of course I remember her." Agnes smiled, feeling slightly relaxed for the first time since she arrived. "Thank you, child. I'm sorry if I seem abrupt, I'm just beside myself with worry. How old are you now?"

"I'm ten, ma'am." Becky smiled warmly. "But you mustn't apologize. I know you are worried about Fanny."

"That I am." Agnes sighed as she watched Becky pour. "But I shouldn't take it out on you. You and your older sister, Ruth, are always so pleasantly polite."

"If only the younger two were as good." Moll grinned. "Lydia and John are much more of a handful. I'm afraid they are spoiled by the older girls...especially John, being the only boy and all." Moll sipped her tea, encouraging Agnes to do the same. "Drink up...the lavender will help calm your nerves."

Agnes tried to steady her trembling hands as they gripped the warm teacup. She found the heat soothing and for the first time felt hopeful as she looked around the unfamiliar room and noticed Moll's black cat, Percy, sleeping in one corner. The room itself was small, but the walls were lined with shelves filled with jars, marked with various herbs and potions. She breathed in the steam from the tea before taking a sip and speaking. "Please, Moll, can you just tell me if my daughter is safe and whether I will live to see her again?"

"I can assure you that Fanny is safe," Moll smiled. "I went up to High Rock last night to guide her myself."

"You went out in that storm last night for my Fanny?!" Agnes slumped in her chair feeling even worse about the many terrible things she'd said about Moll in the past.

"Of course, I did and I called upon St. Elmo and his helpers to bring them all home." Moll patted Agnes's arm. "Now finish your tea."

Agnes took a deep breath before lifting her cup and taking another sip. For the first time since the storm began, she felt a sense of calm slip over her.

"Please tell me what you know. Don't keep me in suspense any longer. I can pay you for your trouble."

"I'll not take money from a friend, Agnes." Moll too sipped her tea then set the cup down. She paused for a moment, thinking.

"Tell me what you see, Moll." Agnes held her breath, waiting for an answer.

"Well…William has been rescued from the prison and they are very close to home now, but I see they are onboard different ships." Moll closed her eyes focusing on what was to come. "I suspect you will find William at your door before another day passes."

"But what about my Fanny? When will I see her?"

"It may take a bit longer for Fanny to find her way home, but have no worries. You will see your daughter within a fortnight."

"But why aren't they together?"

"It's a long story, Agnes…one that should be told by no one, except Fanny herself and I can assure you that she will come home safe and sound with adventures of a lifetime to tell you and your grandchildren."

"Grandchildren?!" Agnes echoed. "Are you saying that Fanny and William will marry and have children?"

"Yes, they will marry soon after their homecoming, but children will wait until the fight for independence is over."

"What does that mean, Moll?" Agnes asked.

"There are dark years ahead," Moll offered. "But we will triumph and become a great nation of power and might. In the meantime, rejoice in your daughter's homecoming. Be glad that she will find her way back to you."

Agnes finally stopped trembling. She couldn't decide whether it was the hot tea or Moll's comforting words, but she felt her body relax and even started to enjoy her drink, as well as Moll's company. The psychic of Lynn had given her hope and restored her faith in Fanny's return. There was nothing wicked about this woman and there were no signs of the devil inside her home. Moll Pitcher had proved herself to be a kind and compassionate person—not a witch at all. She had been totally wrong about Moll and felt very embarrassed by her wicked thoughts.

Due to the Second Continental Congress's ban on trade with Great Britain, which was to take effect on September 10, there had been a flurry of activity in every port along the eastern seaboard, Lynn included. Merchants and sailors alike all tried making one last shipment from places like Pamlico Sound, Charleston, Norfolk, Philadelphia, New York, Rhode Island, and Boston. As a result, before the storm warehouses on the wharfs overflowed with tobacco, lumber, naval stores, corn, salt, molasses, rum, sugar, and other staples. Now, most of these stockpiled goods were ruined, or gone altogether. The once-filled structures had collapsed in place, cluttering the shoreline and much of the valuable goods they once held floated out to sea.

After Agnes's visit, Moll walked to the docks of Lynn where she viewed the destruction. Much had been lost as splintered fishing boats crashed upon the shore, while debris and flotsam littered the harbor. Moll shook her head, overwhelmed by the loss, but as she looked up at the sky, she saw an eagle-shaped cloud pointing toward Beverly Harbor. She realized then that Fanny and William would soon bring their ships to safety there. Moll also knew that just before the storm hit, General Washington, under strict secrecy, had acquired a wharf at that very harbor where his newly formed American Navy would launch. Despite the devastation, the seer of Lynn smiled to herself. All was as it should be. The fallout from the storm would serve as a good distraction while Fanny and William brought their ships home right under the very noses of the British.

Not everyone, however, was as fortunate as Fanny Campbell and William Lovell. In the aftermath of the hurricane and as the storm surge subsided, bodies washed ashore amongst the ship wreckage. The huge swells lasted for days while fishermen, lucky enough to survive, brought in pieces of flotsam and bloated bodies, along with their catch. The massive damage prompted the Provincial Congress to help with disaster relief, but there was no funding for lost ships or rebuilding along the waterfront. Due to an 'Act of God', the Revolutionary Assembly granted an extension to those merchants attempting to ship goods in advance of the September 10 boycott. By the time the great storm finally blew itself out in Newfoundland, many English and Irish ships were lost or damaged. Between America and Canada, more than four thousand lives were snuffed out and this 'Act of God' would come to be known as the Hurricane of Independence.

⚓

Just as Moll promised, William came home after leaving his ships with Colonel John Glover in Beverly Harbor, but it took Fanny a while longer. After heading a mutiny, she rescued William and Samuel from La Cabana, the deadly Cuban prison, captured three British ships, and took on a bevy of cutthroat pirates, all while dressed as Captain Bartholomew Channing. On the sail back to Lynn, however, the three ships were attacked by the *Dolphin*, a British royal cutter captained by Fanny's old suitor, Ralph Burnett. He took Fanny prisoner aboard his ship. Angry at her refusal to be his wife, Burnett assaulted her, causing Fanny to stab him in order to escape, and escape she did. As Fanny found her way to her parents' doorstep, the ocean was still churning up its dead.

Now that Fanny and her ships filled with weaponry were home, Moll Pitcher had serious work to do. It was imperative that these invaluable supplies, weapons, and gunpowder not fall back into British hands. Some of the captured booty from Channing's three ships was easily disguised as stores and cargo at Glover's wharf warehouse. The weapons and gunpowder had to be hidden as quickly as possible in order to keep them from the British. It would be nearly a week before the crew could safely unload the ships, but it gave the men in charge time to make transportation arrangements. Elbridge Gerry, elected to the Massachusetts Provincial Congress, and John Glover, both men of Marblehead, hired freight wagons to carry the munitions to Lynn where Moll's neighboring brothers, Rupert Burchstead, and Elmore Burchstead, helped her. They could always be counted on when Moll called. She and her little crew would hide the goods inside the wolf pits of Lynn Woods and other places such as the old Western Burial Ground.

The two wolf pits lay about twenty feet apart and were located deep in Lynn Woods on the north side of Walden Pond. They measured approximately two feet across and five feet long. One was seven feet deep and the other almost five. Their origins remained murky. Were they really built to trap wolves? Were there even wolves in Lynn Woods at one time? Or were they part of another structure that was long gone? None of this mattered to Moll when she used them to conceal the pilfered weaponry.

Before turning their attention to the task of repairing their damaged cities and wharfs, residents along the Atlantic Coast began their recovery by burying their dead. The increased number of graves being dug provided a perfect cover for hiding weapons in plain view of the enemy until General Washington and his Continental Army needed them.

CHAPTER TWO

Witchery

(1 6 3 8 – MARBLEHEAD, MASSACHUSETTS)

By the time John Dimond sailed across the Atlantic from London to the colonies in 1638, Marblehead, Massachusetts was home to a handful of fishermen. The young man had left his family at St. Dunstan and All Saints in Middlesex, England dreaming of a fresh start. He wanted a place where he could work, maybe even marry, and raise children—a place that was just beginning to blossom. The New England colonies seemed just right for launching a brand-new life and Marblehead, with its burgeoning reputation for fine fishing, appealed to John. Like his father and grandfather before him, he was a fisherman by trade.

Marblehead, at the time, was still within the limits of Salem, which was run by strict Puritans of the Calvinist Church. However, those who preferred a more liberal lifestyle had relocated to the tiny fishing village, where a community was forming—without the benefit of organized religion. Upon his arrival, John found lodging and work with Jeremiah Grant who owned a small fishing vessel that he kept moored in the harbor. Grant lived in a quaint frame house near the shoreline with his wife, Lydia, and two daughters, Johanna and Abigail. He had always felt a certain disappointment concerning his lack of sons, but Grant was fond of his girls and rarely refused them anything—much to his wife's dismay. The sisters worked hard, helping their busy mother, who not only cleaned and dried the fish her husband caught, but also kept a large garden and a pen full of pigs. In addition, Lydia took in sewing to earn a few extra dollars, making her one of the most industrious wives in the village.

Johanna, the eldest girl, was of marrying age, while Abigail was ten years younger; Lydia had lost four children in between them, which accounted for their difference in age. Johanna's azure eyes and thick dark curls assured her no shortage of suitors, but none of the local gents piqued her interest. At least not until this stranger from England entered the Grant household. John was tall and lanky—a bit on the awkward side and Johanna found his shyness endearing. Abigail liked him immediately and after dinner often sat on his lap while he told stories of England and his passage across the Atlantic.

"John, please tell us about the night of the great storm," Abigail said to him one evening.

"But I've already told you about it." John grinned at the child. "Dozens of times!"

"But it's so exciting!" Abigail jumped on his lap as they sat in front of the warm hearth.

"You might as well tell it again, John," Lydia said, sighing. "I'm afraid she won't leave you alone until you do."

"I suppose you're right." He shrugged and then turned to give the little girl his undivided attention. "Well…it was darker than dark outside the ship that night with not a star visible in the sky and the wind was howling like a pack of wild dogs. The seas were so rough that the waves quickly grew to be at least twenty feet tall—"

"But the last time you said that the waves were only fifteen feet high," Abigail interrupted to remind him.

"Well, I've had more time to think about it," he answered with a wink toward Johanna, who blushed at his attention. "And now I am sure they were at least twenty feet."

And so the story would go on with John embellishing and Abigail squealing with delight as he told the tale of the harrowing storm and the escape they'd made—an escape that seemed to get narrower with each retelling.

At the end of the story, Abigail always made the same request.

"Can I please blow your whistle, John?"

"Which one?"

"You know…the curlew-peewit your father gave you."

"Not in the house…the sound is too shrill," Lydia always said, frowning. "If you must blow it, child, please do it outside."

"Mind your mother." John reached into his pocket and pulled out the black whistle and handed it to Abigail. "But once you're outside, give it a good hard blow. My father always said that the sailors could hear it no matter how far out to sea they might be."

⚓

When he wasn't fishing with Jeremiah or telling tall tales to Abigail, John focused on Johanna. He liked the way she laughed and the kindness she always showed to friends and strangers alike. Before long and to Johanna's delight, he asked Jeremiah for his daughter's hand in marriage. Thrilled to finally have a son, Jeremiah gave a grand party to celebrate the union of John Dimond and Johanna Grant. As a wedding gift, he made John a full partner in his fishing business and together the two men reaped the benefits of the sea.

The newlywed couple remained living in the Grant household and, in 1641, celebrated the birth of their first-born—a green-eyed boy they named Edward. Two years later, they welcomed a second son, William, but sadly, that was a difficult birth and afterward Johanna could have no more children. It was probably just as well because even as an infant, Edward proved to be different and demanded much of her attention. Whenever he cried, only the sight of the sea would console him, so Johanna was often seen down by the shore, carrying her firstborn son. It seemed that dipping his toes into the cool salt water was the only way to appease him. Days before a severe storm struck, the child would grow restless as if he sensed trouble in the air. He often paled and refused to eat whenever a fishing vessel was lost in the Atlantic. Johanna thought her son had a sixth sense when it came to the elements and the men who earned a living on the water, and she soon began paying attention to the signs he gave her.

John refused to believe his wife at first until he remembered a story told by his own father about an old uncle who could predict shipwrecks and storms. It was said that the townsfolk often came to him asking whether they should go to sea. If he warned against it, they refused to set sail. Was it possible that little Edward inherited a power that no one could explain? The close-knit family kept what they knew to themselves in an effort to protect the boy, but in 1648, when he was but seven years old, Edward shocked everyone.

"Father is leaving us." Edward announced one bright afternoon as he and his mother walked hand-in-hand to the harbor where the men were due in after a long day of fishing.

"Oh, is he now?" Johanna frowned at her son. "And just where will he be going?"

"He's going to be with the angels," Edward answered in his most matter-of-fact voice.

"That's a terrible thing to say!" Johanna jerked his arm as her heart began to pound and her breath grew short.

"It's not so terrible, mother," the boy continued. "Father will be happy there, but I suppose we will miss him here."

"I'll have no more talk of your father going anywhere!" Johanna narrowed her eyes. "It's one thing to predict the weather, but honestly, Edward, you can't possibly know when a person might...." She couldn't bring herself to even finish the sentence from the fear that lodged in her throat.

"But I do know, mother." The grown-up look in her little boy's eyes caused her to tremble. "You'll see."

Three weeks later, John Dimond collapsed on the fishing boat early one morning as he and his father-in-law prepared to cast off. He was interred shortly after at Old Burial Hill and a shaken

Johanna gave Edward his father's treasured curlew-peewit whistle. That same year, Marblehead was given its independence from Salem.

⚓

As Edward and William grew, so did the small community of Marblehead. Although it remained a fine fishing village, several families settled in the area and obtained farmland. Names like Doliber, Norman, and Bennett appeared among the registrars. Abigail married into the Glover family and had a large brood of her own, while Johanna continued living in the Grant house with her boys who soon towered over her. Like her own mother, she took in sewing to pay the bills while Edward and William worked at the docks as soon as they were old enough. In time, they took over the boat left to them by their grandfather and father.

In 1670, twenty-nine-year-old Edward Dimond married pretty brown-eyed Rebecca Norman, just fifteen, in the home of her father, Lieutenant Richard Norman, who was both a fisherman and innkeeper. Edward and Rebecca stayed at the Grant House along with his mother and brother, but Edward had his eye on a large piece of property at the foot of Old Burial Hill, where a house had been built around 1655 by a local blacksmith. Legend claimed it was made of timber from an ill-fated brigantine that had washed ashore. Hence, the citizens of Marblehead took to calling the place the 'Old Brig'.

Tall and lanky, much like his father, Edward embraced the serenity the cemetery offered, as well as the panoramic view of the water below that soothed his soul. He often went there to think when he wasn't at sea with his brother. Sometimes, his spirit guides, Red Cap and Blue Cap, once ancient mariners themselves, joined him while he walked amongst the headstones of the cemetery. Edward often had visions about upcoming storms, his neighbors, or various lost items that needed to be found. Many residents of Marblehead and nearby communities consulted him about their fishing trips, their delicate health, and the state of their affairs. Well-liked and highly thought of, Edward always did his best to use his intuitive abilities to help them whenever he could—unlike the mysterious Mammy Redd, whom the locals shunned for her odd ways and brisk, unfriendly manner.

When Johanna died, just before the birth of her first grand-child, Edward and William laid her to rest next to their father in Old Burial Hill. Shortly after, Edward had a vision about a great storm that would cause a deadly fire at the Grant home. He felt so strongly about keeping his family safe that he bought the Old Brig and moved his growing brood into it. By now their children numbered three—William, Mary, and Aholiah, or John as he was called. Edward begged William to join him at the Old Brig, but his brother refused to move, insisting that he wanted to die in the same place where he was born. Several weeks later he got his wish when a spring storm passed through New England and lightning struck a tree just outside the Grant home. Before help could arrive, the tree and the house went up in flames with William trapped inside.

Edward withdrew from the outside world as he blamed himself for not doing more to save his brother. Now forced to work alone, he still went to the docks, but rarely spoke to anyone. When a neighbor asked for his help, he claimed his powers had left him—even though they hadn't, since he couldn't completely shut out his guides, the ancient mariners. Through them, he often knew when a local would perish, or when a fishing crew would be lost at sea, but he said nothing to anyone until the fall of 1675 when a mighty storm rocked the colonies, putting many of Marblehead's fishermen in grave danger.

⚓

In 1683, Edward Dimond foresaw the drowning death of his father-in-law, Lieutenant Richard Norman, at what is known today as Norman's Woe. He warned the lieutenant about sailing in his thirty-foot-foot shallop, but to no avail. That spring, Norman's vessel suffered severe damage in a storm off Misery Island and he attempted to swim ashore, but never made it. An inquest was held and his death was officially determined accidental, but that did nothing to appease his family who deeply grieved his passing. Edward once again withdrew. If he couldn't use his powers to help others then what good were they?

In the years that followed, Obed Peach's Three Cod Inn grew its business on Front Street, and Marblehead established the first school, as well as its first organized church. Samuel Cheever was ordained as minister of The First Church of Christ and tended to his flock that numbered just over four dozen parishioners. Edward struck up a close friendship with the good reverend and with Cheever's encouragement, he slowly began to use his mystical powers once again. Soon sailors consulted him regularly about whether they should put out to sea, or lay over in the harbor. If Edward advised against it, most often they would wait until he gave them the all-clear to sail. The women came for advice about whom to marry, or if they were expecting, they would ask Edward if he knew whether they were carrying a healthy boy or a girl. Edward would lay a gentle hand on their growing bellies, close his eyes and simply know the answer—rarely predicting the wrong sex.

If someone came to him with an issue he couldn't readily resolve, he would go up to the cemetery behind his home, where he'd pace and converse with Red Cap or Blue Cap until he clearly saw the answer to their concern. Sometimes he would even hear the shouts of distressed sailors caught in storms far out to sea. On those occasions, he would blow his father's curlew-peewit whistle and holler orders to the men. The bewildered townsfolk shook their heads at his antics, but when their beloved sailors came limping home, telling how they had heard the Wizard's shrill whistle and loud commands during what should have been a deadly storm, they were grateful for his eccentricities. It was their gratefulness that saved Edward from the gallows during the witch trials, when a group of hysterical young girls accused several unfortunate souls of casting spells and doing the devil's work.

Between 1692 and 1693, twenty men and women, including Mammy Redd who was arrested based on accusations by girls she'd never even met, were put to death in and around Salem. Since Mammy Redd's abrasive nature had made her unpopular among her peers, she was tried, convicted, and hung on Gallows Hill in the fall of 1692—the only resident of Marblehead to be executed for witchcraft.

⚓

The Three Cod Inn remained a favorite watering hole for the locals—especially after a hard day at sea, or a long fishing voyage. The Inn's proprietor, Obed Peach, a gray-haired old-timer, always greeted his thirsty patrons with a toothy smile and a shot of whiskey, or a full mug of beer. He knew what his customers preferred and could be counted on to pour their drinks the moment they entered his establishment. Edward Dimond, being a regular, knew a cold brew awaited him when he walked in.

"Evening, Wizard!" Peach greeted him with a grin from behind the bar for it was Peach who had given Edward his nickname. "Come sit down. I've got a tall one ready for you."

"Thanks, Obed." Edward perched on a stool directly in front of Peach.

"Got any news for us today, Wizard?"

"It's going to be a quiet season," Edward said as he lifted his glass. "And I have a feeling that the fish will be plentiful this year."

"Glad to hear it." Peach leaned in closer. "When the fish are jumping so is The Three Cod."

"It will be a prosperous year for Marblehead," Edward said with a sigh.

"That's good." Peach ran his fingers through his thin gray hair. "But you don't seem happy about it. Is there something else, Wizard?"

"Yes," Edward said, frowning. "Death will claim some of our children. They will have to make room up on Old Burial Hill for a Huching and a Sarvant—those babes won't live to see the flowers bloom next spring."

"Poor things." Peach shook his head in sorrow. "Sometimes I wish I could see what you see, but when you come around with such sadness, I don't envy you your powers, Wizard."

"Sometimes, when I see things like that, my heart is heavy, but then Rebecca reminds me that, more often than not, I help the folks around here."

"Well, it seems to me that you help a lot of strangers, too." Peach wiped up the bar with a wet rag and a wink in an effort to lighten the mood. "I've sent a lot of visitors your way—after they've downed a few drinks that is. Yes, sir! Having a wizard in the neighborhood is mighty good for business."

And so it went. The Wizard gave counsel to locals and strangers alike, but he was most revered when he guided a ship back home through a storm that would have otherwise proven deadly. Many a sailor often spoke of hearing that old curlew-peewit whistle blasting through the thunderclaps and the howling winds. They knew that the Wizard's booming voice would soon follow, guiding them back to safety. And those who saw that tall and lanky figure pacing through the gravestones at Old Burial Hill took comfort in knowing that the Wizard was hard at work to bring their loved ones home.

⚓

As the 1600s turned into the 1700s, the Wizard remained a be-loved son of Marblehead, known for his wise counsel and great kindness to anyone that sought him out. His children numbered an even dozen (seven boys and five girls), but none of them seemed to inherit their father's powers, which was a cause of great relief as the Wizard never wanted his offspring to feel the burdens he carried. Unknown to him at the time, however, those things often skipped a generation. Edward Dimond lived out his years in the Old Brig and spent much time on Old Burial Hill when he wasn't patronizing The Three Cod Inn. All but one of his boys became fishermen.

His son, John, chose to work as a cordwainer, or a maker of shoes—not to be confused with a cobbler who simply repaired them. By the time John married Lydia Silsbee in 1735, the Wizard had been gone for three years and had joined Red Cap and Blue Cap on the other side. He was sorely missed by family, friends, and neighbors, but especially by Rebecca, his widow. John, being her eldest surviving son, inherited the Old Brig and with the help of his new wife, cared for his aging mother. When Lydia delivered a baby girl the very next year, everyone took note of her striking green eyes. They named her Mary, but called her Moll, and the townsfolk bowed in reverence whenever they saw her because of her likeness to her grandfather, the late Wiz-ard. Oddly enough, when she cried inconsolably, only the sight of the sea calmed her, and it was Rebecca who was often seen down by the docks carrying the child and dipping her toes into the cool salt water.

Six months later, Rebecca died from a sudden heart attack.

The infant Moll wailed for two days prior to her grandmother's passing. It seemed to her parents that their daughter had anticipated the tragic event, but neither of them spoke of it. The green-eyed infant grew into a beautiful toddler who seemed to possess the speech and wisdom of a much older child.

Moll was soon joined by two brothers, first Sampson and then Richard. One of her favorite playmates was little Johnny Glover—a fatherless boy who lived nearby. He was four years older than Moll, which suited her advanced ways. The two were often seen playing in front of the Old Brig and were always delighted when Lydia called them in for some freshly baked cookies. As much as Moll enjoyed her afternoons with Johnny, she particularly relished nighttime, when Lydia would put her to bed in an upstairs room. To her mother's dismay, Moll never liked to be rocked or snuggled. She usually wanted to be left alone and so, on most nights, Lydia simply kissed her daughter and left her to her curious love of the dark.

Unbeknownst to Lydia, Moll would quietly wait for the tall, white-haired man to come. Stroking her hair with a broad smile, he often stayed until she fell asleep. As Moll grew, she had no idea who he was exactly, but she felt safe in his presence. At first he didn't speak, but one night when Moll was extremely restless, he whispered in her ear. "It's all right, my child. It's just a storm that's brewing. It will pass by morning."

"But I'm afraid of storms." Moll's eyes brimmed.

"Don't be afraid. One day your sense of the weather will save many a fisherman. You have a gift, Moll."

"What kind of gift?"

"You are like me, my girl. Good or bad, we see things before other people do and we must use our gift wisely."

"Like the time I told Mother not to hang out the wash, because I knew it was going to rain?"

Yes, just like that," he said, smiling.

"But she didn't listen to me."

"And what happened?"

"Everything got wet," Moll said, grinning. "And mother had to wash the clothes all over again."

Moll never mentioned the lanky stranger to her parents or her brothers. Instinctively, she knew he came to see her—not them. As she grew, he sometimes told her things that she didn't quite understand, yet his smile was always so kind that she trusted him and there was no reason to be afraid. She didn't know his name, but never felt the need to ask him what it was. After all, they shared the same green eyes, which no one else in her family could lay claim to. In Moll's young world, she believed that everybody had a nighttime visitor who made them feel special.

On Moll's fifth birthday, the kindly old gentleman made his final appearance. "I have something for you." He reached into his pocket and pulled out a small, dark object.

"What is it?" Moll sat up in her bed.

"It's called a curlew-peewit whistle."

"A curly pea-whistle?!" Her eyes brightened with excitement.

"It's a cur-lew-pee-wit not a curly pea," the man said, grinning. "And I want you to have it."

"Oh, thank you!" Moll took the whistle and examined it. "Can I blow it?"

"Not yet." He shook his head. "You'll wake everyone up."

"Can I blow it in the morning?"

"I suppose," he said. "But the real reason I am giving it to you is that it will help you in the future. When people see this whistle, they will know you are special and that they should listen to you."

"No one ever listens to me," Moll grumbled.

"That will change, my child. One day, you will grow into a woman who will be known throughout the land. Great men will seek your counsel and their ladies will curtsy whenever they meet you."

Moll's eyes lit up. "And if they don't, I can blow my whistle loud enough to hurt their ears."

"Oh, Moll," the man said, laughing in delight. "You won't have to do that. You are someone people will pay attention to. The whistle is just a symbol of who you are and where you come from."

"But I'm just Moll Dimond," the girl said, shrugging. "And Mother says we are from Marblehead."

"No." He shook his head. "You are the Wizard Dimond's granddaughter and this whistle proves it."

"Are you the Wizard?" Moll asked.

"I am and you must always remember that we share a gift."

The next morning Moll appeared at the breakfast table clutching her new treasure. Her father and the boys were already eating and her mother was blowing on a bowl of hot porridge to cool it when a loud, shrill sound made them all jump.

"What have you got there, Moll?" Her mother frowned as she carried the steaming bowl in one hand and a spoon in the other.

"A whistle." Moll opened her hand as her mother set the still-steaming bowl in front of her. John caught his breath in one sharp gulp—Lydia's grip on the spoon gave way and it clattered to the floor.

"Where did you get that?!" John squinted at the whistle.

"The Wizard gave it to me."

"Saints save us!" Lydia shuddered before turning to her husband. "I saw you put that thing in your father's coffin before we buried him."

"I most certainly did." John was suddenly as pale as the porridge. "I placed it in his cold, dead hands myself."

Lydia tried to remain calm. "Moll, you must tell us exactly how you got this whistle and don't be making up tales."

"I never make up tales, mother," Moll reminded her. "The Wizard gave it to me last night."

"The Wizard?" John echoed. "And just what does this Wizard look like?"

"Oh, he's very handsome and tall," Moll smiled. "He has white hair and green eyes…just like mine. Do you know him?"

"That's it!" John slammed an open hand on top of the wooden table and looked directly at his wife. "Your father left us land near Lynn and we are going to build a house there and move away from Old Burial Hill as soon as we can."

CHAPTER THREE

Washington's Cruisers

(1 7 7 5 – MARBLEHEAD, MASSACHUSETTS)

oll Pitcher's childhood friend, Johnny Glover, was born in Salem, Massachusetts to Jonathan, a house carpenter, and his wife, Tabitha. He had two older brothers—twins named Samuel and Jonathan, and one younger brother, Daniel. After their father died in 1737, Tabitha moved her young family to Marblehead to be closer to her family. There, Johnny took a liking to the Dimond family—he was especially fond of green-eyed Moll and looked up to her father, who was always a father-like figure to the lad.

As John Glover grew, so did his interest in shoemaking and, like Moll's father, he learned the trade of a cordwainer. In time, Glover gave up his shoemaking for rum trading. After taking on his own ships and the sea, success soon followed. As his wealth grew, the hardworking and ambitious young man acquired several vessels along with a wharf in Beverly Harbor, where he warehoused his inventory. He married Hannah Gale and built a modest, but impressive home in the town of Marblehead overlooking the Atlantic, from which he noted the number of British merchant ships sailing along the coastal waters to and from Boston Harbor.

Glover was not just a businessman—he felt a civic responsibility to the colonies and, since 1759, had been active in the Marblehead militia under the command of Colonel Jeremiah Lee. When Lee, one of the wealthiest members of Marblehead society, died unexpectedly in May 1775, John Glover was elected Lieutenant Colonel of the 21st Massachusetts Regiment from Marblehead. Intuitively, Moll always knew that her childhood friend would find great success no matter what he pursued, and she encouraged him in his private undertakings as well as in his public endeavors.

At Moll's urgings, shortly after his military appointment, Glover marched his men to Cambridge, where he joined George Washington and the Continental Army. Plagued by a severe shortage of supplies and munitions, Washington informed Glover that he must find a way to acquire more stores. Glover remembered all the British ships he'd seen from his home in Marblehead and suggested that Washington create his own fleet of ships, designed to intercept British merchant ships carrying supplies meant for the King's Army, which was lodging in Boston. Once in the hands of the colonists, the spoils could then be distributed to the Continental Army. After conferring with Moll, Glover magnanimously offered up one of his own schooners— the *Hannah*, which then became the first ship in Washington's new fleet.

As commander of the newly formed Continental Army, General Washington authorized the formation of the Continental Navy on September 2, 1775. The Second Continental Congress soon made it official and Glover's wharf at Beverly Harbor was declared their home base. Under Washington and Glover's orders, the *Hannah* was quickly refitted for war and readied to set sail three days after the great hurricane subsided. The ship, under the command of Captain Nicholson Broughton, had orders to "cruize against such vessels as may be found...bound inward and outward to and from Boston, in the service of the (British) army, and to take and seize all such vessels, laden with soldiers, arms, ammunition, or provisions...which you shall have good reason to suspect are in such service."

The *Hannah* did not disappoint. With mostly Marblehead fishermen-turned-sailors for crew, the *Hannah* set sail from Beverly Harbor and soon captured the *HMS Unity*—a sixty-ton British freight barge carrying munitions, making her the first prize seized by the new American Navy.

Encouraged by their success, Washington ordered Glover and his regiment to Beverly where they procured and supervised the refurbishing of five more schooners—the *Lee*, the *Harrison*, the *Lynch*, the *Franklin*, and the *Warren*—along with one brigantine, the *Washington*. Thus, they called their little fleet, Washington's Cruisers.

⚓

While the new fleet was being organized in Beverly, problems arose to the north. English Captain Henry Mowat was ordered to destroy all seaport villages along the coast not loyal to the Crown. For his first conquest, he chose Falmouth (now the site of Portland, Maine). On October 16, 1775, he sailed into Falmouth Harbor and ordered the townsfolk to give up their arms and swear an oath of loyalty to the king. The citizenry refused on both counts. Two days later the British Navy attacked, firing upon the town for several hours. Cannonballs, grapeshot, and musket balls rained down relentlessly, forcing the colonists out. Mowat then ordered a landing party to set the colonists' homes ablaze as well as any other buildings still standing.

This British brutality did not have the desired effect. Instead of spreading terror, it caused an unexpected backlash throughout the colonies, spurring the Massachusetts Provincial Congress to authorize the use of letters of marque. These formal documents gave approved privateers permission to take action against the British Navy. In addition, the Second Continental Congress expedited its plans to broaden the new American Navy. Congressional Delegate John Adams even described the violent incident as "the true origin of the American Navy."

The colonial ships, now part of the new navy, all flew under the pine tree flag. The pennant, designed by Washington's secretary, Colonel Joseph Reed, displayed a lone green pine tree set upon a plain white background with the phrase 'An Appeal to Heaven' emblazoned across the top. This banner not only distinguished them from other ships, but also unified them by ensuring that they recognized each other. The vessels were chartered from their respective owners at one dollar per ton per month and the experienced captains commissioned to sail these ships all hailed from Marblehead. The ships raided British ships up and down the Massachusetts coast, capturing much-needed supplies from the enemy. Although the men were loyal to the cause, the rowdy fishermen that made up the new navy's crews greatly irritated General Washington with their disorderly conduct and constant complaints. In fact, he didn't consider them to be real soldiers. Regardless of Washington's opinion, they somehow got the job done by taking weapons from the British and placing them into the hands of the Continental Army. Glover's good friend, Moll Pitcher, was often called upon to bury their loot deep in the wolf pits of the Lynn Woods, where the redcoats wouldn't find them.

Washington, despite his misgivings about the men who sailed his ships, remained confident that America needed her own fleet of vessels. He was proven right when the *Lee*, a seventy-two-ton topsail schooner captained by John Manley, captured the *H.M.S. Nancy*, a British brigantine, on November 28, 1775. As a result of this conquest, the Continental Army gained what the English lost—two thousand Brown Bess muskets, one hundred thousand flints, thirty thousand rounds of artillery ammunition, thirty tons of musket ammunition, along with a thirteen-inch brass mortar. And as Moll well knew, Washington's Cruisers were just getting started with what would become a successful navy.

⚓

Early that December, Moll Pitcher braved the cold and snow, traveling by wagon to Marblehead, the city of her birth, with a friendly neighbor who had business there. She intended to speak with her long-time friend, John Glover, on behalf of William Lovell, Fanny Campbell, Jack Herbert, and Samuel Breed. She wanted to request that the Continental Congress issue letters of marque to their three captured ships, the *Constance*, the *George*, and the *Wellington*.

John's wife, Hannah, a gaunt, pale woman, greeted her at the door. "Come in out of the cold, Moll!" The thin woman shivered as a quiet cough escaped her throat.

Moll stepped inside just as several children raced by and up the stairway.

"The children are all well, I see." Moll grinned as she took off her cloak.

"They have so much energy." Hannah took the dark green cape and hung it on a large hook near the door. "And no matter how hard I try I can never keep up with them."

"I know," Moll agreed. "My darlings are with their father today so I can rest a bit."

"I don't think coming to Marblehead was very restful." Hannah took Moll's arm. "But we are always happy to see you. John is in his office. I'll take you to him and then I'll bring some hot tea to warm you up."

The two women walked to the back of the house where a small room was set aside for business—both military and personal. Colonel Glover sat behind a large wooden desk with a stack of official-looking documents that needed his review and signature. Hannah left them and disappeared into the kitchen.

"Moll!" He stood up with a smile and embraced his old friend. "You never change!"

"It's so good to see you, Johnny!" For just a moment, Moll let the warmth of his arms wash over her. "Sometimes, I wish we could go back to simpler times."

"Were they really simpler, Moll?" He lightly brushed her fingers with his before letting her hand go.

"Maybe not," she smiled. "Maybe we just remember them that way."

"Tell me how you've been." He gestured toward an empty chair.

"I've been fine." Moll sat down. "But Hannah's not well, is she?"

"I'm afraid not." Glover frowned and a crease appeared across his forehead. "She grows a little weaker every day and I don't know what to do for her."

"I know you worry about her, but she will never regain her strength." Moll leaned forward. "She will be a good wife and mother for as long as she can."

"Sometimes, I feel it's my fault." John sighed. "I leave her alone too often and the children are a handful."

"But your work with General Washington is critical and Hannah knows that."

"Hannah knows what?" Mrs. Glover carried a tray with a tea service and three cups.

"Hannah knows how to make a fine cup of tea," Moll said, winking. "And she keeps the colonel in fine form."

"Someone has to." The woman smiled as Glover moved his paperwork and she set the tray down on his desk.

Hannah poured three steaming cups of tea and after they drank, she handed Moll her cup. "What do you see, Moll? Will John and I be blessed with more children?"

Moll peered into the empty cup and saw death, but her many years of fortune-telling had long since taught her how to handle these unfortunate situations. "I see no more children, but a happy life nonetheless."

"I'm almost relieved to hear that," Hannah said, sighing. "I don't think I could handle anymore little Glovers—as long as John is content, that is."

"John is content." Glover smiled at his wife but glanced at Moll. He knew she'd seen more than children in the tea leaves.

"I'll leave you two to your business." Hannah gathered the cups before leaving the room.

"What did you really see in her teacup?" Glover asked once his wife was gone.

"I think you know, Johnny, but she still has time and you must make the best of it."

"What about you, Moll?" Glover reached for her hand, but she pulled away.

"I am the psychic of Lynn," Moll reminded him. "And I am here on important business. I've come to request letters of marque on behalf of William Lovell, Jack Herbert, and Samuel Breed and the three ships they delivered to Beverly Harbor."

"And a fine catch they are," Glover said. "We were in dire need of the munitions and supplies they brought back. I understand you took care of the extra guns and staples."

"I did and they are buried deep in the wolf pits in Lynn Woods, but I can make them available whenever you need them."

"I'll send word through our old friend, Elbridge Gerry," Glover nodded.

"And when they are ready to be picked up, I'll hang a red tablecloth in the garden. Fanny Campbell and Marion Herbert will get the word out."

"William Lovell's intended and Jack Herbert's wife?"

"Yes, they were all instrumental in capturing the three British ships."

"We are indebted to them for their bravery," Glover agreed.

"I understand that the ships they captured are now in Beverly Harbor under your protection."

"That's right," Glover nodded. "They are being repaired and refitted for service as we speak."

"And will you be granting them letters of marque so they can continue their raids as official privateers?"

"I would be a fool not to," Glover smiled. "I just wish I could have met Captain Channing and thanked him personally."

"Captain Channing is gone for good, I'm afraid."

"I know you, Moll." Glover smiled. "And there's more to the tale of Bartholomew Channing than you've told me so far. As someone who has known you most of your life, I am asking that you enlighten me. What really happened to the good captain?"

"It's a twisted tale, Johnny," Moll said, shrugging. "Are you sure you want to hear it?"

"Of course." Glover lit up a small black pipe. "And don't leave anything out."

Moll smiled at the thought of finally telling the tale of Fanny Campbell's charade as Bartholomew Channing.

⚓

After Moll took leave of Colonel Glover's house, she had one final stop to make before returning to Lynn—Black Joe's Tavern. Joseph Brown, a free black man, and his wife Lucretia, affectionately known as 'Auntie Creese', owned a popular tavern on Gingerbread Hill right across the street from the Jeremiah Lee Mansion. Their inn was a favorite spot of the local fisherman— especially after a hard day at sea. While Black Joe served 'Sir Switchels'—a drink made of water and molasses with just a touch of vinegar to balance the sugary sweetness, Auntie Creese offered up her famous spice cookies, which she called 'Joe Froggers'—named for her husband and shaped like the lily pads that could be found in the nearby pond. Made with molasses, rum, saltwater, and various spices, Auntie Creese's cookies never grew stale since she didn't use milk or eggs. That's why she often packed them up by the dozens for the fishermen of Marblehead when they sailed out to sea.

"Well, if it ain't Moll Pitcher!" Black Joe greeted the psychic of Lynn with a grin from behind the bar. "Come sit down and let old Joe mix you a brew."

"I don't have much time today, Joe." Moll took a seat by the bar. "My neighbor wants to get home before dark."

Joe leaned in close to her. "You know, Moll, most ladies wouldn't come near this place."

"They don't know what they're missing." Moll grinned. "Besides, I can't go home empty-handed. Whenever I come to Marblehead, the children expect me to bring home some Joe Froggers."

"Creese!" Black Joe hollered out to his wife who always seemed to be in the kitchen. "We got a guest here! You got any Joe Froggers ready to go?"

"Comin', Joe!" A stick-thin black woman in an old blue apron appeared holding a tin plate filled with cookies and a neatly folded brown bag resting on top of them. "Oh my, Moll!" Auntie Creese quickly set the dish on the bar and came around front, where the two women exchanged an enthusiastic hug. "What brings you here today?"

"Business with Colonel Glover." Moll winked. "And that's all I can say."

"You're sure I can't interest you in a hot toddy?" Black Joe offered.

"Well, maybe a small one," Moll said.

"Colonel Glover is a mighty important man," Auntie Creese noted as she packed up the cookies. "I hear he's starting up a fleet of ships for General Washington."

"I'm not at liberty to say." Moll winked again.

"Well maybe you're at liberty to tell Auntie Creese why you never married the colonel?" The black woman put her hands on her narrow hips.

"He never asked me." Moll tried to control the blush in her cheeks. "But Mr. Pitcher did."

"The colonel is a good man." Black Joe placed the hot toddy in front of Moll.

"So is Mr. Pitcher." Moll sighed. "And some things are just not meant to be. Johnny and I have been friends for a very long time and we must be content with that."

"That's what I been telling Joe!" Creese frowned. "He should be content here at the tavern, but no! Joe, here, wants to join Washington's army. Do me a favor and tell him he's crazy, Moll."

"Not so crazy, Auntie Creese," Moll said, shaking her head. "The general could use a fine man like Joe."

"But that would leave me to run the tavern by myself," Auntie Creese complained.

"You pretty much run it anyway," Joe said with a chuckle. "I just tend the bar."

"And what am I supposed to do if you don't come back?"

"What do you say, Moll?" Joe set a steaming drink in front of her. "If I join the Continental Army will I come back to Marble-head?"

Moll took his left hand in both of hers and closed her eyes. She could hear the sounds of battle far in the distance. A vision of Joe, unharmed but in uniform, took shape. "You will be fine, Joe, and you'll distinguish yourself as a hero. Many lives will be saved because of you and a certain man from France."

"Did you hear that, Creese?" Joe turned to his wife with a grin. "I have to go so I can be a hero and save lives. There's a Frenchman out there who needs me."

"Hmmph," Auntie Creese grunted. "I don't know why you can't be a hero right here in Marblehead." Muttering to herself and shaking her head, she returned to the kitchen.

"Just who is this Frenchman?" Joe wanted to know once his wife was gone.

"He's very young, but he will be hailed a great hero and he will need a good man beside him that he can trust."

"And you think I'm that man?"

"Joe, you are one of the finest men I have ever had the pleasure to meet…no matter what Auntie Creese says."

CHAPTER FOUR

Life in Lynn

(1 7 5 0 – LYNN, MASSACHUSETTS)

*B*ack in the day, John Dimond had often thought of moving his family to the city of Lynn, Massachusetts, about six miles south of Marblehead—mainly because of the tannery there. Several artisan shoemakers that he knew had already relocated to Lynn and John believed that living closer to the tannery would allow him to expand his home-based shoe business. Knowing this, Lydia's father, Henry, left his son-in-law a large parcel of land in Lynn that was situated directly on the road to Marblehead. The property sat on Essex Street opposite Pearl, right at the base of High Rock—in front of the vast woods that were famous for two things—the wolf pits that lay hidden and the pirate treasure rumored to be buried there.

The five Dimonds moved into their new home before Moll turned six. The new house was much smaller than the Old Brig, but Lydia turned it into a comfortable cottage for the family. Their nearest neighbors, Dr. Henry Burchstead and his second wife, Anna, lived directly across the street. When they married in 1728, Anna, the former widow of Captain John Alden, Jr., already had three children and the good doctor had six so it was a noisy brood that greeted the Dimonds upon their arrival. Moll and her brothers were delighted to find so many playmates at their fingertips, but what intrigued them even more were the two great whalebones that formed an arch in front of the Burchstead home. The large white ribs, culled from a beached whale, were a local landmark and Moll delighted in saying that she lived across the street from the 'bones of the greatest whale'.

Moll was happy in Lynn, but she missed the Wizard, who no

longer visited her. She treasured the curlew-peewit whistle, but her parents forbade her to blow it in the house. On most days she hid it under her pillow not only for safekeeping, but also so her mother wouldn't see it. Moll knew instinctively that the wooden whistle made Lydia nervous. She also missed Johnny Glover and whenever her father returned to Marblehead for business, she went with him just to see Johnny. Sometimes they stopped at The Three Cod Inn, but old Obed Peach had long passed on and his son, Jeremiah was now running the place. Jeremiah always had oranges on hand so he made a fresh glass of juice for Moll whenever she visited. Most days, however, Moll spent with her mother learning to cook and sew, as well as to read and write. Lydia believed all her children needed some form of education and took it upon herself to provide their lessons. Moll was a quick study and usually helped her younger brothers when they struggled with something new. In addition, Lydia showed Moll how to concoct various home remedies that would take care of minor ills and injuries. Selling these herbs and elixirs was a good way to make extra money for the family coffers.

Each spring, mother and daughter planted a garden on the southwest side of the house, where Lydia claimed the sun shone best. Moll liked to watch the tiny sprouts poke through the soil and then become fresh vegetables and herbs. In the fall, she helped can the vegetables and dry the herbs before winter arrived. There was never a shortage of mint, basil, and sage for cooking or yarrow, angelica, and valerian for medicinal purposes.

As Moll grew more familiar with the citizens of Lynn, she began to see things others couldn't. She always knew when a baby was coming—often before the mother herself was aware of it. She saw a sickness as it entered a household and recognized death before it struck. The young girl also had a knack for knowing the weather, sensing blinding blizzards, severe storms, summer droughts, rough seas, and wicked winds. Moll was also a good judge of character and instinctively knew whether someone was trustworthy or dishonest. Her family no longer questioned her abilities, but tried to keep her skills confined to their household. They were afraid that outsiders might not understand, and in their ignorance, lay harm to their daughter.

⚓

John Dimond did his best to provide a decent life for his family. Making shoes, however, took time. The leather had to be pounded and prepared before the actual cutting. Precision was important as the upper part of the shoe was handsewn to the sole ensuring a perfect fit. An insole and outer sole were then attached with a few finishing touches for comfort. The tedious process was not production-oriented and even the best cordwainer could only turn out a small number of pairs in a timely fashion no matter how hard he worked.

As luck would have it, a few years after their move, John brought home a stranger. He was anxious for Moll to meet the man who claimed to be a professional shoemaker from Wales. Moll studied the visitor as he sat across from her at the dinner table. His unruly brown hair fell across his forehead and his dark, deep-set eyes shone with enthusiasm. His gray suit was worn, but clean, and when he first entered the house, Moll made note of his shoes. They were brand new and well-crafted with the finest leather. She watched closely as he buttered a roll and listened intently as he spoke with an accent she'd never heard before.

"I've brought shoes of all shapes and sizes with me from Wales." His dark eyes twinkled with pleasure.

"Everyone knows that the best shoes come from England, Mr. Dagyr." Lydia stabbed a boiled potato with her fork.

"Please call me, John," he said, smiling. "And that is exactly why I'm here. I have learned the business from the best in the trade and I have brought my knowledge to Lynn because of the tannery and the talented lot of cordwainers that live here."

"Mr. Dagyr wants to gather all of the cordwainers in Lynn and teach us to make the finest shoes."

"For a fair wage, I hope," Lydia raised an eyebrow.

"Ah, a smart wife, you have, my friend." Dagyr grinned with a wink. "I will pay a fair wage to any man willing to learn and willing to work. Together, we will make the most excellent shoes the colonies have ever seen."

"And Lynn will be known far and wide as the center of shoe-making," Moll noted with a faraway look in her eyes.

"That's right," Dagyr replied with even more enthusiasm.

"And you will supply many men with boots made for marching," Moll continued.

"If there is a need, of course." Dagyr nodded, a little confused by the child's comment.

"There will be an enormous need," Moll went on. "When the great general calls upon the colonists to come forward."

"You must excuse my daughter," John said. "She is known for her vivid imagination."

"Nothing wrong with a bit of fancy." Dagyr smiled kindly. "It's those of us with imaginations who change the world."

"And whether we change the world or not, we all need a sturdy pair of shoes." John pushed a carrot on his plate.

"Spoken like a true cordwainer!" Dagyr beamed. "So, tell me John, will you come work for me and learn how to make the finest shoes this side of the Atlantic?"

John threw a questioning glance at his daughter who gave a slight nod. "Yes," he said, turning to their dinner guest. "I will be glad to join you and together maybe we can persuade a few more cordwainers to also sign on."

Moll had a good feeling about this venture and later told her father that this man with his odd way of speaking would one day be hailed for his inventive methods. Over the next five years, just as Moll had predicted, John Adam Daygr created a successful shoemaking business. He opened a factory on Boston Street near Carnes and taught the local cordwainers better ways to craft their goods and as a result, their output was greater and their quality much improved. Dagyr was so successful in his shoemaking business that many more cordwainers traveled to Lynn with the hopes of finding work.

Dagyr's shoe factory became known throughout the colonies for its fine workmanship and innovative production methods. Now, instead of making individual shoes, the cordwainers worked together, each one responsible for a specific shoemaking activity. Their joint efforts resulted in a well-made pair of shoes that rivaled any footwear from England. Dagyr married a local girl, Susanna Newhall, and at their wedding, Moll informed them that they would welcome three children to their family—two girls and a boy.

As Dagyr's shoe factory grew in size and prominence, Moll blossomed into a lovely young woman. Many of the townsfolk were aware of her peculiar abilities, and kept their distance. For the most part, the boys were not interested in keeping company with a miss who could foresee the future and the girls came around only when they wanted advice of the heart. 'Who should I marry? When will he ask me? How many children will we have?' But, as with her grandfather before her, some of the fisherman began to consult Moll before setting sail, asking of storms and rough seas. Moll did her best to answer them all, and more often than not, she provided useful, accurate information, thus growing her reputation as the town seer.

Once in a while, someone would come by the Dimond house asking about the pirate treasure supposedly buried in the nearby woods. Local lore told of a buccaneer named Thomas Veale who had lived inside a cave in Lynn Woods about one hundred years earlier. He was said to have hidden several chests of gold and silver coins there. When the Charlevoix Earthquake of 1663 hit Quebec, Canada, it also violently shook the New England area causing a great deal of damage. Legend had it that Veale had been trapped and killed in his cave by the quake. Unfortunately, he took the secret of his treasure with him to his stony grave. It was not uncommon for citizens of Lynn, as well as strangers to the area, to go poking through the woods hoping to discover Veale's booty. When asked if she could 'see' where the pirate stashed his loot, Moll always gave the same reply: "If I knew where the treasure was buried, don't you think I'd dig it up?"

When Moll wasn't preoccupied with hidden booty or helping the neighbors, she maintained a quiet devotion to her childhood friend, Johnny Glover. Glover had grown into a strapping young man, who was working hard to build his own empire in Marblehead. She was proud of his success, but common sense told her that they had no future together. Her heart, however, felt differently. On a rare occasion, when a boy did show her some interest, she made the mistake of comparing him to Glover and the would-be suitor never quite measured up in her eyes.

Lydia mentioned it only once to her daughter and that was after Glover had stopped in to call on Moll's father one summer afternoon. "Is Johnny Glover the reason you discourage the other boys, dear?" Lydia asked casually as she pulled a loaf of freshly baked bread from the kitchen hearth.

"I don't know what you're talking about, mother." Moll frowned, clearing a place on the table for the steaming bread.

"I think you do." Lydia set the loaf down. "I see your face every time Johnny comes around."

"Johnny is my oldest and dearest friend." Moll sighed. "And that's all there is to it."

"But would you like it to be more?"

"Mother!" Moll stamped her foot. "That is ridiculous! Johnny would never settle down with a fortune teller from Lynn."

"Why not?"

"Because he's going to be an important man one day and he needs a different kind of woman beside him."

"You are a fine woman and any man would be lucky to have you."

"Johnny Glover is not just any man," Moll retorted. "He is destined for great things and we are meant to be just good friends the rest of our lives. Nothing more."

"Is that how you see it, Moll?"

"That is exactly how I see it and I should know." Moll narrowed her eyes. "And I would appreciate it if you never speak of Johnny in that way again."

⚓

The French and Indian War was underway and a young Virginian by the name of George Washington was rising up the ranks. While Moll knew very little about the battles that were taking place far from Lynn, she knew that this Washington fellow would one day be hailed the greatest of heroes. She also knew that unrest was coming and that the colonies must unite if they were to survive.

"I see death upon the battlefield," she told her mother one afternoon while the two women tended the garden. "There will be great suffering, but also great joy."

"Moll, I don't pretend to understand the things you say, but I know better than to dismiss your words." Lydia picked a large bunch of radishes and put them in her basket. "But we have no army to speak of, so I'm not sure what kind of battles you think you see."

"The visions come and go." Moll knelt next to her mother. "I don't always understand them myself, but I know that a bloody road is ahead of us and we will be a stronger people because of it."

The Dimonds' good neighbor Dr. Burchstead passed away in his sleep, and the town mourned its loss. His youngest son, Benjamin, who remained in the same house, took over the patient care much to everyone's relief.

The same year that Moll turned nineteen, she had a frightful vision. It was the fall of 1755 when Moll and Lydia were in the kitchen drying a large batch of fresh mint. The mint made a tasty cup of hot tea during the winter months and the pungent smell of the green leaves filled the room. Moll suddenly put her hands over her eyes. "Everything is shaking!" she cried. "And I hear the sound of thunder."

"Moll!" Lydia put an arm around her daughter. "Sit down. Tell me what you see."

"I see destruction," Moll cried. "A terrible force from the north will shake Boston. Houses will fall and churches will lose their steeples. I see great cracks in the ground and damage all around us." The vision passed as quickly as it came, but it left a cold, hard feeling in Moll's very bones—a dread that she couldn't dispel. Something terrible was soon to come, of that she was certain.

Exactly one month later on November 18, 1755, Moll was awakened at 4:30 a.m. by a loud rumbling. In the darkness, her bed began to shake with a frightening violence. She lay there holding her breath and clutching her whistle for what seemed like hours, but in reality was only a matter of minutes. Books fell from her shelf and her old rocking chair rattled and shifted to the opposite side of the room. When it was over, she heard her father calling. "Moll! Moll! Are you all right in there?"

Moll slowly got up and cautiously left her room. John, Lydia, and the boys were standing in the hallway when another tremor shook. They held on to each other until the vibrations subsided.

"What is happening?" Lydia clutched the neck of her nightgown.

"It feels like a quake," John answered. "Is everyone all right?"

"I think so." Sampson's voice cracked in fear.

"I'll go outside to see if the house is damaged," John said as he headed downstairs.

"We'll all go." Richard trailed after him, followed by the rest of the Dimonds.

Once outdoors, they found the Burchsteads, also in their nightclothes, all standing in front of their house. The home itself appeared to be intact, but the two giant whalebones were now leaning to the left. As daylight appeared over the horizon, several more aftershocks rumbled through the area. While most of Lynn was spared, Boston and Cape Ann were not so fortunate. Stone chimneys toppled and falling bricks battered many homes. Various churches, their steeples dangling, were also deemed unsafe. Dishes and glassware were lost, fences had fallen, and many frightened cattle had run off. A local distiller even claimed a business loss when one of his cisterns cracked, causing the spirits inside to leak out into the street.

What would later be known as 'The Earthquake of Cape Ann,' unsettled the colonists. Thankfully, there were no deaths, only minor injuries amid the heavy damage reported. The epicenter is believed to have been about twenty-four miles offshore and to the east of Cape Ann. The tremors were felt as far north as Nova Scotia all the way down to South Carolina with a magnitude of about six point zero on the modern Richter scale, making it the most powerful earthquake to ever hit Massachusetts. As strong as it was, however, it didn't uncover the pirate's booty buried in Lynn Woods, but the fury of Mother Nature that released itself along the eastern seaboard in the fall of 1755 made Moll realize that her ability to foresee the future was indeed a gift—a gift that she must learn to use wisely and with the greatest of care, just as the Wizard had told her.

⚓

As the eastern seaboard cleaned up from the recent earthquake, trouble between the British and the French escalated. While the French wanted to expand their holdings in the New World, the British were determined to keep theirs. For the most part, Native Americans sided with the French while the colonists fought alongside the British. After all, most of the settlers either came directly from England or were descendants of British families and still felt a certain loyalty to the Crown.

The actual fighting, however, took place far west of Lynn along the wilds of the Ohio River Valley and even farther north near the French settlement of Quebec. In 1758, a company of soldiers left Lynn, marching toward Canada to join in the battles there. Many mothers, sisters, and wives came calling on Moll Dimond seeking reassurance of their loved ones' safety. Moll did her best to convince each and every one that fate would be kind to them, but occasionally, she knew that a certain someone would not come home. She did her best to comfort John and Mary Mudge whose nineteen-year-old son, Samuel, was killed while under the command of British General Jeffrey Amherst, as well as the family of Edmund Ingalls, a descendent of one of Lynn's founders, who was also lost. Either way, Moll always sent them off with kind words and an element of hope.

"Is this the war you've been talking about?" Lydia asked her daughter when word of Ingalls's demise reached them. The women sat together near the hearth with a pile of mending between them.

"I don't believe it is." Moll threaded a needle and picked up a pair of her father's trousers. "Honestly, father is a shoemaker, "she said, sighing. "How does he always wear out the knees in his pants?"

"You know your father works hard, Moll." Lydia smiled as

she handed the girl a patch. "But I want to hear more about this war that you see."

"The fighting I see is much closer to home," Moll explained. "The dead lay in heaps in our fields and farms. Our cities are under siege and men in red coats are threatening our very lives."

"The British soldiers?!" Lydia gasped as she dropped her sewing. "How can that be? We are fighting with them against the French right now! How is it we will be fighting against them and how can we ever expect to win a war over one of the world's greatest armies when we have no army of our own?"

"I don't know, mother." Moll shook her head. "I just see bits and pieces, but I know that it will come to pass one way or the other."

"If you are right, I hope I am not alive to see this bloodshed." Lydia shuddered. "And I pray your brothers will be spared."

"It will not be your battle nor the boys'." Moll closed her eyes, for at that very moment she saw herself as the family's lone survivor. "It will be my duty to help the cause."

"But you're a girl," Lydia reminded her. "What could you possibly do in a war?"

"I don't know just yet." Moll began sewing the patch. "But I will figure it out when the time comes."

Moll also had visions of that young Virginian, George Washington. The published account of his firsthand experiences in the Ohio River Valley were read far and wide by both the British and the Americans, making him somewhat of a celebrity and hero. Moll, fascinated by Major Washington's tales, reread his writing many times over, knowing that he would become an integral part of the colonies' future.

"We haven't heard the last of this fellow, Washington," Moll would tell anyone who'd listen. "We will all owe him a debt of gratitude one day when we find ourselves in need of a real leader."

CHAPTER FIVE

A Wedding

(1 7 7 5 – PHILADELPHIA, PENNSYLVANIA)

The Second Continental Congress, including delegates Thomas Jefferson, Benjamin Franklin, and John Adams, had been hard at work managing the war effort. They met in Philadelphia in the spring of 1775 and that fall when King George III proclaimed that a formal rebellion was taking place within the colonies, the Second Continental Congress responded by declaring that, without fair representation, England had no right to maintain authority over them.

In addition, the Congress had recently approved an embargo against loyal British colonies, which prompted Henry Tucker, a Bermudan merchant who traded in the West Indies and was the only representative from the Caribbean, to travel to Philadelphia. There, he presented his plan to raid an unguarded warehouse, which was located just north of St. George—filled with gunpowder. In return, Tucker asked for Bermuda's exemption from the embargo which would negatively impact the remaining British colonies in the Caribbean. Orchestrated by Tucker, the raid was a success providing the Colonial Army with sorely needed gunpowder and giving Bermuda a break from the new ruling.

On November 10, Congress also passed a resolution to form the Continental Marines, who were to serve as onboard security for naval ships in order to protect not only the ships, but also their captains and officers. The other important event enacted by Congress later that month, was to formally establish the navy as an official American military branch. In addition, the Continental Congress appointed a clandestine committee to enlist other European nations to help America obtain its independence from

Britain.

By mid-December Congress had authorized the construction of thirteen new frigates, instead of merely refitting existing merchantmen. Of the thirteen, five (the *Hancock*, the *Raleigh*, the *Randolph*, the *Warren*, and the *Washington*) were rated with thirty-two guns; another five (the *Effingham*, the *Montgomery*, the *Providence*, the *Trumble*, and the *Virginia*) were rated with twenty-eight guns; and three (the *Boston*, the *Congress*, and the *Delaware*) were rated with twenty-four guns. As well-equipped as these ships were, they weren't a real match against the Royal Navy in battle. They were mostly used to raid British goods and guard American supplies. In reality, only eight ever made it out to sea as they were forced to scuttle or burn the rest to prevent the British from capturing them and turning them into an asset for the Crown.

While serious preparations for war were underway in the colonies, the Lovells and Campbells took some time to celebrate their good fortune. Fanny and William were delighted to be back home in Lynn after their great Caribbean adventure and they were anxious to be married as soon as possible. They had waited long enough, so despite the cold weather, they agreed upon a December wedding. Fanny's mother, Agnes, was busy sewing a simple satin wedding gown while Fanny preoccupied herself with making a bridal veil that would hide the fact that her lovely long locks were missing.

Jack and Marion Herbert had settled back into their little cottage at the base of High Rock, near Moll Pitcher's house, where they were busy taking care of Jack's aging mother. To their delight, Agnes had taken such good care of the old woman while they were gone, she was now up and about instead of bedridden as she had been when they left her.

William and Fanny originally planned to be married in Lynn, but after hearing their remarkable story, John Glover insisted they hold their wedding at his home in Marblehead—all expenses paid. It was the least he could do for such brave patriots, he had told Moll before writing a formal invitation to the couple requesting the honor of hosting their nuptials. William and Fanny accepted Glover's generous offer and arrangements were made for an evening ceremony on December 18, 1775—two weeks after Moll's visit to Marblehead.

Early on the morning of the scheduled wedding, Glover sent two fine carriages to Lynn to carry the Campbells, Lovells, and Pitchers along with Jack and Marian Herbert to Marblehead. The colonists were still celebrating the recent capture of Fort Ticonderoga in northern New York, as well as their major win over British troops in Virginia. The mood was light as Hannah Glover oversaw the marital festivities, making sure a fine dinner would be served directly after the ceremony, while the other women helped Fanny dress in an upstairs bedroom of the Glover mansion. The men shared cigars in the parlor and eagerly discussed General Washington's success, hoping that the siege of Boston would soon be over as well.

It was truly a day for celebration since there had been many a sleepless night in the Campbell and Lovell household—fearing they might never see their children again. Especially after Fanny, disguised as Captain Channing, had sailed off on the *Constance* to rescue William and Samuel Breed from certain death in the notorious Cuban prison known as La Cabana Fortress.

"I'll go downstairs and ask Hannah if someone could press this veil." Agnes picked up the white headpiece from the bed. "And while I'm down there, I'll see if the flowers have arrived."

"Thank you, mother," Fanny said. "I don't think I could keep up with all of these details without you."

"That's what mothers are for…worry and details." Agnes opened the bedroom door. "As you well know, we worry over everything, but what you'll never understand is how frightened I was during all those months you were gone to sea…dressed as a man no less." She shuddered as she closed the door behind her.

"Your poor mother." Moll grinned. "I don't think she'll ever forgive me for sending you off as I did."

"But if it weren't for you, Moll, William and I wouldn't be here today." Fanny sighed as Marion buttoned the back of her dress. "It was your brilliant idea to send me off disguised as Bartholomew Channing. And it succeeded in bringing William home to me."

"But it was you who overthrew the *Constance* and saved William," Moll reminded her. "I only relayed what I saw in your destiny. I once told you about it when you were a child. Do you remember that?"

"Yes, and I thought you were quite mad back then." Fanny chuckled. "If I only knew then what I know now.

"Well…some days I feel like a madwoman, but there's no denying that much of what I see proves true."

"Like our wedding?" Fanny was suddenly overcome by her own emotions and a stray tear escaped.

"Now, stop that!" Marion drew a small lace handkerchief from her pocket and handed it to her friend. "Your eyes will be all red before you even make it downstairs."

"You have been more than a sister to me, Marion." Fanny hugged her friend. "You even risked your own life to help us and I can never repay you for that."

"But it's only thanks to you and William that Jack and I are together, so once the two of you are married, we will be even," she said, smiling.

"And despite your own hardships," Moll added. "You all managed to bring back three fine ships with a wealth of provisions for General Washington and his Continental Army, whom, might I remind you, are eternally grateful."

Marion helped Fanny step into a pair of dainty white shoes that were handcrafted by Moll's husband just for this special occasion. "I know I am British-born, but I truly feel that I am an American now and what's right is right. We must all support the cause."

Moll gently tugged on Fanny's gown making sure it fell gracefully from her waist to the floor. "Johnny assures me that General Washington knows that you two women have done more than most men on behalf of our fight for freedom."

"And we are not done yet!" Fanny declared, while Marion nodded in agreement.

"You will be done, once I get this on your head." Agnes, still in a tizzy, rushed back into the room carrying Fanny's freshly pressed veil carefully draped over one arm. "I swear, Fanny Campbell, you may have strong sea legs and be able to sail a ship, but you'd never get along on dry land without me!"

Fanny smiled at her mother who quickly set the veil atop her daughter's head. The three women situated it just right so it seemed as though Fanny's short hair was simply upswept amongst the delicate lace and satin ribbons.

The brief ceremony took place in John Glover's parlor. As the bride and groom repeated their vows, Glover stole a glance toward Moll who was seated along the other side of the makeshift aisle. Always in tune with her long-time friend, Moll looked up at him for just a moment. No one else noticed—not Hannah nor Robert, but Glover saw Moll take a handkerchief from her sleeve and dab at her eyes.

After the newlyweds were pronounced man and wife, a servant passed out glasses of champagne—something Glover had insisted on serving. Jack Herbert held up his glass flute in a toast. "It has been a long road, but here we are blessed by good fortune and good friends. And I believe some words from a fine Irishman named Mooney are in order today. He once raised a glass with me and said: 'May you be poor in misfortune, rich in blessings, slow to make enemies, quick to make friends. But rich or poor, quick or slow, may you know nothing but happiness from this day forward.'"

Always a gracious host, John Glover escorted Fanny to her

seat in the dining room. "I do hope this bloody war ends soon so that you and William can enjoy your new life together. You make quite a couple," he said, winking as he whispered softly to her, "and you make quite a sea captain!"

Fanny gasped! This man was aware of her secret. Neither William, Jack, nor Marion would ever have let that slip. Only Moll could have possibly told him, which meant that she trusted him completely. Still, Fanny remained cautious.

"I can't imagine what you mean, sir." She smiled coyly as she sat down.

"I think you do." Glover patted her hand. "And I can assure you that your secret is safe with me, my dear. I merely wanted to express my respect and admiration and say that I could use a good man like Bartholomew Channing to help run our new fleet."

"Then I am honored, sir." Fanny smiled up at him. "Maybe there will soon be a way that William and I will serve the colonies again."

"Arrangements can be made." Glover nodded mysteriously.

"Why, Captain Glover." Fanny's curiosity was piqued. "What exactly are you getting at?"

"I shouldn't be saying this, but I know of the sacrifices you and your friends have made and the bravery you all have shown." Glover bent down and spoke quietly in Fanny's ear. "It is my understanding that in addition to forming a navy, the Continental Congress may also issue letters of marque this coming spring. Perhaps, you and your friends might be interested in obtaining one for each of your ships?"

"Of course." Fanny smiled, intrigued at the thought.

"I could vouch for you," he offered.

"You would do that?"

"I would be honored." He bowed slightly before taking his leave and sitting next to his wife.

A fine meal of venison and roasted potatoes was served before the bride's cake was cut. As the guests enjoyed the tasty fruitcake, a young male servant entered the dining room and whispered to John Glover who nodded, and said something to his wife before quietly excusing himself. Fifteen minutes later, the servant returned, but this time he approached Moll. "The captain would like to see you in his study."

Without a word, Moll followed the young man down the hall. She stepped aside as he lightly knocked on the study door.

"Captain Glover? Mrs. Pitcher is here."

"Come in, Moll," Glover called out. Once inside, Moll was surprised to find that he was not alone.

"Elbridge Gerry!" She smiled at the sight of a dark-haired man in his early thirties seated on a chair across from Glover. "I didn't know you were back in Marblehead."

"I just got here and I came straight to see the captain," he said. "I had no idea that a wedding was in progress. My apologies if I've interrupted anything."

"No need to apologize." Glover motioned for Moll to sit down. "You are here on important business."

Elbridge Gerry was born into a wealthy Marblehead family in 1744. His father, Thomas, was a former sea captain who reaped great success as a shipping merchant. He was also active in local politics. The third of twelve children, Elbridge entered Harvard College at the young age of thirteen, where he earned his degree before joining his father's business. He also followed in Thomas's political footsteps as an active patriot, as well as a member of the Continental Congress. During the siege of Boston, he had played a crucial role in bringing desperately needed supplies to the colonists via the harbor in Marblehead.

"I'm afraid we must once again call upon you for help, Moll," Gerry began. "And as always, this matter is quite confidential."

"Of course," she said. "What is it you need?"

"Since we've taken over Fort Ticonderoga," Glover said, "we are bringing back weaponry to fight off the British in Boston. General Washington thinks it's high time to end this terrible siege."

"Henry Knox left the fort three days ago and is now on his way here with more than sixty tons of cannon and other arms," Elbridge added.

"But it's winter and he must travel over three hundred miles!" Moll gasped.

"I know it seems impossible, but he's using horses, oxen, and as much manpower as he can muster," Elbridge explained. "And once he arrives, we must be prepared to receive the goods."

"That's where you come in, Moll," Glover said. "We need to distribute the weapons in various places throughout the region. Can we count on you to hide a supply in Lynn?"

"Well, the ground is pretty cold right now in Lynn Woods, but I think with a little help, I can find a wolf pit or two that would be willing to take in your guns," Moll said.

"And when the guns are needed?" Elbridge raised an eyebrow.

"I'll hang my red table cloth on the line as soon as they are ready for transport. No one will be the wiser. Those lobsterbacks who come to me inquiring about their future have no idea they are speaking to a patriot," Moll said, winking.

"Moll, you always amaze me with your clever ways." Glover could not hide his admiration.

"Well, Johnny," Moll teased, "I can only sometimes see the future, but I can always help the cause. It's high time we force those Brits out of Boston and good riddance to 'em, I say!"

⚓

Henry Knox, a volunteer soldier and owner of The London Bookstore in Boston, had so impressed General George Washington with his expert handling of arms at Bunker Hill that Washington soon appointed him chief artillery officer. After the capture of Fort Ticonderoga, it was Knox who recommended that the weaponry stored there be sent to Boston in an effort to end the British siege.

What came to be known as 'The Knox Expedition' or 'The Noble Train of Artillery' included fifty-nine pieces of heavy weaponry weighing close to sixty tons. To accomplish his task, Knox oversaw the building of sixty sturdy sleds and obtained one hundred sixty oxen to pull them. The group left Fort Ticonderoga on December 5, 1775 and traveled to the north shores of Lake George where the arms were then loaded onto a large barge-like ship called a gundalow. The gundalow promptly sank in the lake but was raised and the artillery saved. Knox then continued his trek overland, crossed the frozen Hudson River, and reached Lansingburg, New York on Christmas Day. Heavy snowfall impeded his progress, but he continued eastward, crossing the Berkshire Mountains, before finally reaching Cambridge, Massachusetts on January 27, 1776 with all of the munitions intact.

Shortly thereafter, Moll was in the middle of a reading for a British officer when someone knocked on her front door. Becky greeted the visitor with a quick apology. "I'm sorry, sir, but my mother is busy at the moment. I will have to ask you to come back." Despite Becky's protests, the red-faced and winded man burst in with a shout: "Moll! I need your—"

Elbridge Gerry stopped short when he caught sight of the redcoat.

"Mr. Gerry!" Moll stood up defiantly. "You know better than to come around here unannounced. My husband is next door and could be home any minute!"

"I'm sorry, Moll." Gerry's red face grew even redder.

"And sorry you should be!" Moll continued, scolding him. "How many times do I have to remind you that I am a married woman and you should seek affection elsewhere?!"

"I'm sorry, Moll," he mumbled again and backed his way out the door.

"The nerve of him!" Moll sat back down and faced her guest. "Some men just don't understand the meaning of the word 'no'! Mr. Pitcher would shred him to pieces if he knew that Mr. Gerry was sweet on me."

"Perhaps Mr. Gerry could use one of your love potions." The Englishman smiled. "It might help him turn his attentions elsewhere."

"I will take your suggestion under consideration," Moll said with a wink. "Now where were we?"

"You were about to tell me how my brother would fare in North Carolina," he reminded Moll. "He and his regiment left a few days ago."

"Yes, yes," she said. "Your brother will suffer no harm, but the general he is with will fall ill before they see any action."

"Then there will be bloodshed?"

"Yes, but rest assured, your brother will not be among the dead or wounded."

"And will the British win the battle?" he wanted to know.

"The war will not be decided by any one battle," Moll answered. "There are many more to come and that is all I see for you today."

"Thank you, my dear lady." The man pulled a gold coin from his pocket. "You have eased my worries."

"Always glad to see a soldier of the king." Moll smiled, took the coin, and stood. She then walked the officer to the door. "Have your brother come and see me when he returns. I may have news for him."

"I will do that and perhaps I will return with him."

"Of course." Moll gave a slight curtsy as he left. "I look forward to it."

The fortune teller watched as the man headed back to Boston. As soon as he was out of sight, she sent Becky next door to Marion's house. A few minutes later, the girl returned with a still-flustered Gerry.

"Really, Elbridge," Moll scolded him. "You can't just come in here and interrupt me when I have a paying British soldier at my table."

"I am truly sorry, Moll, but did you have to tell him that I was trying to steal you away from your husband?"

"You being single and all, I just couldn't think of anything else to say." Moll shrugged and offered him a chair. "I certainly didn't want him to think that I might be consorting with a patriot!"

"You are a fine woman, Moll Pitcher." Gerry grinned. "But I'm afraid I have no romantic notions at the moment…for you or anyone else."

"So why did you barge in here like that?" Moll took the chair opposite Gerry.

"I just wasn't thinking," Gerry began. "It's just that it was imperative we talk. I never imagined that you were entertaining one of the king's men."

"How do you think I get my information about upcoming battles my dear?" she asked. "Those lobsterbacks will say anything as long as I can assure them that they are not marching to their death. All I have to do is listen."

"Ahh…you are brilliant, Moll. By them believing you to be a loyalist you have their trust. So did this lobsterback give you some important news?"

"That he did and since you're here, you can get word to Johnny and to General Washington that British troops are on their way to North Carolina as we speak. Something about Moores Creek."

"I will pass that information on today, but before I do, I need your help." Gerry leaned in closer to Moll. "Henry Knox has returned from Fort Ticonderoga with tons of weaponry. Can we count on you to hide the smaller arms in Lynn Woods?"

"Yes, of course," Moll agreed. "How much do you have for me?"

"About six trunks' full."

"What about the larger pieces?"

"General Washington plans to set them up around Boston and end this damn siege once and for all."

"Will you be seeing the good general?"

"I will be going to Cambridge tomorrow to assist with the dissemination of arms and I should be back in three days with the load for you."

"Very well. I will make plans to bury the trunks nearby and when you are ready to use them, get word to me. Oh, and one more thing, Elbridge...."

"Yes, Moll?"

"Please tell General Washington that Moll Pitcher predicts those atrocious redcoats will be driven out of Boston before the Easter celebration."

"Is there anything else, Moll?"

"Yes," she said, smiling. "Tell Lady Washington that I will join her for tea very soon."

Once Gerry left, Moll called upon Elmore and Rupert Burchstead and they all went into Lynn Woods to find a spot to bury the treasure.

CHAPTER SIX

From Dimond to Pitcher

(1 7 5 9 – LYNN, MASSACHUSETTS)

ack in the spring of 1759, the good people of Lynn momentarily forgot about the French and Indian War that was waging in the distance when a few farmers lost some cattle and another a horse. Soon, chickens were missing, and the ones left behind were so traumatized that they stopped laying eggs. There was talk of a monster lurking in the woods and fear for their children gripped the community. Some came to the now-grown Moll, seeking information about their disappearing livestock. Moll quickly assured them that an animal—not an ogre—was to blame for all the trouble. One afternoon, Dr. Burchstead's widow, Anna, spotted an enormous black bear lumbering toward the woods behind the Dimond home. She almost fainted from fright, but managed to run inside her house for help. Everyone knew that bears and other animals lived in the nearby woods, but no one in Lynn had ever before seen such a huge creature.

Young Dr. Burchstead called upon his neighbors to arm themselves and join in search of the beast. The very next day, a group of ten men, including Moll's father and brothers, went into Lynn Woods. While the women kept their children close and prayed, their men tracked the oversized bruin through the trees. Several hours later, the group emerged from the woods dragging a gigantic black bear carcass behind them. Word spread quickly throughout the town and everyone came out to see the huge animal that Dr. Burchstead believed weighed over four hundred pounds.

"Poor boy." Moll knelt over the bear and gently ran her hand along its fur.

"That poor boy tried to eat me," a young man spoke up.

"Well, I see he didn't succeed." Moll stood, recognizing Robert Pitcher, a local young man whom her father had recently hired as an apprentice. He had very dark eyes and a mop of black curly hair that fell across his brow as if he hadn't combed it.

"Look at my leg, Moll." He lifted his right foot. It was bloody and his pants were torn from the knee down. "That monster grabbed me and dragged me away…a good fifty feet before I managed to get out from under him. I believe he planned to have me for lunch."

"Robert Pitcher!" Moll's brother, Samuel, appeared at his sister's side sporting a frown. "I saw you trip over a dead branch and fall into a briar patch long before we caught sight of that old bear."

"Even if I did, I like my version better." Robert winked at Moll.

"He's been trying to talk to you for months now, Moll," Samuel rolled his eyes. "Why do you suppose he took that apprenticeship with father?"

"I needed a job," Robert said, shrugging, but he had mischief in his eyes. "And why not work for the man who has the prettiest daughter in town?"

"You should be ashamed of yourself for telling tall tales," Moll said, but she couldn't help but grin.

"Well, I'm not!" Robert took her hand. "And if you had any decency, you would tend to my wounds no matter how I got them."

"Come into the house," Moll said, laughing. "I'll fix up that leg of yours and send you on your way."

"If he gives you any trouble," Samuel called after them, "just holler."

But Robert Pitcher gave Moll no trouble at all. He sat quietly while she cleaned his cuts and applied some healing ointment on them. As she bandaged his leg, she felt self-conscious knowing he was staring at her. Except for Johnny Glover, she wasn't used to a man's attention. Most of the local men her age only came around when they wanted advice or their fortune told. They would never consider marrying such a peculiar girl. She couldn't help her unique gifts and if a man refused to accept who she was, then she preferred to be alone. The role of an eccentric spinster suited her just fine, she thought defiantly. But deep down, she truly wanted a man who could love her for who she was.

"There you are." Moll, still kneeling, pulled his pant leg down. "Good as new. Except for those trousers," she said, shaking her head.

Robert stood up, took her arm, and drew her to her feet. "Tell me what you see when you look at me, Moll."

"I…I'm not sure." She tried to catch her breath, surprised at her own unexpected feelings.

"Then I'll tell you what I see," Robert said, smiling. "I see a happy life with children…maybe three."

"I see four," she quipped without thinking. There was something different about Robert Pitcher, and for once, she didn't compare the man with Johnny Glover.

⚓

Robert Pitcher wasted no time in wooing Moll. He turned up at the Dimond home on a regular basis—often with flowers for Moll, as well as for her mother. He ingratiated himself not only into the family, but also into Mr. Dimond's business of shoemaking. As for Moll, she was never happier. She had finally found someone who wasn't put off by her perplexing abilities. Of course, the fact that he was a loner helped immensely.

An only child, Robert's parents were gone and he had no siblings to dissuade him from marrying this unusual, but amazing woman. A few of the townsfolk whispered their displeasure, but these were the same folks who came to Moll when they needed help. Besides, Robert Pitcher knew a good woman when he saw one and paid no attention to his neighbors' idle gossip.

Spring turned into summer and summer fell into fall while Robert continued learning the shoemaking business and calling on Moll. Moll enjoyed his attention and took her younger brothers' teasing in good stride. She even encouraged them to find mates, but both were shy and spent most of their time working with their father. "Shoes! Shoes! Shoes!" Moll would tell them with a grin. "No wonder you can't find a girl…you are always looking down at their feet instead of up at their eyes!"

By the time Christmas came, Moll knew two things for certain: she and Robert Pitcher would be married by the end of next year; and the city of Boston would soon be ravaged by flames. Her first notion of the great fire came one night in a dream right after the New Year. She awoke to the smell of smoke and a choking sensation deep in her throat. At first, she thought her own house was on fire, but soon realized her family was safe and the smoke had been only a dream. For the next week, she saw darkness, ashes, and a large flame shaped like an angel—or maybe it was the devil. She couldn't be certain which it was, but when she saw a smoldering heap of wood in Boston Harbor, she finally confided in Robert.

"I fear for Boston," she told him one night as they sat together in front of the hearth.

"Why, my dear?"

"I've been having dreams and visions." Her face paled at the memories. "I see a great fire burning throughout the city of Boston. Homes destroyed. Businesses gone. And worst of all, the harbor—even the water looks aflame."

"You know as well as I do that fire is always a threat." Robert took her hand.

"But this is unlike any fire we've ever seen before." She pressed her lips together in a grim fashion.

"Will many die?"

"I see no death," she replied. "Just destruction on a massive scale."

"Do you know when this will happen?"

"Just as spring arrives," she said, "but before the garden is planted."

Over the next several weeks, Moll's dream recurred on a regular basis and her uneasiness grew until the early morning hours of Wednesday, March 20, 1760 when the Dimond family awoke to a burning smell and smoke hanging heavy in the air.

"It's happening," Moll murmured, feeling a weight in her chest as she made her way to the kitchen. "The fire is here! God help them all."

"It looks like Boston is burning!" Samuel called from just outside the front door. The sky was filled with a bright flickering light as Dr. Burchstead, still in his nightclothes, stood beneath the great whalebones—his eyes fixed on the rising black smoke.

"We should go help," he called over as Richard joined his brother, all now gazing in the direction of the blaze. "I'll change and get my horse. If you want to come, be ready in five minutes!"

"It's no use." Moll shook her head, but stayed inside the doorway. "Nothing can be done. It will just have to burn itself out."

"But there may be people who need us." John pulled on his coat. "Come on, boys. Let's get our horses. We can ride to town with Dr. Burchstead. The least we can do is try."

"Be careful!" Lydia called after them, but her words were drowned out by a tremendous explosion that rocked the very ground beneath them. High Rock seemed to shudder in place.

"The munitions!" Moll gasped as she reached for her mother and tried to steady herself.

"It's the end of the world." Lydia wrung her hands in anguish.

"No, mother," Moll said. "Just the end of Boston as we know it."

By the time the good doctor and the Dimond men reached Boston, several smaller fires still burned, but for the most part, they found smoldering ruins where homes and businesses once stood. The blaze had broken out in Boston's west end at the home of the widow Mary Jackson and her son, William. Together, they ran The Brazen Head, a popular general store that was attached to their dwelling. The shop and their household had gone up in flames in a matter of minutes. Mary and William were lucky to be alive.

The strong winds pushed the flames eastward, burning most of the structures in their path along King and Congress Streets. The blaze progressed to Boston Harbor where it consumed ten ships moored there. While most able-bodied citizens fought the fire, a few brave souls realized a British store of gunpowder and wea-ponry was in the direct path of the firestorm. The men worked frantically to move the volatile matter in an effort to prevent a disastrous explosion, but they were only partially successful as the flames grew closer, forcing them to flee. The remaining gun-powder caused a tremendous blast that was felt as far away as New Hampshire—the very same explosion that rattled Lydia and Moll back in Lynn.

When it was over, the people of Boston claimed it was the worst blaze the city had ever seen. While there was no loss of life and injuries were few, the damages were excessive with three hundred forty-nine homes and businesses gone, leaving more than two hundred families homeless.

And like her grandfather before her, Moll Dimond felt weighed down by the unusual powers that fate forced her to car-ry. If only she could have done something to prevent the disaster. What good was her gift, she thought, if she could not use it to stop such terrible things from happening?

Robert Pitcher was genuinely touched by the depth of Moll's

feelings—especially the internal conflicts she often suffered when dealing with disturbing news. To predict the birth of a healthy baby was one thing, but to see the angel of death hovering over a neighbor was something altogether different. It was Robert that brought Moll a book about the art of reading tea leaves, hoping it would help her to channel her powers. She studied it with great interest and soon purchased a set of four white teacups—each with a blue rim and gold handle— matching blue-rimmed saucers. She kept the teacups above the hearth and family members knew that they were not to be used for a casual drink.

At first, Moll practiced only on herself. She would drop a pinch of tea leaves in the bottom of her cup and then pour some boiling water over them. When it cooled enough, Moll drank all but a teaspoon or so. Holding the handle in her left hand, she would ask a question and then turn the cup three times in a counterclockwise motion. She would then invert the cup over the saucer for a minute or two allowing all the liquid to escape. Then she would turn the cup upright and begin her reading. She was always pleased to find a heart shape near the handle—the closer to the handle the sooner the event she learned from her book. The further from the handle, the later the occurrence. So, it came as no surprise when Robert Pitcher asked Moll for her hand in marriage, after obtaining her father's blessing and permission, of course. The small wedding ceremony took place in the Dimond home on October 2, 1760 and a radiant Moll took on the name that would bring her world-wide fame.

The newly married Mr. and Mrs. Pitcher stayed at the foot of High Rock in the Dimond home. It was a good arrangement for Moll continued helping her mother with household chores and Robert continued working with her father and brothers. At first, all were content, but a few weeks after their marriage, a foreboding feeling crept over Moll. She tried to shake it but couldn't. Robert had watched his new wife with great concern and one night as they lay together in bed, he spoke up. "What's been troubling you, my dear?"

"Nothing, I can be sure of, Mr. Pitcher," she whispered, clutching his hand. "But I feel a change is coming and not necessarily a good one."

"Now that we are married, my girl, don't you think it's time you call me Robert?" he said, grinning.

"No, I prefer Mr. Pitcher," Moll replied. "It sounds so much better than just plain Robert."

"What is the change that you see? Is it the war with the French?" Robert asked.

"No." Moll shook her head. "This war will end, but another…a much greater one will follow."

"What does that mean?" Robert propped himself up on an elbow.

"I'm not sure," Moll said. "But the war is some years off while this feeling I have seems more imminent."

"Perhaps you should have a cup of tea tomorrow," Robert suggested. "See what the leaves reveal."

"Perhaps, I will," Moll whispered as Robert kissed her neck.

"In the meantime, maybe I can find a way to lift your spirits." He caressed her.

The very next morning before anyone else arose, Moll boiled some water and took one of her blue-rimmed cups down from the mantle. She crumbled a few tea leaves in it and poured the water from the kettle, then sat in front of it watching the steam rise. Once it cooled sufficiently, she picked up the cup with her left hand and gave it the three obligatory turns before drinking the brew. She then laid the cup upside down on its saucer and waited for it to drain.

When Moll turned the cup upright, she gasped at the sight of a crown shaped by the tea leaves sitting near the handle. The crown looked to her as if it were covered in darkness.

"What do you see there, Moll?" Her husband's voice startled her. She had been so deep in thought she hadn't heard him enter the kitchen.

"Nothing good." The color drained from her face as she looked up at him.

"Tell me." He sat down next to her and took her hand in his.

"The king will soon die."

"The King of England?"

"Yes, and since Prince Frederick is already gone, King George's grandson will sit upon the throne."

"Will he be a good king?"

"Not for the colonies." Moll's eyes brimmed with tears. "I fear the worst. King George the Third will become our enemy."

"Not possible," Robert tried to assure her. "We here in the colonies are almost all Englishmen by birth or descent. The Crown could never be our enemy. Check your tea leaves again."

Moll peered into the cup once more and noticed a single unfocused eye that sat opposite the handle. She pushed the cup away.

"What is it, Moll?" Robert felt his wife trembling.

"It's madness," she whispered. "Madness will plague our new king."

⚓

True to Moll's visions, the seventy-six-year-old monarch of England, King George II, collapsed and died unexpectedly on October 25, 1760. Since his eldest son, Frederick, had preceded him in death, his grandson, George William Frederick, had been crowned the Prince of Wales and it was that young man who took over the throne at the tender age of twenty-two. He called himself King George III. It took several weeks for the royal news to reach the colonies, but Moll Pitcher was not surprised when she heard the official report.

The Seven Years War, or The French and Indian War, as it was known in the colonies, was raging and the new king inherited all of the trouble left by his grandfather. As far as the colonies were concerned, the war ended on November 29, 1760 when the French officially surrendered Fort Detroit to the British, but other headaches awaited King George III as 1761 unfolded. Two earthquakes struck England that spring and in April, a deadly flu epidemic ravaged London.

But it wasn't all bad news. On September 8, the twenty-two-year-old king married the teenage Charlotte of Mecklenburg-Strelitz as his advisors and his mother insisted he needed a wife. They were not officially crowned King and Queen of England until two weeks later. The new king told his bride not to meddle in his political affairs and she gladly obliged, leaving the running of the empire to her spouse.

Closer to home, residents of Lynn, Massachusetts grieved over the death of Reverend Nathanial Henchman, a highly respected clergyman, who had served them well as a preacher for over forty years. He left behind a wife and five children. Mourners included Robert and Moll Pitcher who continued to live in the Dimond household with Moll's family.

Robert still worked with his father-in-law plying his trade as a cordwainer much like Moll's brothers, Samuel and Richard—neither of whom took a wife. Moll herself lost two babies that year, but knowing that children lay in her future, she didn't despair. Instead, she focused on improving her skills in the reading of palms and tea leaves. She also dried herbs and leaves, making potions with the crumbled foliage that she sold to the locals—some herbs for their healing abilities and others for their persuasive powers. The extra income she earned went a long way in helping her family—especially during the severe draught of 1762 when the gardens and farms in the Boston area were barren. It was so bad in fact that on Wednesday, the 28 of July, the entire community observed a day of fasting and prayer. A few days later, their invocations were answered when a much welcome rain soaked the local earth. While the adults gave thanks, young children like Fanny Campbell and William Lovell took to the streets dancing as the downpour soaked their very skin.

It was the day of the miraculous rain that Moll took a second look at her father. John seemed slightly bent as he walked, and his steps appeared a little slower. At sixty-two, his wife believed that age was catching up to him, but Moll saw things differently. She even woke Robert up one night after a disturbing dream.

"Mr. Pitcher!" She poked her husband. "Mr. Pitcher! Get up!"

"What is it, my dear?" He rubbed the sleep from his eyes.

"It's father!" She sat up. "I fear for him! His days with us are numbered."

"You can't know that."

"But I can," she said, tearing up. "The Wizard told me."

"Your grandfather?!" Robert suddenly gave her his undivided attention.

"Yes," she said. "He just came to me in a dream. He said that in a fortnight he is coming to take father home."

"Maybe it was just a nightmare, Moll." Robert tried soothing her.

"No, it's been years since I've seen the Wizard, but I'm telling you he was here tonight. He wanted me to know that father is going to leave us, but we mustn't tell mother, or the boys. They would worry so and there is nothing they can do to change it."

"Maybe in the morning you should brew some tea and see what the leaves have to say," Robert suggested.

"I can't wait till morning." Moll got up. "I must make tea now."

"Well then...I'll join you." Robert followed his wife to the hearth where he built a small fire and Moll boiled water.

She took down two of her special cups and saucers and the

couple savored their aromatic beverage in silence, so as not to disturb anyone else. When her cup was almost empty, Moll completed her usual ritual and Robert did the same with his cup.

"Shall I read yours first?" she whispered to her husband.

Robert shook his head. "No need. I already know my fortune…a long and happy life with the loveliest girl in Lynn. Turn your cup over and tell me what you see."

Moll drew in a deep breath and picked up the blue-rimmed cup. She looked inside and caught her breath—a cross had taken shape near the handle. Robert reached for her hand before she could speak. "It will be all right, my girl. We will manage somehow. We always do."

Exactly two weeks later, John Dimond sat with his family around the dinner table. They enjoyed a simple meal together and then afterward John went outside to stroll around the garden. Moll knew when she saw the door close behind him that her father would never come back. Robert's hand grasped hers and together they followed him just in time to see him clutch his chest and collapse in front of the house.

"Father!" Moll's screams brought out her mother and brothers, as well as their neighbor, Dr. Burchstead. He dropped to his knees and tried to revive John, but it was no use. After several agonizing moments, Dr. Burchstead rose to his feet. "I am so sorry, Lydia. John was one of the finest men I have ever had the privilege to know."

Lydia collapsed in Samuel's arms while Richard, along with the good doctor, tended to John's now-lifeless body.

"I knew, but I couldn't save him," Moll whispered to Robert as angry tears escaped down her cheeks.

"You were a fine daughter." Robert held Moll tightly against his chest. "But it was his time. There was nothing you could do."

"What will become of mother?" Moll gasped. "How will she cope with the loss?"

"I don't need a cup of tea to see that," Robert said, smiling.

"We give her a grandchild to love."

And exactly nine months later, Robert's prediction came to pass. Moll gave birth to a fine baby girl and named her Ruth.

CHAPTER SEVEN

Common Sense

(WINTER 1 7 7 5/1 7 7 6 – LYNN, MASSACHUSETTS)

On December 23, 1775, King George III issued a royal proclamation. As of next March, the American colonies would be closed to all commerce and trade. This would hit the colonies hard, but the patriots also knew that the lack of trade from America would be equally detrimental to the Crown. On the bright side, however, the Continental Congress received the welcome news from France that they would back the patriots and support them in their war against Britain—at least in an unofficial light.

In addition, fighting between the Americans and British had recently begun in South Carolina near Charleston Harbor when an army of colonists attacked a loyalist camp inside Cherokee territory.

On New Year's Eve, the Washingtons worshipped at Christ Church in Cambridge. The very next day, General Washington ordered the raising of a new banner—the Union Flag. Its thirteen red-and-white stripes represented the thirteen colonies and in the upper left-hand corner was a Union Jack—the red cross giving a nod to the British. Hung high on a seventy-six-foot pole, the flag could be seen as far away as Boston and defiantly symbolized the colonists' dedication to the American cause. They were determined to fight to the finish and never again be loyal to the Crown, regardless of the war's outcome.

That very same day, as the Union Flag billowed in the New England wind, the British launched a vicious attack on the southern town of Norfolk, Virginia. From the harbor, they cannonaded the town well into the evening, then sent landing parties ashore to burn the remaining buildings. By the time it was over, much of the town had been destroyed, mirroring the recent assault on Falmouth. When the deadly news reached General Washington and the Second Continental Congress, they dispatched some of their own ships from the newly formed navy to act as a coastal patrol to protect these seaside towns from the British. The *Andrew Doria,* sailing under William Lovell's friend, Captain Nicholas Biddle, was one of them.

Despite the difficult times, the Campbells and Lovells celebrated their good fortune that Christmas, but Fanny's joy was short-lived. Just as the New Year began, a nervous William insisted they walk over to see Jack and Marion.

"Are you keeping something from me, William Lovell?" Fanny demanded as she tried to keep up with his quickened pace. "You haven't been yourself the past few days. Even your mother has noticed something different."

"You know me too well, Mrs. Lovell." William didn't look at her as he continued walking.

"You and Jack are up to something." Fanny frowned as she sidestepped an icy patch. "And whatever it is, Marion and I aren't going to like it, are we?"

"Probably not," William quipped, taking Fanny's hand. "That's why Jack and I thought it best that we tell you both together. Strength in numbers, as they say."

"So, you are going to keep me in suspense until we get there?"

"I'm afraid so," he said. "But it won't be long."

They walked the rest of the way in silence and the dread inside Fanny grew. Whatever William and Jack were planning had to be dangerous; after all, they lived in perilous times.

Despite the cold, Jack was waiting for them on the front porch, hands inside his coat pockets. "It's about time you got here. I had to come outside to get away from Marion. She was peppering me with questions."

"Go on in, Fanny." William held the door. "Jack and I will be right there. We just have a few details to discuss first."

"Marion and I expect answers…honest answers," Fanny said, frowning. "So, I suggest you two be quick about it."

Once she was inside, William and Jack stayed near the door quietly talking while Marion and Fanny exchanged worried glances.

"Do you have any idea what our husbands are up to?" Fanny hung up her cloak.

"Not a clue." Marion shook her head as she poured four cups of hot coffee. "Jack refused to talk to me until you and William got here. Something about strength in numbers."

"Hmmmmmmmmmm.…" Fanny picked up her cup letting the steam warm her face. "They are definitely plotting something."

Just then, the front door opened and the two men stepped inside.

"Jack," Marion said, wasting no time. "We're all together now. I think you and William best let us in on your little secret."

It was Jack's and William's turn to exchange nervous looks.

"William?" Fanny put her cup down. Suddenly, the room seemed very warm. "We are waiting."

William and Jack both took a deep breath before coming to the table. Each claimed a chair opposite his wife.

"Fanny, Marion," William began with some hesitation in his voice, "I am not sure if you are aware that there has been some fighting down south."

"It's more important than ever that we protect our harbors along the entire Atlantic coast," Jack chimed in.

"Just what are you getting at?" Marion demanded.

"While we are waiting for our letters of marque," Jack began, "Colonel Glover has asked us to sail with the *Andrew Doria* under Captain Nicholas Biddle."

"It's only as harbor patrol, that's all," William added, trying to diminish the danger. "And we won't be gone long."

"I assume women aren't allowed onboard," Marion said, stiffening.

"You know very well women aren't allowed on Washington's Cruisers," Jack reminded her.

"Maybe Bartholomew Channing should return." Fanny put her coffee cup down with a bang. "If I am not capable, he certainly is."

"Now Fanny," William said, "you know Channing can never come back. He is wanted by the British. He…you would be hung for treason."

"How long will you be gone?" Marion asked, attempting to keep her composure.

"Just a few weeks." Jack reached for her hand. "You have to understand, Marion, that William and I need to do something for the cause. You ladies are at least working with Moll hiding guns and carrying messages while William and I only work on our ships."

"And who will work on the ships while you are gone?" Fanny demanded.

"Samuel will oversee what is being done," William answered. "Of course, if you two find the time in between your work with Moll, you could always assist him."

"It's no use arguing." Fanny looked squarely at Marion. "It seems our men have made up their minds. They sail away and we stay here because we are incapable women."

"Far from incapable, Fanny!" William's voice grew louder. "No one knows better than Jack and me just how capable you ladies are, but right now Moll needs you and Captain Biddle needs us. We promise you we won't be gone long."

It was settled. No matter how much Fanny and Marion disliked the idea, William and Jack caught a fishing sloop and headed to Philadelphia that very afternoon.

A few months earlier, the Second Continental Congress had purchased the brig, *Andrew Doria*, often referred to as the "*Black Brig*," and converted her to a warship in Philadelphia, intending to add her to their coastal patrol fleet.

On January 4, 1776 under the command of Captain Nicholas Biddle, the fourteen-gun brig set sail with William Lovell and Jack Herbert on board as the captain's first and second mate, respectively, based on recommendations from John Glover. Biddle, a Philadelphian, was an experienced sailor who had first gone to sea as a ship's boy at the age of thirteen. The *Andrew Doria* was one of five newly fitted warships led by Esek Hopkins, the only Commander and Chief of the Continental Navy. The small fleet also included the *Alfred*, the *Cabot*, the *Columbus*, and the *Providence*. They headed for the Chesapeake Bay with orders to cruise the Carolina coasts. Three smaller ships, the *Hornet*, the *Wasp*, and the *Fly* joined the fleet in February. It was all routine sailing until General Hopkins decided differently.

⚓

Shortly after William's and Jack's departure, Moll Pitcher found herself watching as General Washington spoke with a mysterious dark-haired man at his headquarters in Cambridge. Washington was a good five or six inches taller than his visitor, but something about this stranger disturbed her. She saw an aura of danger surrounding him and his grey eyes shone with a wicked light.

"Come, Moll!" Washington beckoned to her. "Come meet our newest general."

Moll stepped forward with a quick curtsy, still not sure what to make of this man.

"Your fabled reputation precedes you, Mrs. Pitcher." The stranger reached for her hand with a quick nod of his head. "Perhaps one day you will honor me with a reading."

The moment he touched her, a burning sensation ran up Moll's entire arm and before she could form any words in response, she screamed in pain.

"Moll! Moll" Someone was shaking her. "Moll! Wake up. You're home with me. You're safe. It's just another one of your bad dreams."

Moll's eyes flew open as she gasped for breath, her arm now completely numb. She looked around the familiar bedroom and finally recognized her husband who was trying his best to soothe her. "Are you all right, my girl?" Robert caressed her cheek.

Moll took a deep breath trying to compose herself. "There's a traitor in the ranks, Mr. Pitcher!"

"A traitor?"

"Yes, and General Washington trusts him completely. I must warn him of the danger."

"The general is a wise man," Robert said. "He knows whom he can trust."

"Not this time." Moll drew the blankets around her, suddenly feeling a chill. "This man is a turncoat…I'm not sure when or how, but eventually he will side with the king and betray our army."

"Are you sure about this?"

"I knew it the moment he touched me." Moll rubbed her arm that was now beginning to ache.

"But it was a dream, my girl. He never really touched you."

"Thank goodness!" Moll closed her eyes. "I would rather face the devil himself than be in the same room as that wretched soldier who calls himself a gentleman!"

"Go back to sleep, Moll. See how you feel in the morning. Things may seem different then."

"No." Moll swung her bare feet to the floor. "I must write to the general and warn him."

"Can't it wait till morning?"

"I won't be able to sleep until I do."

"And if he doesn't believe you?"

"I'll write to Lady Washington and Johnny, too, if I have to," she insisted. "They must listen before it's too late." And with that, Moll left her husband to sleep alone, while she sat at her Queen Anne table composing a letter to be sent to Cambridge at once.

Moll wasn't the only one wielding a pen that night. Patriot Thomas Paine was in the midst of writing his soon-to-be-famous commentary, *Common Sense*. His ideas were clear—the American colonists must fight for equality, independence, and an end to British oppression once and for all. *Common Sense* was soon published and made its way across the thirteen colonies. It was read at town hall meetings in cities large and small, inspiring all who heard it. Paine called for all colonists to unite in favor of a revolution. His words held mass appeal and stirred the spirit of rebellion like nothing before. If the British wanted a fight, by God, they would get one.

Dressed as men, Fanny and Marion first heard about Paine's pamphlet at a gathering in Lynn shortly after it was published. They routinely attended these assemblies disguised as men since women were not allowed inside. The two women felt it was important to stay informed about the latest events concerning the war, the army, and the newly formed navy—especially since their husbands were on active sea-patrol. The women wanted to hear the latest news in person and not receive it second-hand before passing what they learned on to Moll. The evening that the pamphlet was read aloud, both women noted a shift in the atmosphere. Men who had previously resisted the thought of war now became open to the idea. It was all true—Americans were not treated fairly by the British. Perhaps a revolution was the only way the colonists could gain their freedom. Perhaps war was inevitable. After all, look what the lobsterbacks had done to

Boston. Maybe it was time for the colonists to unite and take charge.

With their men away, Fanny and Marion were more determined than ever to take an active part in the revolt. They helped Moll hide many of the smaller weapons that Henry Knox so bravely delivered from Fort Ticonderoga. Moll knew well the wolf pits deep in the Lynn Woods, where she buried the pistols, sabers, and rifles along with the ammunition that she separated from the guns. In the unlikely event that the British might discover part of the stash, they would not get everything. Guns without bullets, or bullets without guns, would do the redcoats little good, but one word from Elbridge Gerry and the Continental Army would be armed and ready to take back Boston when the time was right. Moll would see to it.

Fanny and Marion also delivered messages from Moll directly to Elbridge Gerry whenever one of her readings produced meaningful intelligence that General Washington, the Continental Army, or the navy might use. Before long, it seemed that the three clever women had indeed created their own covert spy ring. Between Moll's many visions and predictions, as well as the wealth of information she gleaned from her unwitting British patrons, there was always plenty of information to pass on to the Sons of Liberty—especially when high-ranking officers of the Crown came calling on the famous psychic of Lynn.

One such patron walked briskly along the path to High Rock, on an unseasonably warm afternoon in late February of 1776. The sword at his side glinted in the bright sunlight as he strode past the whalebones in front of Dr. Burchstead's house. The tall, dark-haired man in his forties hesitated for a moment before knocking on Moll's door. Her daughter, Becky, answered the door, concerned to find a British general standing there. The high-ranking officer removed his hat and bowed. "Might this be the home of Mrs. Moll Pitcher?"

"And who might be calling?" Becky asked even though she

recognized the general. She had seen him in and around Boston several times over the past year, but she was unsure whether he posed a threat or came as a paying customer.

"I am General William Howe." The man gave another slight bow, before tucking his hat under his arm. "I understand that Mrs. Pitcher is quite skilled at seeing the future."

"My mother has been known to make accurate predictions." Becky stepped back, relieved to learn he had come for a reading.

"I was wondering if she might have some time to spare for me." Howe gave Becky a hopeful smile.

"Mother," she called out. "General Howe is here. He would like a reading if you are up to it."

"I'll be right there, dear." Moll answered from the back of the house, where she was busy mixing potions. A moment later, she appeared, wiping her hands on a stark white apron that was tied around her waist. Percy trailed behind her. She pointed to an empty chair next to her small Queen Anne table. "Please sit down, general. My daughter, Becky, will make you a cup of tea. The leaves will help us to see what your future might hold."

Visibly uncomfortable, the general took a seat across from Moll while Becky crumbled tea leaves into one of the blue-rimmed china cups before ladling some steaming hot water on top of them. She set the cup and saucer in front of General Howe.

"Thank you, Becky," Moll said, dismissing her daughter. "That will be all."

"Yes, mum." The girl gave a quick curtsy. "I'll go tend the potions for you."

"There's a good girl." Moll smiled as Percy crept silently into the room and meandered over to General Howe, who bent over to scratch the cat's head. Percy arched his back and swatted at Howe's hand with a loud screech.

"Percy!" Moll scolded. "That's no way to treat a servant of the king and an honored guest in our home! Shame on you!" She then turned to Howe. "You mustn't hold that against poor Percy.

He dislikes most folks that come here. I guess it's his way of protecting what's his." The black cat then ambled over to Moll and curled around her feet. He settled in and closed his eyes, not feeling the least bit bad about his shameful behavior.

"I'm sure he's harmless." Howe looked directly at Moll. "The question is…are you?"

"I'm a simple woman who happens to be gifted," Moll replied. "Like my grandfather before me."

"Of course, the Wizard," Howe said. "Both General Burgoyne and General Gage told me about your family."

"What else did they tell you?"

"They said that you could see the future." Howe sat back in his chair. "And if I had any questions about mine, you might be able to help me."

"That I can." Moll gave her most winning smile. "But first, tell me, sir, how are things in Boston? Will the good Brits be staying a while longer?"

"We are prepared to fight if we must," Howe answered. "But we prefer not to do battle here again if it can be avoided. There are more important places that need our attention."

"What places could be more important than Boston?" Moll asked. feigning disbelief.

"New York and New Jersey to name two," the general told her frankly.

Moll leaned forward. "But general, you don't think that the lazy men who make up the Continental Army will ever defeat the British, do you?"

"Of course not." He grinned at the very thought of the British losing their hold over the colonies. "But tell me, Mrs. Pitcher, are you really a loyalist as they say you are?"

"I am ever so loyal." Moll smiled again. "That's why I encourage the king's soldiers to come to my table. Their secrets are safe with me. Now, swirl your cup and drink your tea so we can see what the leaves have to say."

Howe did as Moll instructed, sipping the hot liquid as quickly as the temperature allowed. When he was done, Moll circled the cup turning it upside down into the saucer. She then picked it up and studied the leaves. Her face grew serious, quickly making the general uncomfortable as he shifted in his seat.

"I see a trip to Canada coming quite soon for you." Moll grew quiet for a spell before continuing. "But most importantly, you will join your brother in New York by the end of summer and there will be a siege on the hillside there."

"And we will win the battle?" The general held his breath.

"The odds will be in your favor and a British victory declared," Moll announced. "And you will be rewarded for your valor. But remember…" she said dramatically, "do not to push your troops too hard. They will need rest and nourishment. To deny them this might prove deadly and I'm sure you would not want that on your conscience."

"Of course not." Howe's smile broadened. "I assure you that my men will always come first."

"See that they do." Moll smiled back at him, happy that he was pleased with her predictions.

At the end of the reading the general compensated Moll quite handsomely for her services, but just as he was about to leave, Moll had one more thing to say.

"Oh, general." The sharp sound of her voice stopped him as he opened the front door.

"Yes, Mrs. Pitcher?" He turned.

"No good will come from a table of gambling," Moll warned him. "Or from the company of a married lady."

Howe paused guiltily stiffening—clearing his throat. "I will take that into consideration." General Howe then turned and abruptly stepped outside.

Moll reached under the table for Percy who purred contentedly at her gentle touch. "He's not a bad man for a lobsterback," she whispered to the cat. "He just doesn't know that what he told me today about New York and New Jersey will soon reach General Washington's ear."

The very next day, Moll received word from Elbridge Gerry that the small arms she had hidden in Lynn Woods were now needed. Moll, Fanny, and Marion, along with the neighbor boys, went to the wolf pits under the cover of darkness and unearthed the guns and ammunition. When the cache was ready, Moll hung a red tablecloth in her front yard. Gerry sent wagons to Moll's little cottage at the base of High Rock. They were directed as to the location of the weaponry and the goods were retrieved from the woods and delivered to the brave men who made up the Continental Army. With any amount of luck, Boston would soon be back in the hands of the Americans.

CHAPTER EIGHT

The Acts

(1 7 6 4 – LYNN, MASSACHUSETTS)

By the time Moll's daughter, Ruth, reached her first birthday in 1764, Moll's standing as the 'Psychic of Lynn' was on the rise as people from neighboring towns like Boston and Marblehead sought her counsel. She rarely turned anyone away from the house at the base of High Rock and always graciously accepted whatever donation they might leave. The extra money helped feed her growing family, which included her widowed mother, Lydia, and her two brothers, Samuel and Richard.

The city of Lynn had also established its reputation as New England's finest place for shoemaking. The *Boston Gazette* even heralded John Dagyr as 'the celebrated shoemaker of Essex County.' As far as Robert Pitcher was concerned, this was very good for business, but that same year two unfortunate events also occurred. First, the British Parliament passed the Sugar Act, which adversely affected trade in the colonies, hurting local economy and threatening American industries—especially the highly lucrative rum trade. Companies closed their doors. Jobs were lost. Ships sat empty in the harbors. Boston businessman and lawyer, Samuel Adams, formally denounced the Sugar Act to the Massachusetts Assembly. He claimed it was an infringement upon the colonists' rights.

Moll found it necessary to travel to Boston one summer day with Dr. Burchstead. He had patients to see and Moll needed a few items for some of her potions. She was at the market near Boston Harbor when a small dark-skinned girl caught her eye. The child was with one of Boston's wealthiest women, Susannah

Wheatley, whom Moll recognized immediately. It was the little girl, however, that made her stop and stare. An aura of bright yellow and blue surrounded her.

"Mrs. Wheatley!" Moll called out and the well-dressed woman turned abruptly.

"Why, Moll! How nice to see you!"

"And you," Moll said. "And who might this beautiful child be?"

"We call her Phillis," Mrs. Wheatley smiled. "I'm afraid she came over on a slave ship. I saw her at the market and I couldn't bear the thought of anyone harming her so I bought her and named her after the ship she was on."

"You bought her?!" Moll repeated. She had never gotten used to the idea of people being sold like cattle.

"Yes, I did," Mrs. Wheatley replied. "But she's well cared for and my children have taken quite a shine to her. They are teaching her to read and write. She's very bright, you know."

Up until now the girl had not said a word but stood staring at Moll as if she could see right through her. Moll reached out and stroked her thick dark hair. "You are destined for greatness, my girl. Use your words and you will be received by kings and queens. Your pen will be your greatest asset and your words will be heard around the world for many years to come."

"What does that mean?" Phillis asked Mrs. Wheatley with just the tiniest bit of fear in her voice.

"I'm not sure," Mrs. Wheatly answered. "But take heed when Moll Pitcher speaks. She sees things we don't."

⚓

A few weeks later, a second unfortunate event occurred when Moll's mother, Lydia Dimond, unexpectedly passed away in her sleep at the age of fifty. It was Moll who found her mother's life-less body lying in bed one September morning. Her screams brought her husband and brothers into the room. Samuel dashed over to Dr. Burchstead's house, but Lydia was already cold and there was nothing to be done for her. While Lydia's death was peaceful, Moll was inconsolable.

"How did I not see this?" Moll tearfully asked her husband after laying her mother to rest next to her father, John, on a bright fall day.

"My girl, it's probably for the best, you didn't." Robert gently draped an arm around his wife as they returned home from the cemetery.

"But maybe I could have saved her."

"How?"

"I don't know." Moll swiped at a stray tear. "Maybe there was a potion I could have made or a prayer I could have said."

"And maybe it was just your mother's time."

"How will we ever get along without her?" Moll choked back a sob.

"We will take it together a day at a time, as we always do."

And so, the Pitchers did just that. The house itself went to Samuel—Moll's oldest brother who lived with them. Robert carried on with his shoemaking business and Moll resumed her readings. It wasn't long before she found herself expecting again. The news was bittersweet as Moll ached for her mother's company, but she also looked forward to bringing new life into their home. After all, Moll believed that the birth of a baby signified hope. However, as 1765 emerged, the colonists were finding it hard to be hopeful when it came to dealings with the British.

Shortly after the New Year, Moll gave birth to her second daughter, a fine, healthy baby she named Rebecca. The first time Moll held her, she saw an aura about the girl and, although she loved Ruth dearly, she knew that it was Becky who would be her closest. Robert had been hoping for a son, but after seeing the newborn babe, he whispered a prayer of thanks that both his wife and child were in good health. He had known far too many good women who had died in the throes of childbirth, sometimes taking a stillborn infant with them.

Coinciding with Becky's birth, Parliament passed the Stamp Act dictating that any printed materials used in the colonies (magazines, newspapers, playing cards, legal transactions, etc.) must be produced on specially stamped paper that was manufactured in London and carried the royal seal. The colonists were also forced to pay for this paper with only British currency—colonial money was not acceptable to the Crown. It was the Crown's way of making the colonists financially responsible for the English military troops that took part in the French and Indian War, as well as those that now occupied Boston. The Americans were incensed at the idea of 'taxation without representation' and the spark of unrest struck further. Then to make things even worse, the British legislature followed the Stamp Act with the Quartering Act, ordering the colonists to provide food and shelter in their own homes to the redcoats.

The irate colonists retaliated on August 26, 1765. They believed that British Provincial Governor Thomas Hutchinson was a Stamp Act supporter. Even worse, they also thought that he appointed his brother-in-law, Andrew Oliver, to the position of stamp master to ensure the new rulings were enforced. That was not the case, but there was no talking to an angry mob fueled by alcohol. The rowdy group gathered in Boston's North End on Garden Court Street and stormed the governor's three-story mansion. They smashed through the front door with an axe and then looted the place, destroying china, burning books, and slashing rugs. The colonists even set fire to irreplaceable historical papers that Hutchinson had collected in his efforts to write a history of Massachusetts Bay. What wasn't destroyed was stolen and once the men had ruined the interior, they demolished the exterior. By morning, only the foundation remained along with parts of the walls. Even the garden fence was trampled. The governor and his family had barely escaped with their lives.

Two days later, Hutchinson's daughter, Sarah, turned up at Moll Pitcher's door, frightened and out of breath.

"Oh, Mrs. Pitcher!" The dark-haired girl began to cry once Moll let her inside. "I've heard about your great powers and I am desperate! Can you please help me? My home, the house my great-great-grandfather built, is gone and I'm so afraid of what will happen to my father!"

Moll took pity on the trembling girl and escorted her to a chair next to her Queen Anne table. "There's a good girl." Moll's tone was soothing as she took two blue-rimmed cups from the mantle. "Let's have a cup of tea while my children are napping, and I will see what I can do."

Sarah found solace in the warm drink, as well as Moll's company. "I am so sorry for coming here unannounced," she apologized. "But I had to see you."

"I understand that you had a good scare the other night." Moll took her hand. "But it's all over now. You and your family are safe."

"But the damage---"

"Houses can be rebuilt, child," Moll interrupted. "And everything in them can be replaced sooner or later."

"I am so glad that my mother did not live to see the destruction," Sarah said, frowning.

"Margaret was a fine woman," Moll spoke softly.

"You knew my mother?" Sarah seemed surprised.

"We met a few times when I was very young," Moll said. "But what impressed me most about Margaret was how devoted she was to your father."

"It's my father I'm worried about," Sarah admitted. "What's to become of him?"

"Finish up your tea and we'll take a look."

Sarah drank the rest of her tea and Moll tipped the cup over to drain. When she looked inside, she saw a snake. "I'm afraid there's more trouble ahead. Lives will be lost, but your father will try to be fair. He will be torn between the colonies and the Crown and eventually leave Boston, but that is in the distant future."

"And then what?"

"A long voyage by ship that will take him to the king."

"Will he ever return?"

"No, child, I'm afraid he won't be buried next to your mother."

"I see." Sarah cast her dark eyes downward. "And what of his book?"

"He will write his books." Moll smiled. "But it will take some time. Now, do you have a question about yourself?"

"No, ma'am." Sarah smiled for the first time. "I prefer not to know what might be in store for me."

"You're a good daughter." Moll smiled too, happy to see the girl's relief. "Your father is lucky to have you, but pay attention to that Oliver boy. You may find him to your liking."

"Yes, ma'am." Sarah pulled a coin from her pocket and laid it on the Queen Anne table.

"You keep it." Moll placed the money in the palm of Sarah's hand. "I'll not be charging you for my services today. Now run along to your father, child. He needs you, and remember what I've told you."

⚓

When the British ultimately repealed the Stamp Act, the colonists took it as a good sign. The fine people of Lynn and other colonial towns celebrated the news by ringing their church bells and building bonfires. The officials in Lynn even set aside the first Saturday in May for a special event to mark what the colonists saw as a decisive win. The Crown had finally heard them.

Moll's eldest brother, Samuel Dimond, volunteered to help prepare the fireworks scheduled as part of the victory celebration that evening. He left the house near High Rock after breakfast, heading toward the docks. As he closed the front door behind him, Moll suddenly smelled smoke and an anxious feeling washed over her. She ran to the door just as Samuel rode off on his horse. "Samuel! Samuel!" she hollered, but he never heard her over the clip of the horse's hooves on the cobblestones. As Moll watched him leave, she saw a strange black cloud swirl around him and just as quickly as it came, it disappeared. She took a deep breath, closed her eyes, and said a quick prayer.

At noon, Robert, Moll and their two girls walked down to Lynn Harbor where the local ships proudly displayed their vibrant colors. It was a picturesque scene set against the bluest of skies and a warm spring breeze welcomed the jubilant crowd. Neighbors greeted each other with happy shrieks and laughter. It had been a long time since the hardworking townsfolk had something to cheer about. Moll eyed the docks, looking for Samuel, but only spotted her younger brother, Richard, who was loading one of the many cannons set up along the waterfront. She left the girls with their father and approached him. "Have you seen Samuel?"

"No, Moll, I haven't." Richard squinted in the bright sunlight. "But I think he's down by the warehouses with a few other men. They are readying the gunpowder for tonight's fireworks. Is something wrong?"

"Maybe." Moll frowned as that uneasy feeling returned.

"I'll go look for him after we shoot off the cannons," Richard offered. "Go back to your family and enjoy the fun. God knows we don't have enough of it."

Moll forced a smile and looked around once more for her older brother. Unable to find him, she rejoined Robert and the girls, but she couldn't take part in the revelry. Something was wrong and despite all the smiling faces that surrounded her, she remained on edge. Excited conversations turned into deafening babble. The exuberant crowd closed in on her and the sunlight dimmed. Moll didn't even hear the cannons fire their shells, but she saw Ruth cover her ears in protest, and the acrid stench of gunpowder burned in her nostrils.

As the smoke cleared, a powerful blast shook the earth beneath them. All heads turned toward the warehouses where a plume of black smoke spewed forth as wood, brick, and ash rained down around them. Parents grabbed their screaming children, running for cover. Robert pushed Moll and the girls under a tree and shielded them with his body. Two more explosions rocked them and then all was quiet.

While the women and children anxiously waited, the men rushed to the warehouses to see what could be done. They pulled several wounded men from the rubble. James Talcott and John Cook were badly burned, while Nathaniel Ledyard and William Gardiner suffered broken bones. Scores of others bore minor injuries that day, but it was Levi Jones, John Knowles, Richard Lord and Samuel Dimond who lost their lives. Moll grieved for them all, but she mourned her brother for months afterward, always wondering if she could have somehow forewarned him of the impending doom.

Their joy about the Crown was short-lived, when, to add insult to injury, the colonists received word from England that even though the Stamp Act had ended, Parliament had passed the Declaratory Act in its place. The British government now proclaimed that it had the same authority in America as it did in England, giving them the power to enact laws in the colonies with or without the colonists' consent. Enraged Americans knew that this meant they would soon be subject to more unwelcome taxes. Enter the Townshend Acts.

⚓

While Robert and Moll welcomed their third daughter, Lydia, the Townshend Acts made life even more difficult for the colonists. The British government-imposed taxes on imported goods such as glass, lead, paper, and tea. The revenue earned was meant to pay the wages of colonial governors and other officials of the Crown residing in America. In response, Bostonians Samuel Adams and James Otis, Jr. wrote the Massachusetts Circular Letter proclaiming the Townshend Acts unconstitutional as the colonists had no representation in Parliament. The Massachusetts House of Representatives approved the letter and passed it along to other colonies as well. In retaliation, Colonial Governor Francis Bernard dissolved the Massachusetts Assembly and forbade them to meet.

But it wasn't only the political issues that troubled Moll that year. Swollen with her fourth child, she began having visions about a local girl named Fanny Campbell. The visions were so vivid that she actually invited the girl to her home so she could warn her of the future and offer help when the time was right. Once that was done, Moll had even more disturbing visions and dreams about the hardworking fishermen of Marblehead. She became so troubled that she barely ate or slept and finally confided her greatest fears to Robert. Concerned for his wife's well-being, he suggested that she speak with her old friend, John Glover. Perhaps he might be able to help. She would have ridden to Marblehead herself, but her time of confinement was near so she wrote a letter instead:

My Dearest Johnny,

If I were able to come to Marblehead, I would have taken the fastest horse, but being so close to delivering my baby, I must be content with this letter in order to unburden myself.

All of the mighty fishermen in Marblehead are in grave danger. I fear for them as I see a large black cloud hovering over the entire city. I am not sure when or where exactly, but mighty storms are coming to the north and they will take many ships in their wake. Dozens of good Marblehead women will be widowed and their children left fatherless. Mothers will mourn their sons and a great sadness will surround the entire village.

You have to warn them, Johnny. Convince them that they must not set sail for the next two seasons if they want to save themselves. I am so sorry to put this burden on you, but I had no one else to turn to. The men of Marblehead respect you and they might listen to what you say.

Tell them, Johnny, tell them that their voyages will end in disaster. Tell them that their friend Moll Pitcher will pray to St. Elmo for their safety, but they must take heed of my words.

I pray it is not too late to save them.

Blessings to you and your family,
Moll

Several days later, Moll received Glover's answer:

My Dearest Moll,

I read your recent letter and I must say, found it disturbing. I know that you can see things the rest of us can't, but the thought of so many men in danger leaves me cold.

I have done your bidding and warned as many as I possibly could, but fishing is their livelihood and the only way most of them can support their families. Several ships have already left our harbor and more will follow. There may be a few men who stay back, and you can take credit for saving their lives when the time comes, but the vast majority are gone or will leave shortly regardless of my words.

Let us both pray to St. Elmo that he will bring them all home safely and with a good catch, but if your words are true then we must pray for their souls and the families they will leave behind.

Your good friend,
John

Moll collapsed on the floor, still clutching Glover's letter. "Is this how you felt, grandfather?" she cried. "Is this how you felt when you knew what was coming, but you couldn't change it?!" Only silence ensued and then Moll grew angry. "Why did you pass this affliction on to me if I am powerless to help the very people who need it?" Angry sobs washed over her like furious whitecaps jarring her entire body and the child within her.

Moll's deadly predictions for the doomed fishermen of Marblehead came true. Between 1768 and 1769, a total of twenty-three fishing vessels and their crews were lost at sea amidst violent storms off the coast of Newfoundland. The battered ships that managed to return brought fewer men home as many sailors were washed overboard by the angry waves. In all, one hundred sixty-two men and boys were lost, leaving seventy women widowed and one hundred fifty-five children deprived of a father. The entire city of Marblehead went into a deep period of mourning as there was not one family left unaffected.

As for Moll Pitcher, she delivered a healthy son without incident. After welcoming three daughters, Robert was overjoyed with his long-awaited boy, a handsome babe with dark eyes and a head full of dark curls. Without discussing the matter with her husband, Moll named him John in honor of her father. At least that is what she told her family and friends, but in her heart, Moll was honoring another man that she cared deeply for—John Glover.

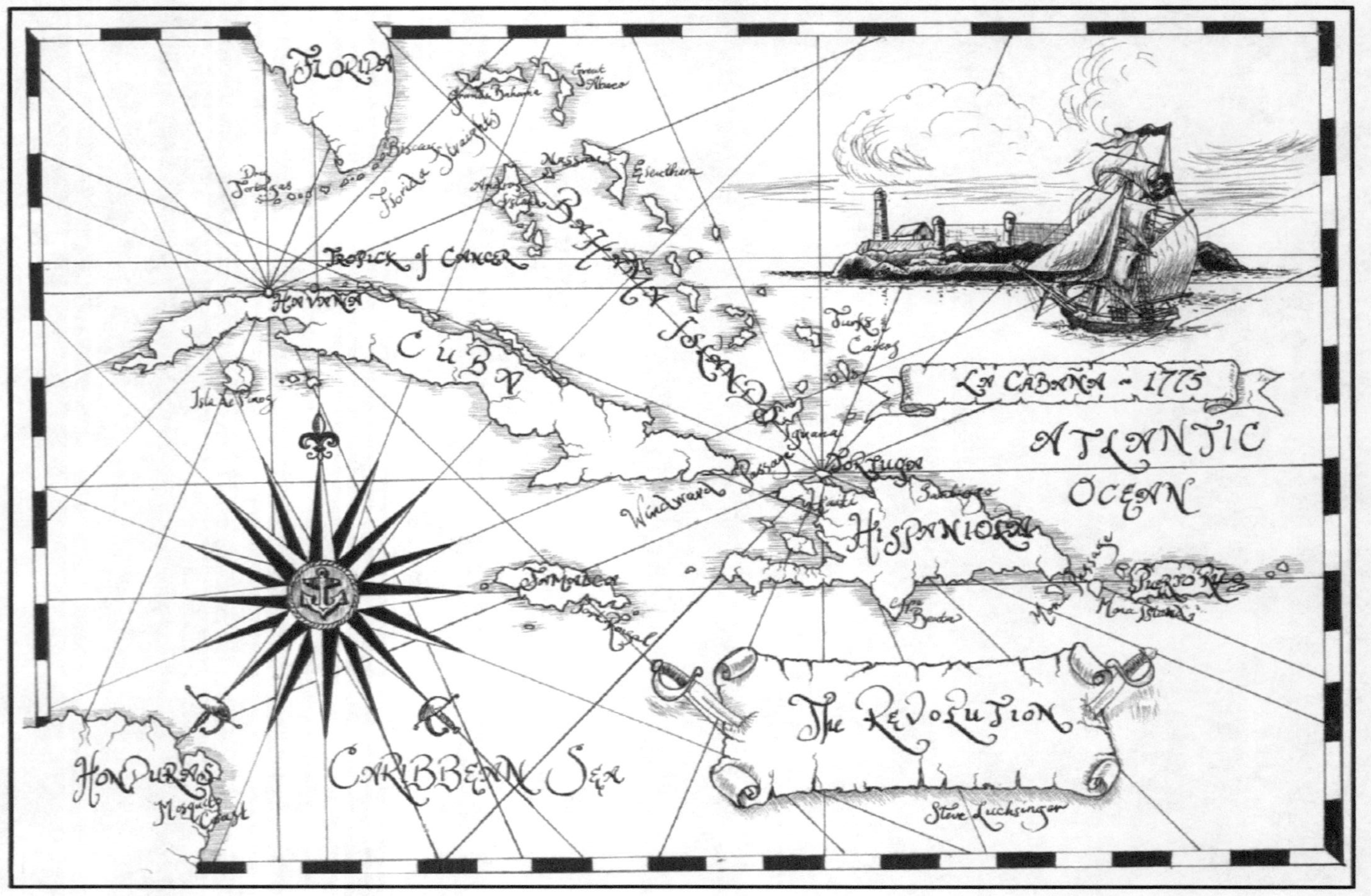

FLORIDA
Dry Tortugas
Biscayne
Florida Straights
Great Bahama
Great Abaco
Nassau
Eleuthera
Andros
BAHAMA ISLAND
Turks Caicos
Tropick of Cancer
HAVANA
CUBA
Isla de Pinos
Guana
Portugos
Windward
Haiti
Santiago
HISPANIOLA
Puerto Rico
Mona Island
Jamaica
St. Bartus
LA CABAÑA ~ 1775
ATLANTIC OCEAN
The Revolution
Steve Luchsinger
HONDURAS
Mosquito Coast
CARIBBEAN SEA

CHAPTER NINE

The Battle of Nassau

(JANUARY - MARCH **1 7 7 6** – NASSAU, BAHAMAS)

*I*nstead of cruising the coasts of the Carolinas, as he was commissioned, Commander Hopkins took it upon himself to order his ships to the British-controlled Bahamas for a raid on the island of New Providence. He intended to seize a large supply of gunpowder stored in the two forts, Montagu and Nassau, that protected the town of Nassau. The Colonial Army had a dire shortage of powder and Hopkins had learned that the Virginia governor and redcoat, Lord Dunmore, had ordered his sailors to take the gunpowder stored in Williamsburg to the Bahamas. That way, the colonists could not steal it—or so Lord Dunmore thought.

Hopkins's fleet was comprised of eight ships: the *Alfred,* the *Hornet,* the *Wasp,* the *Fly,* the *Cabot,* the *Providence,* the *Columbus, and* the *Andrew Doria*—the newly-fitted brig that William and Jack sailed on under Captain Biddle. The group hit rough swells and gale force winds causing the *Fly* and the *Hornet* to separate from the group. When calmer waters finally prevailed, the six remaining warships continued southward, flying not only the Union Jack, but some, like the *Alfred,* sailed under the yellow Gadsden Flag as well. The banner, recently designed by patriot Christopher Gadsden and adopted by the new Colonial Navy, depicted a coiled rattlesnake ready to strike with the words, "Don't Tread on Me," blazoned across it.

Although William and Jack had little local knowledge of the Bahamas, they knew that the small atolls were brimming with British cruisers—pirates being unlikely for that very reason. However, with their little armada of well-armed ships, they felt they had the strength to take on any buccaneers or redcoats that might fall in their path. Should they overtake a British cruiser or merchantman or two, that would mean less provisions for the British. It would also mean more profit for their own crew, even though payment for captured vessels was often delayed. To the men aboard the warships fear was not an option. As far as William and Jack were concerned, they knew that if Fanny had bravely taken on three British merchant ships and the British cruiser, the *Dolphin,* without an ounce of fear—surely, they could do the same.

Hopkins's fleet arrived at the island of Abaco on March 1, 1776, shy of the *Fly* and the *Hornet*, which had badly fouled their riggings, causing major damage. The remaining ships captured two loyalists' sloops—pressing the owners to serve as pilots. A local captain managed to escape and notify the Bahamian governor, Montfort Browne, of the pending attack from the rebels. The little armada's landing forces were transferred to the two captured ships along with the *Providence.* The plan was to enter the port at dawn on March 3 and take control, but they were unaware that the British already knew of their plan.

The *Andrew Doria,* the faster of the ships, found it necessary to lay hove-to, allowing the other ships to catch up. When they arrived and the warning guns at Fort Nassau were heard by the rebels, they rejoined the fleet six miles east of Nassau in Hanover Sound. Regrouping with the *Wasp* for cover they made an unknown landing on a point south of Fort Montagu, taking over the fort with two hundred marines under the command of Samuel Nicholas, and then waited there overnight.

Realizing that the rebels had them outnumbered, the island officials sent a messenger with a truce flag to the fort. The rebels made clear that their mission was to secure the gunpowder stored on the island, and if this demand was not honored they would attack the town. Hopkins then proceeded to pass out leaflets throughout the town with their intentions clearly stated and Nicholas's marines were allowed to occupy the area. The community leaders even gave them the city's keys. During the night however, Governor Browne, being forewarned, had ordered most of the gunpowder removed from the island and boarded onto the *Mississippi Packet*, sending one hundred sixty-two barrels to St. Augustine, Florida, a British stronghold. The ship slipped right past the rebels in the unguarded harbor.

Even though much of the gunpowder was now gone, the marines stayed on the island for two weeks dismantling the guns at the forts and loading as much of the ordnance and weapons as they could find onto their ships, including the remaining thirty-eight barrels of powder. Hopkins pressed one additional Bahamian ship, the *Endeavor*, into service to help carry the extensive munitions they had obtained while Governor Browne was arrested and taken aboard the *Alfred*.

A rampant mosquito-borne virus, known as breakbone fever *(dengue),* infected many of the crew onboard the eight American ships. However, William and Jack had already contracted the disease while in La Cabana prison, which made them immune—sparing them a second bout of it. Unfortunately, there was also an outbreak of smallpox aboard all the ships except the *Andrew Doria*, since Biddle had the foresight to inoculate his crew before leaving Philadelphia. As a result, his ship was used as a hospital for the entire fleet, with William and Jack assisting as makeshift medics. It was a long two weeks for the two men and the foul smell of illness brought back all the dreaded memories of La Cabana.

For the most part, Captain Biddle was kept away from the sick men. No one wanted to risk his health or his presence at the helm. Early one morning before William and Jack began their rounds of administering to their patients, they were summoned to the bridge where Captain Biddle awaited them.

"You're fine men." The young captain put his hands behind his back and smiled. "And I just wanted to personally thank you for the good work you're doing. I do realize you signed up to be sailors on my ship, not medics taking care of so many sick soldiers."

"We work where we are needed," Jack said, shrugging. "If that means fighting the lobsterbacks or tending to those less fortunate than that is what we do."

"Tell me something, boys. Why is it that the two of you don't seem to fall ill like the rest?"

"It's from when Jack and I were incarcerated at La Cabana," William offered.

"In Cuba?!" The captain was obviously surprised to hear this. "And you survived?! I knew you had had a run-in with pirates, but La Cabana. Word has it that's a hellish place that most never leave."

"Yes…we were there for over a year," Jack said.

"While we were there, we suffered from so many different diseases we lost count. Breakbone fever…typhoid to name a few," William added. "I think it made us stronger…immune in some way. Neither of us seem to get sick very often so maybe something good came of the whole nightmare after all."

"You have certainly gone above and beyond the call of duty," Biddle said. "I'm proud to have you as crew. When we get back to a safer harbor I plan on writing commendations for both of you."

"That's very kind, sir," Jack said, smiling.

"You've earned it." Biddle reached out and shook hands with both William and Jack before dismissing them. "Now carry on with your duties and by all means, stay well."

Governor Browne and other island officials were taken prisoner onboard, and the armada set sail for Block Island off Newport Rhode Island. As they reached the northern coastline east of Long Island they spotted and pursued two British ships, the *HMS Hawk* and the *Bolton*, which were both laden with stores, powder, and armament. Those two additional prizes resulted in copious amounts of weapons that would also be given to Washington's army.

As successful as Hopkins had been in avoiding resistance until that point, things changed. On April 6 the lookout aboard the *Andrew Doria* spotted two ships twenty nautical miles southeast of Block Island—one being the *HMS Glasgow*, a grand prize. The *Glasgow* hailed the *Cabot*, which was commanded by Hopkins' son, John Burroughs Hopkins.

When notified of the sighting, Hopkins ordered the fleet to pursue Her Majesty's vessel in hopes of taking her. Unfortunately, a grenade was thrown onto the *Glasgow's* deck by an overzealous sailor, causing the *Glasgow* to immediately engage the American ships in battle. The *Cabot* fired the first heavy broadside into the *Glasgow* and due to the fleets' unprepared positioning they were unable to fight a coordinated effort. Trying to avoid a return attack from the *Glasgow*, the *Cabot* fell off the wind, crossing in front of the *Andrew Doria's* bow, forcing William, who was at the helm, onto a port tack to avoid a T-bone collision with the *Cabot*. This unplanned tack took a furious William out of firing range, leaving only the *Cabot*, the *Alfred* and the *Columbus* to mount an attack on the enemy.

The two ships valiantly pounded the British with their cannons, however, they fared worse than they inflicted. During the battle, major damage was rendered upon the *Cabot,* setting her adrift and wounding Captain John Burroughs Hopkins, and the *Alfred's* tiller line was severed by fire rendering her steering useless. After repositioning his course, William fired successfully at the *Glasgow* with a vicious salvo, making the enemy run from his engagement. Giving chase, the black brig stayed on the enemy's heels as they retreated toward Newport Harbor to avoid being boarded. Hopkins stopped the chase and recalled them to the fleet, his orders infuriating Captain Biddle, William, and Jack who were confident they could have easily taken the vessel as a prize with their fast and heavily armed brig.

All the ships ultimately managed to escape; however, eleven of the American sailors were killed in the battle, which would become known as the Battle of Block Island. Captain Biddle would later describe the conflict as, "helter-skelter", feeling it was poorly planned. The fleet returned successfully to New London, Connecticut on April 8 just in time for William and Jack to find their way back to Beverly with a local fisherman. The Bahamian Governor Browne was later successfully traded for the captured American general William Alexander, Lord Stirling. Hopkins was praised for his successes, however his failure to capture the *Glasgow*, as well as his refusal to follow orders, resulted in several court-martials.

⚓

William and Jack always had mixed feelings about the fact that their wives had not joined them on that journey. All had agreed, however, that Fanny's and Marion's roles within Moll's homegrown spy ring was too important to leave while Boston remained under siege. In the meantime, Colonel Glover provided cover for the three ships Fanny had taken under the guise of Bartholomew Channing. They now sat at anchor off his wharf in Beverly Harbor. The ships' names, of course, were changed to disguise their origins as stolen British merchantmen. Respectively, the *Constance* was changed to the *Fanny*, the *George* was now the *Marion*, and the *Wellington* was renamed the *Mary of Lynn*, in honor of Moll.

Word finally came just before the spring thaw that the three ships would receive their letters of marque any day. Fanny only hoped that William and Jack would return by the time that happened. The repairs on the vessels, progressing at Glover's Wharf, were funded by Samuel Breed's wealthy family for their new venture, the West Indies Shipping Company. The plan was to use the ships for trade purposes in the Caribbean. Their role as merchantmen would provide their needed cover to ultimately succeed as privateering vessels. Fanny arranged for most of the original crewmembers, including the Irishman Terrance Mooney and his friend, Tom O'Hara, and the British-born Edward Finch, to sign on to sail—all wishing that Captain Channing would still have been with them. They, of course, believed the story that Channing had been swept out to sea, never to return, after escaping from Captain Ralph Burnett on board the *Dolphin*.

Channing was a hero to these men, however the British still considered him a pirate and wanted him hung as a criminal if captured. William and Jack encouraged the rumor of Channing's demise, ensuring that the infamous captain would be mainly remembered as a tall tale of the sea. Even Terrance Mooney, who felt indebted to Channing for helping with the burial of his sainted mother, never suspected the truth. Mooney, however, was taken with William Campbell's lovely young wife, and he swore that the spirit of Captain Channing had somehow gotten into her.

Fanny and Marion both found time to look in on Hannah Glover and her children as well as to travel to Beverly Harbor to make sure that all was commencing as contracted on the refit of the ships. They also worked with Samuel Breed at Glover's Wharf. Samuel was in charge of managing the daily efforts and issuing checks for work completed. Since so many naval ships were returning to Beverly with prize vessels, Washington grew worried that the British would soon discover where their ships were being taken and attack the harbor, which was now the new American Navy's home base. Earlier in December 1775, he had dispatched the Marblehead Regiment from Cambridge and stationed it in Beverly to defend the harbor.

For the most part, Fanny was pleased with the progress being made, but not happy with her husband's absence—especially when her mother dropped hints about grandchildren. Fanny and

William wanted children, but they both believed that this was not the time to bring an innocent child into such a chaotic world. Marion and Jack agreed on that count and with the help of one of Moll's potions, the women avoided any unplanned pregnancies. There would be plenty of time for a family once the fighting was over, even if Agnes begged them to reconsider.

"Fanny, child," Agnes complained one afternoon as she and her daughter prepared a meal. "You've gone and done your adventuring. Once William returns from patrol, don't you think it's time to have a baby, or is that another womanly trait that displeases you?"

"Of course, it doesn't displease me, mother." Fanny sighed, stirring the large pot of stew that simmered over the hearth. "But if we are given letters of marque, we have to do our part as privateers for the colonies."

"I don't understand you, Fanny." Agnes frowned, dropping a few peeled potatoes into the pot. "A lady has no place fighting a war and chasing British ships...or for that matter sailing one! Why it's downright disgraceful that any daughter of mine would even consider such nonsense. I blame Moll Pitcher for putting such foolish ideas in your head."

Fanny waved her ladle. "Must I remind you, mother that if it weren't for Moll Pitcher, William would be dead right now and I would have no husband and we wouldn't be standing here talking about babes!"

"It's not just babes." Agnes wiped her hands on her apron in an effort to hide the trembling. "What if something terrible happens to you while you're off on the high seas? What if this time you don't come back to us?"

"I think I've already proven that I can take care of myself." Fanny narrowed her eyes. "Haven't I?"

"You're a stubborn girl." Agnes shook her head. "And if you ever do have children, I may not live long enough to see them because you just may put me in an early grave."

Fanny's face softened. "I promise you, mother, you will meet your grandchildren, each and every one, in due time. Besides, I am not afraid of a battle at sea, but having a baby without you here to help me is terrifying. I can't even bear the thought so you best not be going anywhere!"

"You just remember that the next time you make my heart race so fast I can't catch my breath!"

⚓

Moll and her daughters took turns checking on Mrs. Herbert whenever Marion was away, and Agnes made daily trips to the Herbert cottage to bring fresh vegetables and meat to the old woman. Agnes even grew comfortable enough around Moll to stop in for a cup of tea now and then and to check to see that the future was still on track for her promised grandchildren.

Since early November, General Washington had been quite concerned that most of his army's enlistments would expire on the first of the new year. He had been hard-pressed to assemble an entirely new army before the old one became extinct. He would have to recruit minutemen and local militia who did not have his current army's training and hard-earned discipline. By the middle of December, he had only enlisted five thousand nine hundred seventeen men, knowing that many more were holding out for bonuses. By the end of December, Washington had miraculously signed up nine thousand six hundred fifty men. This number included his new naval troops, which were much harder to fill due to the biting winds and bitter cold sea they would have to endure. Due to the need to entice more enlistments, on November 2, 1775, Congress had resolved that men who served on continental vessels would share in one-half the value of a captured man-of-war as well as one-third of its transport, which gave potential recruits an extra incentive to join the new navy. General

Washington knew he still did not have nearly enough men he required for their planned assault on Boston. Their numbers, however, were great enough to counter a British offensive and Dorchester Heights would be the perfect place to occupy.

In the midst of the madness, General Washington had received a poem written by a young dark-skinned girl, Phillis Wheatley. She called it 'His Excellency General Washington'. He was so touched by her words that he took the time to personally write her a letter inviting her to Cambridge where she was graciously welcomed.

⚓

On March 7 1776, just days after Moll's meeting with General Howe, the Americans, under the command of General Washington, worked overnight to strengthen their fortification at Dorchester Heights, which overlooked the city and the Port of Boston. Washington's objective was to quietly erect fortifications against the British Army and catch them unawares. From this elevated vantage point, the Continental Army could fire upon the enemy below, and the redcoats would be hard-pressed to retaliate as their cannons could never reach such high ground.

In the dark of night, General John Thomas and his two thousand men quietly marched up Dorchester Heights with tools and fortifications. Washington himself was there to oversee the endeavor and to encourage his men. He also had enough boats and floating batteries prepared to carry three thousand of his troops. Under silence and secrecy, Washington's men moved the cannons and other heavy artillery that Henry Knox had delivered from Fort Ticonderoga into place on Dorchester. They used oxen, timber chandeliers, and fascine (bundles of wood held together with wood braces) to haul their equipment up a hill overlooking the city of Boston.

The men cut trees and used them to build walls for protection from British artillery. They also laid bales of hay in front of their cannons to minimize the noise. They even filled large barrels with rock, intending them as weapons to roll down the hill against attacking British soldiers.

The next morning, the Continental Army began its surprise attack on the British in Boston. The astonished General Howe is reported to have said: "My God, these fellows have done more work in one night than I could make my army do in three months." The barrage continued, forcing Howe and his officers to make a decision—stay and fight or retreat from their occupation of the city. But Howe knew that somehow he had to disarm the colonists and end the insurgence once and for all. He planned an attack.

Howe's plan, however, was ultimately foiled by an Act of God when a late winter snowstorm hit the east coast. Inclement weather and snow squelched Howe's counteroffensive. Howe then decided to save his army and abandon the siege on Boston. By mid-March, as the weather grew more favorable, the English troops began moving out. On March 17, 1776, the Royal Navy was forced to evacuate the British Army and formally withdraw from Boston. General Washington prevented the redcoats from burning the city by agreeing to let them go unharmed as long as they went peacefully. He did, however, capture several British supply ships from the outer harbor.

Moll Pitcher, along with many other locals, came to the harbor that day to watch the British soldiers take their leave. Just as the lobsterbacks were boarding the ships that would carry them off, she eyed the general and called out. "General Howe!"

He turned in her direction at the sound of his name, squinting in the sunlight.

"Don't forget what I said!" Moll shouted with a wave. "Make sure your men have good rest!"

Howe tipped his hat in reply, then boarded.

General Howe and his army sailed out of Boston Harbor heading for Halifax, Nova Scotia, with a fleet of one hundred twenty ships carrying more than eleven thousand British soldiers and one thousand loyalists who fled for their lives. After eleven long months, the Siege of Boston was finally over and the Americans cautiously reclaimed the city. It was a decisive win for General Washington and the Continental Army.

Afraid the British would now attack New York, Washington left Cambridge and moved his army to Manhattan, marking the start of the New York and New Jersey campaigns, as Moll's intelligence from Howe indicated.

Although no further military action occurred in Boston, the city remained the center for Revolutionary Naval and marine activity. The ports of Boston, Marblehead, and Beverly continued as vital locations where warships and privateers were fitted, and all of Washington's fortifications in the Boston area were maintained for the war's duration.

CHAPTER TEN

Anger and Rebellion

(1 7 6 9 – 1 7 7 0 – LYNN, MASSACHUSETTS)

ack before the siege of Boston had become a crisis for the colonists, they did their best to survive the harrowing winter of 1769 with its record snowfall. The good people of Massachusetts looked forward to spring despite the seven hundred uninvited British soldiers who patrolled the streets of Boston to ensure that the colonists behaved during the early days of what would soon to be classified as their insurgence. While the Americans grew accustomed to the sight of redcoats in their city, their presence remained unwelcome. Quite familiar with her famous reputation, many of these lobsterbacks were eager to consult with the great psychic of Lynn, since many of their superiors had taken counsel from the world-renowned seer. Moll, however, was not seeing many customers during this time. Devastated not only by the fatal marine losses from Marblehead, she struggled with the death of her remaining and youngest brother, Richard.

Moll hadn't needed a vision or a dream to know that Richard had been ailing. His coughing fits from consumption rattled his body and his face grew more ashen every day. Dr. Burchstead did his best to care for Richard, and Moll made up her finest elixirs, but nothing seemed to help. Gasping for breath, he passed away in his sister's arms on a bitterly cold winter night as icy winds rattled the windowpanes. He had died at the young age of twenty-nine. The little house at the base of High Rock once again went into mourning and Moll's depression deepened. Serving tea to local girls hoping for news about prospective husbands no longer seemed important, nor were neighbors seeking help to find a lost purse.

With both her brothers gone, the house now belonged to Moll and, to her credit, she tried to make it a happy place for her husband and four children, but it was a struggle. Some afternoons when her house was quiet, she raged at her grandfather for passing on such a crippling skillset. Robert often reminded her that she possessed a gift, but she proclaimed that lately it felt more like a curse. While she temporarily stopped reading tea leaves, she still sold potions to the locals when they came to her with real, as well as imaginary angsts. Moll would put on a pleasant enough facade and always sent them off with a word of encouragement and hope. Even though her heart wasn't in it, she knew she needed to keep her clientele. After all, making ends meet was a daily challenge for the Pitcher family and they needed any extra income that she could bring in.

Before the ground could properly thaw, a British captain arrived at Moll's door one sunny afternoon at the end of February 1770.

"I'm not presently taking customers," Moll firmly told him before he had a chance to speak.

"Please, Mrs. Pitcher," his voice held a hint of an Irish brogue, "Sarah Hutchinson thought I should see you. She tells me that you helped her once when she needed it."

Moll remembered the frightened young girl who had called upon her almost five years before and her demeanor softened. "And who might you be?"

"I'm Captain Thomas Preston." He offered his hand. "And I would appreciate it if you could spare me some of your time. I can pay you for your efforts."

Moll took his hand and suddenly, the room went dark despite the brightness of the day. She heard several shots and smelled gun powder as it lingered in the air. Gasping for breath, she placed her free hand across her brow in an effort to clear her head.

"Mrs. Pitcher?" She heard Preston's voice in the distance and felt his hand squeeze hers. "Are you alright?"

Moll couldn't speak.

"Maybe I should come back another time." Preston tried to pull his hand away, but Moll's grip tightened.

She gulped for air. "No, please stay. Come in and I'll make some tea before my eldest two come home from school and the little ones wake up from their naps."

"If you're sure—" Preston hesitated.

"Yes." Moll stepped aside to let him in. "It's important we talk."

Preston removed his hat and sat at the Queen Anne table while Moll quietly prepared tea.

"Are you sure you're all right, ma'am?" Preston asked once again.

"Yes, but I need to know why you've come here." Moll set the steaming brew before him.

"Mrs. Pitcher, I must be honest." He placed his hands around the cup to warm them. "It is quite obvious to me that the people of Boston do not want the king's soldiers in their city. We are only following orders, but they dislike us and make no amends for it."

"The colonists are unhappy with the Crown," Moll reminded him. "Your presence serves as a constant reminder of their many differences."

Preston leaned in towards Moll. "And their discontent is what concerns me. I am worried about my men if there is any unrest."

"Drink your tea…then we shall see what the leaves tell us," Moll insisted. She watched him closely as he lifted the cup and downed the steaming brew in a few gulps. He had a handsome face and beneath that red coat, she sensed a man who did his best to be fair. Moll tipped the cup, then closed her eyes trying to prepare herself for what she might see. Quietly she studied the leaves. "There's trouble ahead," she said, seeing a gun and a devil.

"What kind of trouble?"

"A crowd with bad intentions. Violence. Death. You and your men will soon face terrible woes if you aren't careful."

"I don't understand." Preston was clearly upset.

"There will be circumstances beyond your control," Moll tried to explain.

"And what shall I do to avoid this trouble?"

"Unless you leave the colonies, this trouble cannot be avoided."

"But I can't leave unless I am told to."

"Then whatever you do," Moll whispered, "do not order your men to fire. It will be the only thing that saves you."

⚓

Within a week of Preston's visit to Moll, a young wigmaker's apprentice, Edward Garrick, taunted a British captain, John Goldfinch, about failing to pay his bill to the wigmaker. Goldfinch ignored the boy who was not aware that the debt had been settled the day before, but Garrick continued his harassment. Private Hugh White, a redcoat on guard duty at the customs house on King Street, heard the trouble. He chided the boy for insulting Goldfinch whom he believed to be a gentleman, but the boy persisted. White lost his patience and struck Garrick with his musket.

An angry crowd soon gathered and yelled even more insults at White who called for help. His superior, Captain Thomas Preston, arrived at the scene intending to escort White back to the barracks and alleviate the trouble, but by now the crowd had turned into an unruly mob. Total chaos ensued. Someone lobbed a club that hit one of the redcoats. In retaliation, the soldier yelled

'Damn you, fire!' and after a moment's hesitation the soldiers did exactly that. The entire incident lasted no more than five minutes, but three colonists were killed that night: former slave and dockworker, Crispus Attucks; rope maker Samuel Gray; and sailor James Caldwell. Seventeen-year-old Samuel Maverick died the next morning and two weeks later Irishman Patrick Carr succumbed from his wounds. Another man, Christopher Monk, was seriously hurt. He died a decade later and his death would be attributed to that night of violence.

Preston rallied his troops and Governor Thomas Hutchinson was summoned. He calmed the crowd by assuring them that he would seek justice. True to his word, Hutchinson arrested Captain Preston and eight of his men the very next morning. After consulting with the Sons of Liberty, Boston attorneys John Adams and Josiah Quincy, Jr. agreed to defend the redcoats. As men of honor, they believed that even the lobsterbacks deserved a fair trial. It was decided that two separate trials should be held—one for Captain Preston and the other for his men. Preston's defense was based on the fact that he never gave the order to fire. Several eyewitnesses claimed that he did indeed utter the word 'Fire!' while others who were there claimed he did not. It was impossible to prove exactly what happened and, because of the discrepancies in eyewitness testimony, Preston was acquitted by the jury. But only Moll knew for sure that he would have never given the order to fire. Of the remaining eight soldiers, six were found not guilty and two were convicted of manslaughter as the jury was convinced that they had fired into the crowd. As punishment, these two had the letter 'M' branded on their right thumbs.

Despite the outcome, however, the colonists were stirred and the incident now known as the Boston Massacre was a turning point in their dissatisfaction with the Crown. Paul Revere did not help matters when he engraved a picture that he called 'The Bloody Massacre on King Street'. It depicted a troop of bloodthirsty British soldiers callously firing upon a crowd of innocent Bostonians. It was hardly a realistic representation of the actual event, but the engraving was seen throughout the colonies. The sight of it enraged the Americans, making the etching an important piece of propaganda in support of a potential rebellion.

⚓

By the time the trials were all said and done, Moll had resumed her readings on a steady basis, realizing that her services were sorely needed in these volatile times. Neighbors once again called on her for help and paying British soldiers of all ranks visited her home. Potions were sold to would-be lovers and elixirs were administered to those who felt poorly. The Pitcher home was known far and wide for its hospitality and kind assistance to a sundry of needs.

The afternoon of January 9, 1771 was cold and dismal in Lynn. Dark clouds threatened another snowfall. The bone-chilling air stung the cheeks and noses of anyone who ventured outside. A fresh layer of snow covered the roads and settled along the tree branches outlining each in a sleeve of white. With more snow to come, the branches would soon grow heavy and break, harming anyone or anything unlucky enough to be in their way.

After feeding her children lunch, young Rebecca Hadley twisted her blond hair into a knot and reached for her heaviest black cloak.

"Maybe you should stay home, my sweet," her husband, Thomas, said, picking up the baby who was beginning to fuss.

"I promised my sister, I'd come." She placed the hood over her head. "She's due with the baby any day now. It's her first and with mother gone, she needs me."

"But it's so cold and it appears another storm's coming. Maybe you should wait."

"I won't be long." Rebecca first hugged the squirming baby girl and then her husband. "She's just across Mill Pond and I'll be back in time for dinner." She beckoned her two small boys over and kissed them as well. "I expect you both to behave while I'm gone and keep your father out of trouble." They giggled as she opened the front door and a gust of cold wind rushed through the room.

Thomas, rocking to and fro with the baby, watched his wife from the window as she disappeared down the street, trying to quell the apprehension that suddenly washed over him.

As Rebecca Hadley walked toward Mill Pond, Moll Pitcher was tending to her own children. Ruth, the eldest, was now almost eight and a little headstrong. Becky, two years younger, was already showing a fascination for Moll's unusual line of work. Three-year-old Lydia was a dainty little thing whose favorite companion was her little brother, John. For the most part, the older girls doted on John and loved to spoil him as much as they could—despite their mother's protests.

"Stop babying your brother," Moll often scolded her daughters. "You'll make him into a lazy no-account if you keep doing everything for him." Suddenly, Moll's face paled and she stopped talking. Her breath came in short shallow gasps. She clutched at her chest as a wave of dread washed through her very soul. And as quick as it had come, the feeling disappeared. Moll's breathing returned to normal and the color returned to her cheeks, but she couldn't shake the feeling of something terrible to come. Unfortunately, something had already happened. Moll grew sure of it. For the next several days, the snow came down hard and fast, blanketing Lynn and the surrounding area—locking most residents in their homes.

As the winter blizzard continued, the older children stayed home from school and Moll busied herself with their lessons so they wouldn't fall behind. As she sat reading to them, the wind whistled and rattled though the windows. It was so loud they almost didn't hear someone knocking at the door. Moll stopped reading and peered outside wondering who could possibly be out in this terrible weather. Poor Thomas Hadley was near hysterics as he stumbled into the house, begging for the psychic's help.

"Rebecca has been missing for days!" Thomas stood covered in snow and shaking from both cold and fear. "My brothers and I have been looking everywhere, but we can't find her. She's out there somewhere in this terrible storm! Please, Moll, can you help us? She'll die in this weather. Can you help us save her?"

Moll herded her children into her bedroom, as was her custom when callers came asking for help. She put Ruth in charge and closed the door.

"Give me your hand." Moll reached out for Thomas once the children were gone.

"Please, Moll, I am at my wits' end with worry," he said, barely able to speak as he tried to choke back his sobs. "The boys keep asking for their mother. I…I don't know what to tell them."

Moll took Hadley's cold hand and closed her eyes, remembering the ominous feelings that had come over her the week before. The icy air returned, making her gasp as a sharp pain sliced through her head. It was all she could do to stay on her feet.

"What is it, Moll?" The man held tight to her hand. "What do you see?"

"I'm sorry, Thomas, but Rebecca is at peace. She's beyond harm now."

"No, Moll!" Thomas' dark eyes spilled over with tears. "It can't be. If you just help me find her—"

"Listen to me, Thomas," Moll interrupted him. "Rebecca is gone. She slipped on the ice and fell into the water. I promise you she didn't suffer, but you'll find her near Mill Pond."

"I came here for help!" Thomas raged. "My children need their mother!"

"Your children need you now," Moll said quietly. "And Rebecca needs a proper burial. Pull yourself together and go to Mill Pond once the storm clears. I assure you that Rebecca is waiting there."

"She must be so cold." He nervously ran his thin fingers through his black hair. "I must take a blanket to cover her."

"Go and seek your brothers' help. Take them to the pond's east side, and I'll come by to check on you and the children."

Rebecca Hadley's body was pulled from the stream just above Mill Pond at the end of January when the snow cleared enough for the search to resume. She had slipped and drowned while attempting to cross the icy waters. She was twenty-four years old and left behind three children who mourned her passing, along with her heartbroken husband. Moll continued to look in on the Hadleys throughout that spring and summer. Her heart especially ached for the baby who would grow up with no memory whatsoever of her mother.

⚓

Moll also kept a continued interest in Fanny Campbell. By now, the girl had blossomed into an attractive young woman who remained devoted to William Lovell, the son of her father's fishing partner. Fanny still avoided Moll at all costs. Moll understood her fears, but she also knew that fate had plans for the young girl who had always yearned for adventure. One day soon, she would come seeking Moll's help and Moll would be ready. In the meantime, Moll conducted readings for her neighbors, the British soldiers who came calling, and she sold potions to those in need of a little helpful magic.

When the weather permitted, she traveled to Marblehead where she sometimes conducted her business at Black Joe's Tavern, reading tea leaves and offering encouragement to those who needed it. Auntie Creese always sent her home with a boxful of

Joe Froggers for the children. Moll often called on the Glovers as well. She brought herbal medicines to Hannah who, despite poor health, was a devoted wife and mother. It pleased Moll that her dearest friend, Johnny, had such a faithful partner. She reminded him time and again of Hannah's fragile state and gently scolded him for his many absences from home.

A record snowfall covered the area in March 1772. According to town records, between March 11 and 20, thirty-four inches of snow fell. In some areas, the drifts measured nearly five feet. While the residents of Lynn and the surrounding towns dug themselves out, Samuel Adams laid out his plan for a Committee of Correspondence, which would help the colonies unite, communicate, and address issues that affected them all. One such concern was the Tea Act that became effective in the spring of 1773.

Prior to the passage of the Tea Act, colonists were buying less-expensive tea from the Dutch. The British considered this 'smuggling' and in order to help out the financially struggling East India Company, which now had more tea in their warehouses than they could handle, Parliament agreed that the company could export their tea from London duty-free. In essence, the Crown gave the East India Company a monopoly on the North American tea trade. In return, the colonists would have to pay a hefty tax in order to enjoy the brew.

It didn't take the psychic powers of Moll Pitcher to see that Americans were not about to tolerate another mandatory tax from the king. Moll's clairvoyant senses were on high alert, however, when William Lovell, Jack Herbert, and Samuel Breed set sail from Boston Harbor on the *Royal Kent* shortly after news of the Tea Act came to New England. The three young men were looking for adventure, but they had no idea of the horrors that awaited them as they made their way to the the warmer waters of the West Indies. Moll knew the time would soon come when Fanny Campbell would seek her help.

⚓

Four months after William Lovell's departure, Benjamin Franklin wrote 'Rules By Which A Great Empire May Be Reduced To A Small One'. The satirical piece admonished the British for mistreating the colonists with unfair taxes that financially benefited only England—not America. He put into words what was on the minds of many and stirred up disgruntled feelings. An unhappy restlessness loomed over the colonies and they vowed that English tea would no longer be a part of their daily routine.

Another kind of restlessness claimed Fanny Campbell. With no word from William Lovell, day by day she grew concerned for his safety. She drummed up her courage and on a cold November afternoon, she paid a visit to the psychic of Lynn. Moll was ready for her. She assured Fanny that William was alive, but now was not the time to take action. Instead, she instructed Fanny to learn all she could about the sea and that is exactly what Fanny did, studying books and spending as much time as possible on her father's fishing vessel, *Love of the Sea.*

About the same time that Fanny called upon Moll, four ships left England heading to America. The *Dartmouth*, the *Eleanor*, the *Beaver*, and the *William* each carried more than one hundred chests of East India Company tea that would be subject to the new act. The *William* was lost at sea in a storm, but the other three ships made it to Boston Harbor. The first to arrive was the *Dartmouth* on November 28, followed by the *Eleanor* on December 2. The last ship to reach the harbor was the *Beaver*, which sailed into port on December 15.

On the 16 of December, a town meeting was held in Lynn and the following resolutions passed:

1) That the people of the British American Colonies, by their constitution of government, have a right to freedom, and an exemption from every degree of oppression and slavery.

2) That it is an essential right of free men to have the disposal of their own property and not to be taxed by any power over which they have no control.

3) That the parliamentary duty laid upon tea landed in America, is, in fact, a tax upon Americans, without their consent.

4) That the late act of parliament allowing the East India Company to send their tea to America on their own account, was artfully framed, for the purpose of enforcing and carrying into effect the oppressive act of Parliament, imposing a duty upon teas imported into America; and is a fresh proof of the settled and determined designs of the ministers to deprive us of liberty, and reduce us to slavery.

5) That we highly disapprove of the landing and selling of such teas in America, and will not suffer any teas, subjected to a parliamentary duty, to be landed or sold in this town and that we stand ready to assist our brethren of Boston or elsewhere, whenever our aid shall be required, in repelling all attempts to land or sell any teas poisoned with a duty.

That same night, Robert Pitcher, William Lovell, Sr., and Henry Campbell joined a group of colonists disguised as Native Americans. The men carried axes and climbed aboard the three British ships docked at Griffin's Wharf. They hacked open three hundred forty-two wooden chests and dumped forty-six tons of tea into Boston Harbor. No ships were damaged in the process, no other cargo touched, and no injuries incurred. The colonists even swept the decks clean before they departed. No damage was done other than a broken padlock, and that was replaced the very next day.

Moll Pitcher was pleased that her husband had taken part in such a rebellious enterprise. If women had been allowed, she would have gone herself and showed those Brits just what Americans thought of their tea. Even when clumps of tea washed up along the shore, they were burned to ensure that no one might dry them out for personal use. When one filled trunk was found, it was taken to Boston Commons and set on fire, sending a clear message to the lobsterbacks that the colonists weren't happy.

And the anger spilled over into 1774, when an unruly crowd from Boston tarred and feathered John Malcolm, the British customs collector. Malcolm, a vocal loyalist, was disliked by the colonists and often faced verbal abuse, but on January 25, 1774, that abuse turned physical. Shoemaker and patriot George Ewes found Malcolm threatening a young boy with his cane. When Ewes came to the child's defense, Malcolm knocked him out with his walking stick. That night, a mob pulled the customs collector from his home, stripped him to his waist and then tarred and feathered him. Malcolm survived, but he gave up his post and returned to England.

When news of the colonists' uprising reached the Crown, Parliament passed the Intolerable Acts, which took away the Americans' rights to self-govern. Next, they instituted the Boston Port Act, which effectively shut down Boston Harbor. None of these new rulings endeared the king to the colonists. They only served to unite the colonists in their quest for liberty.

One thing that did please the Americans was the removal of General Hutchinson from his position as Governor of Massachusetts Bay. He was replaced by General Thomas Gage who sailed into Boston Harbor on May 13, 1774. The locals were glad to see Hutchinson off, but they gave Gage a cool reception. Eventually, their feelings turned even icier as he officially established a naval blockade around the Port of Boston. No one was allowed in or out. All goods coming to and from the city had to travel through other smaller ports such as Marblehead, Salem, or Lynn. Boston relied heavily on its port for its very livelihood and quickly suffered a serious economic crisis. Businesses closed and jobs became scarce. Many desperate people moved away as Gage enforced each new act.

CHAPTER ELEVEN

Changing Gender Again

(APRIL 1 7 7 6 – LYNN, MASSACHUSETTS)

*W*illiam Lovell and Jack Herbert arrived back in Lynn in early April aboard the *Andrew Doria*. Biddle did his best to recruit William and Jack back aboard his ship for his next mission patrolling the coastline from Connecticut to Virginia, but, since their letters of marque were ready, Jack and William chose to sail on their own ships to the West Indies. Their goal—to obtain munitions and gunpowder from one of the Danish or Dutch islands, which so far had remained neutral as merchants during the war between England and America.

Those neutral islands relied on trade with the Americans as well as the British and they felt no need to choose sides and ban trade with either country. Biddle valued William and Jack as crew and was disappointed they were unable to join him again, but he understood that with their own letters of marque they could add that much more value to the Continental Army with three new ships for their growing fleet of privateers. Besides, Fanny and Marion wouldn't hear of them leaving again without their wives—disguised as men of course—even though the men tried to talk them into staying safe at home.

As both strong-minded women pointed out, they were likely in more danger carrying messages for Moll as spies, than sailing aboard the *Fanny* and the *Marion* with their men protecting them. Should the two women be caught by the British Army while delivering messages, they would likely be hung for espionage. As Fanny reasoned, she would rather die in a sword fight next to her beloved than at the end of a rope at the hands of the British. Marion was quick to second that regard, putting an end to the debate.

The women would be part of the crew. Fanny would serve as first mate under William and since Marion was not a seasoned sailor, she would navigate the galley onboard her namesake with Jack at the helm. It was her intention to keep the men aboard well-fed. William and Fanny would, of course, have Edward Finch and Tom O'Hara aboard, knowing they were loyal, reliable seaman.

So, Fanny and Marion sought out Moll's help to aid them in dreaming up their newest, convincing male personas. Fanny could take no chances in resurrecting the now deceased Captain Bartholomew Channing, since he was still considered a wanted criminal by the British Navy. Even William and Jack agreed that a new disguise would be in the best interest of all. It didn't take Moll long to create a new believable charade for Fanny, however Marion was so fair and beautiful it would take some doing to hide her maidenly attributes as a truly convincing man. Moll avoided darkening Fanny's skin this time since Fanny's time spent at sea and on the road delivering messages had created natural coloring for her face and hands. Marion, however, required a light application of silver nitrate to make her, or him, appear as a seasoned seaman from the West Indies, as well as adding a dark tint to her hair. Although she wouldn't require too much "seasoning" disguised as a cook down in the galley.

Moll managed to arrange documents through her contacts to provide the two women with the proper sailing credentials— Marion becoming Jean LeDee, a French merchant sailor from the small French island of Saint Barthélemy, in the Leeward Islands. After all, she had studied French and could be a great asset in dealing with any French islands from which they might wish to acquire provisions or cargo. Her accent was amazingly believable and even impressed Fanny, the true master of disguise. Her cover story was that LeDee's family had been members of the early French mariners who'd founded a settlement on the island in the mid-seventeenth century.

The island of St. Barth's, as it was known, had eventually

proven itself an economic failure as a spice-producing island or trade port for King Louis XVI, thus he failed to provide protection for the small French colony, which made it prey for the local pirates as well as the British. The island had eventually been sold to the French West Indian Trading Company and later became part of the colony of Guadeloupe. Jean LeDee's story was that he'd sailed to America aboard a French merchantman delivering provisions to the Continental Army and was looking for a new ship, offering his local knowledge of the Leeward and Virgin Islands trade routes.

Due to her red locks, Fanny was given the name Franklin Connors, a Scottish fishing captain who had come from Scotland with his father some years before. His story was that although Scotland was part of a political union with England forming the United Kingdom, Connors despised the British and was thrilled to be sailing for the colonists. Fanny quickly started practicing her Scottish brogue and brushing up on Scottish history and its participation to date in the new American war. She made numerous visits to the library to comb through recent newspapers to see what contributions her supposed countrymen had made to their efforts, if any. What she'd learned was that Patrick Henry, who'd shouted, "Give me liberty or give me death!" at the Second Virginia Convention in Richmond, the year before, was of Scottish blood, as was Henry Knox, who'd organized and led the Noble Train of Artillery from Fort Ticonderoga in New York to Boston.

Another Scot, John Paul Jones, had been appointed first lieutenant of the *Alfred*. William had brought back stories of Jones from the battle of Nassau and the battle of Block Island. He had been greatly impressed by Jones' brazen command and knew he'd go far in America's new navy. Jones had fled to America from Scotland due to trouble with the British and had been quick to join the Americans in their fight for freedom.

Samuel Breed stayed on at the new port in Beverly to continue running the West Indies Shipping Company—managing the incoming bounty of privateers' spoils from captured British ships. Those spoils included the ships as well as captured seamen who wished to sail with the newly formed Continental Navy. Those who chose to remain loyal to their homeland were graciously escorted ashore in the closest safe port that was not protected by the British Navy. After all, the last thing the Americans wanted was for the British to learn about the Continental Navy's privateer stronghold at Glover's Wharf. So, they were cautious not to bring any questionable sailors to the secret home base of America's new navy.

Moll aided Samuel in hiding and dispersing many of the captured munitions with her little network and the help of Fanny and Marion to carry messages. Moll decided that if she were to lose Fanny and Marion as her primary messengers, she would enlist the young neighbor boys, Elmore and Rupert, who'd always helped her bury munitions in the wolf pits deep in the Lynn Woods. She knew she could trust them and she felt they were far too young to serve the Continental Army as soldiers. Their participation in these important affairs would make them feel as if they were playing their part to aid the patriots in winning the war. Fanny and Marion took the young men with them on several of their last deliveries and taught them how to casually blend in and avoid attracting the suspicion of the British Army, or any loyalists. The four were nothing more than a group of young men traveling on their wagon selling vegetables and herbs from their Lynn gardens.

Fanny had enlisted her father, Henry Campbell, and William's father, William Lovell Sr., to use their fishing vessel, *Love of the Sea*, to carry Moll's and the Sons of Liberty's messages from port to port along the coast. They traveled as far as it was practically safe to fish those waters and avoid attracting the attention of the British. After all, the British didn't own the ocean nor the fish in it—at least not as far as they were concerned. Upon the start of the Revolution, cod was king and the Campbells and Lovells not only supplied salted cod to their trade routes, as well as to the army, but they often secretly carried munitions south to provide the army with much-needed weapons. By day they delivered fish and by night, munitions. Sarah and Agnes fretted terribly when the men were away on a delivery, but they worked relentlessly cleaning and drying fish for their husbands to trade. Due to their industrious business and hard work, the two families flourished financially during a time that many others found it hard to put food upon their tables. It was especially difficult for the wives and children of soldiers and sailors left at home to fend for themselves. That's where Agnes and Moll grew close—aiding those families with food for their hungry children. Moll always made certain to render her visions of Fanny and William's safety when they were at sea to Agnes, lending her friend much comfort in knowing that they would indeed return to them.

Fanny had learned through Glover's network, that William's friend, Hugh Montgomery, had been given the command of the brig the *Nancy*. So, William, Jack and the women laid out their plan—follow the *Nancy*, which had left some weeks before in March, to the West Indies. The *Nancy* had originally been a British merchantman captured the year before by John Manley, and it provided several thousand muskets with over thirty tons of musket shot and seven thousand round shot for cannon. An American Financer of the war, Robert Morris of the Pennsylvania Committee of Safety, had recently chartered the brig for Congress and hired Montgomery to sail to the Virgin Islands in the West Indies to purchase much-needed gunpowder. Montgomery had been assigned specifically to sail the *Nancy* to the Spanish island of Puerto Rico in the Virgin Islands and the small Danish islands of Saint Thomas and Saint Croix to supply munitions to the Continental Army.

Samuel's wealthy family had generously funded the start of their newly formed enterprise—the West Indies Shipping Company—and it was allotted enough investment funds to fill its three ships with munitions and provisions to sell to the Continental Army back at home. Of course, should they be lucky enough to seize one or two British ships full of weapons along the way it would serve as icing on the cake.

When the men returned in early April, the women had everything prepared for their first foray in their new venture. The detailed planning and ingenuity by their wives and partner Samuel Breed, impressed William and Jack. They not only had their letters of marque and documents ready, but a strong, reliable, and skilled crew for all three ships. The young boys, Josh and Levi, that William had saved from the *Crimson Blade,* were hired to man the galley of the *Mary of Lynn.* William praised the boys for all the help they'd been to Fanny and Samuel in readying the ships for their passage. On Moll's recommendation, they had also found a qualified captain named Joseph Clement for the *Mary of Lynn,* Moll's namesake. The man was a skilled seaman as well as a good friend of William's. They even had the ships fully fitted out and provisioned—ready to sail as soon as the men had time to visit with their families and prepare themselves for their next adventure. It was spring and there were nor'easters still blowing steady so it would be a relatively quick trip to reach the Virgin Islands—barring any trouble with the British or pirates, God forbid. At that point, there was little difference between the two types of seafaring scoundrels—both species of criminal now classified as fair game to the colonists.

Of course, there was no way the four would sail without Moll's visions and blessings, so they made a visit to her cottage for the psychic of Lynn's seafaring reading to see if their voyage would be successful and safe, or a doomed one. Moll and Marion sat at Moll's table with Jack and William standing behind them.

They passed the blue-rimmed teacup around for all to drink from the psionic brew. Then Moll turned the cup the required number of times and inverted the last teaspoon of liquid and leaves into the saucer. Quietly, she studied the remains of the leaves scattered throughout the cup and let out a long sigh.

"What is it Moll…what do you hear?" exclaimed Fanny hearing concern in Moll's expression.

"Well dear, I see a very prosperous voyage for all including the American Army from the fruits of your labor. She paused looking directly at William. "However, you will have to confront the enemy in order to save my namesake."

"You mean they will capture the *Mary of Lynn*?" William questioned, concerned.

"Yes, and it will seem hopeless. However there are two very young men aboard who will ultimately save the ship from the British as well as themselves from a life of slavery."

"You mean Josh and Levi," Marion said with certainty.

"Yes, the boys will prove to be brave and loyal crewmen. They owe their lives to you, William, and they will prove themselves worthy of your respect and kindness."

The four paused, digesting Moll's words.

"Is it safe for us to sail on the full moon and the high tide?" asked William.

"Yes, it is a fortuitus time to begin your journey, but you must stay vigilant and do not let the *Mary* lag behind you. However, you will not be able to do battle for her when the time comes. It will be the cunning imagination of the two boys that will outsmart the British crew."

The four sailors sat quietly for a moment digesting her prediction.

"Will we capture any British ships along the way?" asked Jack.

"You will capture your attackers should the boys succeed in their effort to undo the British crew and outwit them."

The four left Moll's with both confidence and concern that afternoon. And against Agnes's and Sarah's wishes, the three merchant ships sailed out of Beverly Harbor early the next brisk spring morning—past Salem Neck into the Salem Sound. William's local knowledge of the area provided them a safe exit from a port that most British ships would not attempt to navigate. From offshore the safe harbor did not appear navigable due to the many rocks and shoals blocking its entrance. The draft of the ships required a deep channel out and only the local fishermen knew the waters well enough to safely maneuver a large vessel—or a small one for that matter—into the harbor. They hoisted their canvas and sailed out through the narrow cut between Little Misery Island to the north and Baker's Island and House Ledge shoal to the south, confident of a steady wind of fourteen knots that morning as the sun climbed out of the golden ocean to greet a new day. Aside from a few mares' tales in the sky, their weather and wind prospects looked promising for a strong steady wind to carry them quickly to their destination, more than twelve hundred nautical miles to the south. William estimated that at an average of five to six knots it would take around twelve to fourteen days to make it to the Virgin Islands. They would arrive sometime in mid-May barring battles or hurricanes. Battles were not something that could be discounted or predicted; however, William was confident that it was too early in the season for a tropical storm to hamper their passage.

⚓

Upon his return, Biddle had immediately begun preparations for the *Andrew Doria* to return to sea on a reconnaissance cruise ordered by Commander Esek Hopkins. He had been commissioned by the Continental Congress the previous December as

Commander-in-Chief of the navy and Biddle served directly under him. The *Andrew Doria* was ready to sail shortly after mid-afternoon on the day of her arrival, however, light wind, fog, and a grounding at low tide kept the brig from sailing until April 9. It was not a smooth start to his cruise and Biddle had an ominous feeling, wishing he had consulted the psychic of Lynn before he sailed. On April 12, a cry from his watch reported the sighting of a sail near Montauk Point, New York and a chase ensued with the *Andrew Doria* on the heels of a schooner which flew British colors. After an hour's chase, Biddle was abeam of the *John and Joseph,* which was on its way to Halifax, Nova Scotia. The ship was originally owned by Nathaniel Shaw of New London, but the schooner had been captured by the British frigate, *Scarborough,* off the coast of Georgia. Biddle and his crew made quick work of recapturing the *John and Joseph* and headed back to New London, New Hampshire with her, reaching port by mid-April. While there, Biddle unloaded the ordnance from Nassau and careened the ship, grounding her broadside on a steep beach, to scrape the barnacles from her bottom. Relieving her of the unwanted growth would surely add several knots of speed to her, making her more agile and nimble while navigating in chase with the enemy, or, fleeing from them for that if that be the case. After waiting for the high tide, Biddle was able to refloat her on May 4 to join Hopkins once again, who had continued on with the rest of his fleet to Providence, Rhode Island.

A few days later, on May 19, Hopkins issued Biddle further orders to sail, escorting the *Cabot.* Within hours of leaving they found themselves running from the Royal Navy frigate *Cerberus.* Separating the two ships, the faster *Andrew Doria* turned south, quickly losing her pursuer. The *Cabot* sailed east to the safety of Nantucket Shoals. On the twenty-first, Biddle spotted and captured the sloop, *Two Friends,* which was filled with rum, salt, sugar, and molasses from the Virgin Islands—bound for Liverpool. Installing his own crew aboard and locking up the British crew, Biddle sent her to Newport, Rhode Island to be sold as privateer goods.

He continued his mission on a northeasterly course in search of British transports with reinforcements for the British Army. He proceeded to capture, with little effort, the *Oxford* from Glasgow and the *Crawford* from Scotland—both carrying, not only troops, but the wives and children of some of the officers and soldiers. Placing his own crew onboard, the three ships headed home in convoy until five British ships appeared on the horizon from the northwest. Once again Biddle scattered his ships and never saw his two prizes again.

Escorting the *Fly,* Biddle headed out to sea ten days later bound for New London—arriving the afternoon of June 26 after taking another prize, the merchantman, *Nathaniel and Elizabeth.* The ship's hold was filled with sugar and rum bound for London. After putting a crew aboard to sail her to the nearest non-loyalist port, he continued on with the *Andrew Doria* to Newport, Rhode Island. Unfortunately, a chase ensued between the *Nathaniel and Elizabeth* and the British *Cerberus* which forced the ship to run aground, leaving her a total loss. Such bad luck had conspired to make Biddle's latest mission to bring his prizes safely to port a failure. He swore then that he would not set sail again without first visiting Moll Pitcher.

CHAPTER TWELVE

Breed's Hill

(**1 7 7 4** – LYNN, MASSACHUSETTS)

Within a month of General Gage's arrival, he visited Moll Pitcher at his wife's urging. Margaret Kimble Gage was born and raised in New Jersey, where she grew up hearing about the great fortune teller of Lynn and she thought her husband and his new position might benefit from a reading. Moll usually welcomed the lobsterbacks to her Queen Anne table as they often revealed things that proved useful to the Sons of Liberty, but Gage was the exception. Frowning, she allowed him in with a brisk wave as Percy dashed away from the officer to hide.

Gage took a seat "Mrs. Pitcher, we've never met, but I get the distinct feeling that you and your cat dislike me."

"I dislike the way your men and your ships are choking Boston." Moll frowned as she sat across from him. "And Percy isn't sociable to most of my visitors so don't take it personally."

"So…you are not a loyalist as I have heard?"

"General Gage, I am a simple woman trying to take care of a husband and four children. That is where my loyalties lie. No more. No less."

"Are you going to make tea?" Gage tried to change the subject. "My wife tells me that you read the leaves."

"Not today." Moll shook her head. "Today, I will look at your palm and see if you are the cause of my recent visions."

"Visons?"

"Yes, now give me your hand."

Gage laid his right hand on the table palm up and Moll studied his lines. "Well?" he asked when she didn't speak.

"Boston will suffer greatly if you continue this persecution." Moll looked him straight in the eye. "There will be serious consequences."

"You see all that in my palm? But I have orders directly from the king," he said, raising his voice.

"And those very orders will be the cause of bloodshed."

"Ma'am, I mean no harm to anyone. I have a duty…that's all."

"Keep telling yourself that and when the first shots are fired, remember what I've said."

"Is that all you have for me?" Gage seemed disappointed in Moll's brevity.

"I have said all there is to say for now." Moll pressed her lips together and let go of the general's hand. "And there will be no charge today."

Gage rubbed his hands together as if to erase her touch. "If that is all, I have a personal question about my wife."

"Go on."

"As you may know, I married an American girl," Gage said. "And I am not sure if she is trustworthy. Is she loyal to me or to the colonists?"

"Your wife is a fine lady," Moll answered. "You should talk to her when you are in doubt. Confide in her and perhaps one day she will grace this table. I think I would like to meet her."

"I will let her know." Gage smiled for the first time. "And maybe I will come back when you are in a better frame of mind."

"End this siege in Boston and you will find me much more congenial." Moll also smiled for the first time since he arrived.

⚓

A month after Gage's visit, Moll received another British caller. This one came accompanied by Fanny Campbell. Lady Marion Ashton had made her way to Boston by way of the *Crim-*

son Blade—the pirate ship she was rescued from. While on board, she met William Lovell, Jack Herbert, and Samuel Breed who offered her protection from the buccaneers they had been forced to join. She brought with her a letter from William Lovell and news of the men's fate. Her presence was the sign that Moll was waiting for. Fanny, with Moll's help, must now prepare for her greatest challenge.

Marion, along with Jack Herbert's mother, moved into a house near High Rock. Moll welcomed her new neighbors and did not seem to mind in the least that Marion was British. Besides, the girl validated Moll's claims that William Lovell was still alive. She was also touched by the tenderness Marion lavished on the Widow Herbert. If Jack made it home, he would indeed be indebted to this girl who showed such kindness to his ailing mother.

While Moll guided Fanny and Marion, General Gage continued tightening his rein on Boston. On September 1, he ordered British soldiers to seize stores of gunpowder from Charlestown and bring them back to Boston. As word of the incident reached Philadelphia where the First Continental Congress assembled, the colonial delegates were dumbfounded and frightened for their families. Whatever happened in Boston could happen anywhere. Their fears were allayed when Paul Revere rode into Philadelphia with the news that there had been no violence. He also assured the men that large supplies of gunpowder and ammunition were still safely hidden.

When the northern lights made an unusual appearance over the Boston area in late October, the townsfolk were thunderstruck. Moll took it as a sign from the heavens. She prayed she was wrong, but she knew that it was inevitable—bullets and bloodshed were in store—especially after the First Continental Congress sent its Declaration of Colonial Rights to Parliament. The delegates outlined their grievances and listed their own Bill of Rights and threatened to boycott English goods. The king was not moved and while many colonists remained loyal to the Crown, a growing number of Americans demanded independence.

Shortly after the New Year, Parliament officially declared that the Province of Massachusetts Bay was in rebellion against King George III. Statesman Patrick Henry, who hailed from Scotland, spoke loud and clear at St. John's Church in Richmond, Virginia, when he said: 'Give me liberty or give me death!' His words became a rallying cry throughout the colonies, inspiring many to take up arms against the British soldiers. Minor skirmishes erupted, intensifying the bitterness between the foes. General Gage was ordered to quash the rebellion by any means necessary.

British Major John Pitcairn visited the Pitcher home on a cold spring day in early April 1775. Pitcairn, now in his fifties, appeared to be a reasonable man and for that the colonists tolerated his presence. Nonetheless, he was still a redcoat and Moll, as usual, pricked up her ears as he spoke.

"Mrs. Pitcher," he began as he sat at Moll's Queen Anne table, "there is trouble ahead and I would like to know my fate."

"Let's see what the tea leaves say." Moll ladled hot water into his cup.

"And just where did you get this tea?" Pitcairn frowned.

"I dried the leaves myself from herbs I grew in my own garden." Moll returned his frown. "Has the king made gardening illegal now?"

"Of course not." Pitcairn shifted nervously in his chair. "It's just that tea has become an intolerable issue on both sides of the Atlantic."

"Well, you can't blame me for that," Moll said. "Now drink up so we can get on with it."

Pitcairn followed her orders and swallowed the brew. Moll tipped the cup and let the remaining drops drain out and then studied the leaves. "Well?" Pitcairn demanded. "Can you see whether I will be hailed a hero?"

"You will be a hero to some, Major, but just one shot will spark an eternal fire of liberty. I would caution you to be very careful."

"You can see all that from inside this tiny cup?" Pitcairn's voice carried his doubt.

"That and more," Moll replied.

"Then you must truly be a witch as they say."

"Oh…is that what they say?"

"Some say it."

"What do you say?"

"I say that my troops have been ordered to take the supplies at Concord at all costs and we shall be victorious!" Pitcairn pounded the little table with his fist, upsetting the teacups. "The Yankees will pay for their insolence and their illegal tea parties very soon."

"And blood will be shed."

"Rebel blood," Pitcairn promised with a sneer.

As soon as the major left, Moll went to work. She hung her red tablecloth on the clothesline and a representative from the local Sons of Liberty quickly paid her a visit. She relayed the information that Pitcairn had revealed and then organized a group of neighbors including the Burchstead boys, Elmore and Rupert, to help her dig up the guns and ammunition she had hidden inside the wolf pits deep in Lynn Woods. She even convinced Fanny and Marion to disguise themselves as boys and act as messengers. The two girls made several trips to Saugus, Boston, and Marblehead passing information and detailing where and what specific arms Moll had hidden, making arrangements for their retrieval.

⚓

On the night of April 18, 1775, the colonists prepared themselves for trouble. Armed with the knowledge that a British invasion was imminent, the Sons of Liberty designated messengers to meet in Charlestown where they could clearly see the steeple of Boston's Old North Church. If one lantern was hung, the British would arrive by land, but if two lanterns were hung, the British would come by sea. The silversmith Paul Revere and the tanner William Dawes were just two of many night riders who waited for the signal. As soon as they saw two lanterns hung in the church steeple, they set off on horseback to warn the patriots of the coming danger.

By dawn the next morning, seven hundred British troops were gathered at Lexington. Only seventy-seven minutemen had arrived, but they put up a gallant fight. Nonetheless the British stormed past them and marched on to Concord. To their surprise, however, the vast majority of arms had been moved and in a short amount of time, thousands of minutemen from Boston and the surrounding areas arrived on the scene including a contingent from Lynn. A great battle ensued and the Americans succeeded in driving the British back to Charlestown.

Four men from Lynn gave their lives in what is now called The Battle of Lexington and Concord: William Flint who left a wife behind; Thomas Hadley, a widower; Daniel Townsend, a father of five; and newlywed Abednego Ramsdell, the younger brother of Shadrach and Meshech. Among Lynn's wounded were Joshua Felt and Timothy Munroe. It is said Munroe counted thirty-two bullet holes in his clothes, which he liked to show off to his neighbors. Samuel Breed's distant cousin, Josiah Breed, was one of five prisoners of war taken that day. He was held for thirty-three days before being released and returning home to Lynn.

For the first time, the clouds of war that loomed over the colonies were a reality. The good men of Lynn formed a safety committee and organized a company of alarm men. Three watches were established—one at Sagamore Hill, one at the south end of Shepard Street, and one along the Saugus River at Newhall's

Landing. No one could leave town without permission and most citizens carried their guns to church. Even Reverend John Treadwell took to his pulpit with his sermon in one hand, a loaded musket in the other and a cartridge box under his arm.

Moll, herself, became preoccupied with visions of bloodshed—at least until Jack Herbert showed up. Against all odds, he had escaped Cuba's La Cabana prison and returned to Lynn. His unexpected appearance was the catalyst Moll needed to launch Fanny Campbell's mission. And so, Fanny's masquerade as Bartholomew Channing began in earnest while the tension in Boston had heightened since the Battle of Lexington and Concord. The lobsterbacks in residence now grew to six thousand men. Their leader, General Thomas Gage, had orders to prepare for war.

The Second Continental Congress met in Philadelphia and named John Hancock as their president. Volunteer troops rose among the colonies and a makeshift army was formed. More skirmishes throughout the Boston area ensued, and as May turned into June, the threat of war deepened. Moll's visions became increasingly vivid, leaving her with headaches and little appetite. It had been a long time since Robert had seen his wife so preoccupied with dark things and he grew concerned.

"What is happening to you, my girl?" He brought his wife a cup of tea once the children were in bed. "You haven't been yourself these past few weeks. Is it the Campbell girl?"

"No, not Fanny." Moll took the steaming cup from her husband. "Fanny will be just fine. She has worked hard and is ready to embark on her mission."

"Then what is it?"

Moll sipped her tea as if to take courage from the warm liquid before she answered. "I have had some terrible visions, Mr. Pitcher."

"Tell me about them."

"There is blood...so much blood." Her green eyes grew moist. "Sometimes, I can even smell the scent of death in the air."

Robert grasped her hand. "Here in Lynn?"

"No, not here." Moll shook her head. "Along Breed's Hill in Boston. Oh, Robert, I see so many men lying there slaughtered."

"War is never pretty," Robert reminded his wife.

"But this is just the beginning." Moll shivered despite the warm tea. "It will be a long, hard fight against the Crown. Thousands of lives will be lost and families shattered on both sides."

"But will we be victorious?" Robert asked.

"We will break free from England," Moll said with a sigh. "But we will pay a very high price for that victory."

⚓

As the number of British troops swelled in Boston, tensions in the city rose. While the New Englanders planted their gardens and tended their businesses, they did so under an ominous threat of war. Even the spring sun couldn't brighten the dark cloud of fear that surrounded them. By mid-June, the colonists became aware that the lobsterbacks were planning to fortify the hills surrounding the city, ultimately giving the redcoats control over Boston Harbor.

Under the cover of darkness, over one thousand colonists, with Colonel William Prescott in command, stealthily built fortifications along both Bunker Hill and Breed's Hill on the Charlestown Peninsula in an effort to defend the harbor. They believed that the elevation would give them an advantage over the British. Since Breed's Hill was closer to Boston, they concentrated their efforts there, building redoubts six feet high with a platform inside that allowed a man to stand on it and fire at the enemy. Word had already been sent to Moll to dig up the small arms and ammunition that she had hidden in the wolf pits.

On June 15, 1775, Fanny, Marion, and Jack prepared for their voyage to Cuba while Moll hung a red tablecloth in her front yard signaling to the Sons of Liberty that the weaponry was ready for them. That same day, Major Pitcairn strode past the tablecloth and paid a second visit to Moll.

"You're back!" Moll exclaimed when she found the British officer standing at her door.

"Yes, ma'am!" He removed his tricornered hat in an apologetic fashion. "I've come to ask you for a reading."

"I've already told you all I know." She glanced at the red tablecloth that was billowing in the wind.

"Please, Mrs. Pitcher." He gave a slight reverent bow. "I would be forever in your debt if you could just spare me a few minutes of your time."

Moll shook her head, but stepped aside to let her visitor in. "Have a seat at my table, but let's be quick about it. I don't have all day. There's not time for tea. Instead, I'll have a look at your hand."

"My fate is written in my hand?"

"Let me have your right hand and we shall see."

Pitcairn turned his hand, palm up on the table and Moll examined it. She intently studied the lifeline and the heart line before she spoke. "What is it you want to know?"

"How will my son and I both fare in battle?" he asked.

Moll studied his hand a little longer. She saw death, but her disciplined manner gave nothing away. "Your son will live to see England again and he will watch over you until the end."

"Will he see me as a hero?"

"He will," Moll said, nodding. "Now I'm sure you have much to tend to, now, you need to go."

Pitcairn stood up. "Mrs. Pitcher, "I am sorry I called you a witch."

"I've been called worse," she said, forcing a smile. "Now be off with you."

"Yes, ma'am." He dropped a gold coin on the table. "Thank you, ma'am."

Moll watched Pitcairn as he strode past the tablecloth and onto the road that led away from her cottage. Within thirty minutes of his departure, a messenger came for the arms and ammunition. Moll's visions of bloodshed were about to prove accurate.

⚓

When British General Thomas Gage saw what the colonists had accomplished in just a few short hours, he was amazed, but he firmly believed, along with his fellow generals William Howe, Henry Clinton, and John Burgoyne, that the ragtag Americans were no match for their professional English soldiers.

On June 17, 1775, the British troops received orders to march up Breed's Hill. American Colonel William Prescott worried about the patriots' low supply of ammunition. He commanded his troops, "Don't fire until you see the whites of their eyes!" His men obeyed his order by doing exactly that, and as a result, many of the king's men were injured or killed, and the British forces were repelled for the first time that day.

The redcoats soon regrouped and began to ascend Breed's Hill once more, but this time they were forced to march over their own fallen comrades through puddles of blood and broken bones. Again, the colonists held their ground and forced the British to retreat.

On their third try, the lobsterbacks met with success. The Colonial Army was running out of ammunition and the British were able to break through their fortifications. Hand-to-hand fighting ensued with the British having an advantage as they carried bayonets. While the English soldiers overpowered the Americans and declared a victory, they paid a terribly high price for their win, with none higher than that paid by Major John Pitcairn who had already suffered two bullet wounds. Bleeding, he led his men directly into the battle, where he was shot in the head as he stood next to his son, Thomas, also a British officer. Thomas caught his father and gently lowered him to the ground while his men openly wept at the sight of their fallen leader. Just as Moll had predicted, Major Pitcairn was carried off the battlefield an English hero and died several hours later in Boston. He was buried at the Old North Church.

The carnage that Moll had seen in her visions rang true. Erroneously called the Battle of Bunker Hill, it was actually Breed's Hill where broken bodies lay in the aftermath and where the grass turned a bright crimson red as both English and American blood mingled in the soil. The English lost two hundred twenty-six men and counted eight hundred twenty-eight wounded while four hundred fifty patriots were killed and three hundred five wounded. One British officer was heard to say that 'a few more such victories would have shortly put an end to British dominion in America.'

Moll was not able to dwell on the battle for long because a few days later Fanny Campbell needed her undivided attention. Fanny, disguised as Captain Bartholomew Channing, sailed away from Lynn, Massachusetts accompanied by Jack Herbert and his new wife, Marion Ashton. The trio were on their way to Cuba to rescue William Lovell and Samuel Breed—the beginning of their amazing adventure.

⚓

In early July, when General George Washington officially assumed command of the Colonial Army, Moll traveled to Cambridge at the invitation of her old friend, John Glover. It was there on July 3 when Moll was first introduced to the General and Lady Martha Washington. Glover referred to her as the 'daughter' of his Marblehead regiment and as the festivities began, Moll had her first of several visions that day proclaiming she saw a great victory for America. Lady Washington took a liking to the psychic of Lynn and a friendship of sorts, as well as a mutual respect, developed between the two patriots.

Visions of a long and bloody war, however, were not the only ones that plagued Moll that summer. After her trip to Cambridge, she began having dreams of a great storm that would soon arrive along the coastline taking many lives. She feared not only for the local fishermen, but for Fanny Campbell, as well. A hurricane, later to be known as the Hurricane of Independence, was brewing far away in the Atlantic and aimed at the island of Martinique in the Caribbean. It would be a one-hundred-year storm not unlike the hurricane of 1675 that forced her grandfather, the Wizard, up to Old Burial Hill where he called upon his helpers, Red Cap and Blue Cap, to bring the sailors home to safety.

The
Caribbean
Sea
The WEST INDIES
Steve Luchsinger
San Juan
PUERTO RICO
VIRGIN
ISLANDS
Virgin Gorda
ANEGADA PASSAGE
ANGUILLA
St. MAARTEN
St. BARTH
BARBUDA
St. CROIX
SABA
St. EUSTATIUS
St. KITTS
NEVIS
ANTIGUA
MONTSERRAT
La Désirade
GUADELOUPE
DOMINICA
MARTINIQUE
St. LUCIA
St. VINCENT
Bequia
The GRENADINES
GRENADA
TOBAGO
VENEZUELA
TRINIDAD
W
E
S

The Nancy flying the flag of Independence.

CHAPTER THIRTEEN

The First Salute

(JUNE 1 7 7 6 – VIRGIN ISLANDS)

Thanks to a contract obtained from the Spanish government, the *Nancy* made stops in both Puerto Rico and St. Thomas in the Virgin Islands to procure ammunition and arms by night and fruit and vegetables by day to elude British suspicion. The munitions had previously been sailed into those ports from St. Eustatius in smaller boats in order to fulfill the prearranged contract. By early June, Fanny's little armada of three sailed into the harbor at Christianstead, St. Croix and moored a few hundred yards from the *Nancy*. When William spotted her in the harbor, he quickly launched a tender to hail Captain Montgomery, alerting him that they were sailing as privateers for the colonies. Their intention was to purchase the same cargo Montgomery planned to carry back to Washington's Army. By that time, the *Nancy* was fully laden with with goods and he aided Lovell in steering him to possible merchants—including those underground purchases to be surreptitiously secured— keeping them from spying British eyes.

Word had just arrived from the colonies that independence had been declared as well as the intended colors of the newly formed country, and a flag was quickly fashioned by Thomas Mendenhall to replace the British ensign on the *Nancy*. Upon Captain Montgomery's orders, the British colors were struck and replaced by the new American flag with three stars surrounded by a circle of ten upon a blue background in the corner as well as red and white stripes below. It would be the first display of the American colors in a foreign port and a salute was sounded—hailing from the cannons at Fort Christiansvaern as well as Fort Frederiksted.

Shortly following the first salute to an American vessel, the *Nancy* set sail for Turtle Gut, New Jersey, leaving the *Fanny,* the *Marion,* and the *Mary of Lynn* to fill their holds with provisions destined for Washington's Army.

Shortly after the *Nancy* sailed northwest to return to the colonies, and after the three ships had managed to purchase and load as much cargo as they could obtain from the two tiny islands of St. Croix and St. Thomas, they headed back to Port San Juan on the north coast of Puerto Rico to fill their holds with any additional provisions the Spanish had allotted for the Americans. Food and produce were in short supply in the Virgin and Leeward Islands since they had always relied on British North America for provisions, however rum and sugar were abundant. The arid islands in the Virgins and Leewards were smaller and grew few crops, except for Puerto Rico, which grew rice, sugarcane, corn, and coffee. Saint Christopher was an exception in having fertile soil but it was controlled by the British due to its valuable sugar cane plantations. Few other crops were grown there—only enough to feed their slaves who worked the cane fields. All the drier islands were struggling to feed their slave population, since the North American food chain had been redirected to feed Washington's army.

A few days after arriving in Puerto Rico the three ships were filled with all they were able to procure and made ready to set sail for Beverly and Boston to sell their cargo. William and Jack knew they weren't home free since several of the surrounding islands in the Virgins remained British strongholds. British cruisers vigilantly patrolled those waters due to the open trade practiced by the Dutch and Danish islands. Captain Clement had proven himself as knowledgeable and adept at navigating and serving as master aboard the *Molly of Lynn.* Both Josh and Levi, who now spoke fluent English, had expressed to William how much they respected Clement and felt that they were as fairly treated as they had been sailing under Captain William Lovell himself. The four who had been apprised of Moll's visions regarding her namesake, had warned John Clement of her premonition, but he quickly laughed it off as a fortune teller's tall tale. Fanny/Franklin Connors, Marion/Jean LeDee, William, and Jack knew better, however. They knew of Moll's accuracy and how her predictions had saved William's life, not to mention the many lives in the American Army in at least three battles so far. Wisely they also shared her prophecy with Josh and Levi. While in port on the three islands the two boys and Marion had spent a great deal of time ashore foraging and provisioning their galleys, to be certain to have enough food stores for the return voyage. There was nothing more dangerous than hungry sailors and their job was to keep the men satiated with full, happy bellies so they remained true to their patriotic cause. Of course, the Lovell and Campbell families had made certain to supply the ships with enough dried fish to feed an army. But then, who would eat salt fish every day and not complain?

It was a late June dawn that the three ships weighed anchor and sailed out of Port San Juan—setting a course just shy of due north at 355°. The summer winds set them on a comfortable beam-to-broad reach towards their homeland. But Fanny knew in her gut that it was far too early for the trio of ships to become complacent and both she, William, and Jack kept a keen lookout for prowling British ships. For reasons of subterfuge they flew the British ensign, instead of their new American colors. Marion had spent much of her time in the galley working as Jean LeDee, the French cook from St. Barthelemy, but on occasion she would take a break topside to visit with the captain. She would use the excuse that she needed to confer with Captain Herbert regarding the men's meals, or take him a cup of tea and rum on a late night's watch. Because Fanny, or Connors. was sailing as first mate and quartermaster aboard the *Fanny*, William managed to spend a great deal of time with her at the helm. That was unless O'Hara or Finch was relieving Connors from quartermaster duty.

Then, Fanny and William were careful to not spend too much time together in front of them in case they might find the couple's exchange a bit too familiar.

It was past sunset when the lookout on the Marion spotted sails far off the *Mary of Lynn's* port quarter. When Jack looked through his spyglass he knew immediately that it was a British warship on a convergent course with their three ships. Even though he could not see how many guns she carried, her sheer size told him to beware. The *Mary of Lynn* was the slowest of the three vessels and Jack and Terrance decided it best to take in some sail area to slow the *Marion* to the *Mary's* pace. That way, if the ship needed to be defended, their Long Tom, as well as the *Marian's* guns, would aid in the battle. His reefing of canvas also sent a signal to the *Fanny* that something was awry on the horizon. It didn't take long for the lookout on the *Fanny* to spot the pursuing ship quickly licking at the heels of the heavily laden barque. It was well past sunset and rapidly growing dark, so William quickly decided to harden up into the wind in order to confer with both Captains Herbert and Clement.

Safety in numbers was their first thought, however as they had learned in the past, it might be best to separate the ships so that at least two would escape capture and make it to their intended destination. The *Constance,* now the *Fanny,* had been known to use its Long Tom guns to out-battle a number of smaller ships, but the other two ships were not as well equipped to do battle against a large crew and much heavier artillery. After a quick conference between the three captains it was decided that they would scatter on differing courses with the lighter, better-equipped *Fanny* heading further west, making her the easiest prey for the British warship. As night fell it was becoming increasingly clear to William and Jack that the British ship had chosen wisely and set a course for the heaviest, slowest, and least equipped of the three. They had set their mark on the *Mary of Lynn.*

It was a dark night with a new moon and a fair amount of

cloud cover blocking the stars, so it was hard to tell exactly where they lay or even the position of the rest of their armada. Although they had agreed to separate, both William and Jack could not desert their companions and both independently made the decision to go in search of the *Mary*. It was around midnight that the British warship, *Victory II,* caught up with the *Mary of Lynn,* firing a single warning shot across her bow. From the sound of the shot Jack and William were able to ascertain the approximate heading of the capture and set a course in that direction. Since the ship was no match for the ninety-eight-gun, thirty-five-hundred-ton schooner, Captain Clement gave the order to heave-to as a boat was launched from the Victory *II* with crew to take command of their new prize. Their crew was ordered to board the vessel, take prisoners and secure the cargo, then sail their newest prize back to British territory.

When the British soldiers found the two slave boys in the galley, Josh and Levi wisely convinced the British crew that they cared little for whom they cooked and that they were happy to continue their duties preparing meals while the ship was returned to port—a British stronghold in Florida. The rest of the crew of the *Mary* were taken to the hold and bound to casks of their own gunpowder. It was fortuitous that Josh and Levi had gone ashore in San Juan to purchase produce for the men's meals since they had spotted a manchineel tree with its small ripe apples just waiting to be picked. Having spent much time in the West Indies they knew immediately how dangerous the fruit was, as well as every other part of the tree. If one should even simply stand under its leaves during a rainstorm, the sap upon one's skin would cause severe burns. The Spanish conquistadors had called it *la manzanilla de la muerte*—'the little apple of death.' It was so lethal the Indigenous people had used it to poison their arrowheads to use against the invading Spaniards. Thinking quickly, the two boys carefully made a brew using the manchineel fruit to put into the grog they planned to serve to the British crew that had been positioned onboard to return the barque to their home port. The boarding crew had found evidence that the ship had indeed been the British merchantman the *Wellington* prior to being privatized as an American vessel by the colonists. So, not only would the generous stores of produce and weapons aboard serve as a rich prize, the vessel itself would be an attractive windfall for the British Navy.

The British warship had orders elsewhere so they left the *Mary* in the hands of their select crew and turned back to the shores of the mainland to patrol for other looting privateers. Once the ship was out of sight, Josh and Levi saw their chance to serve their brew to their captors, while pretending to give the same concoction to their fellow crewmen, so as not to raise suspicion. Having mixed the poisonous fruit with lemon and beer, the men weren't alerted at first taste to the toxicity of their treat. At least not until they had finished imbibing a tankard full. It was at that point that their lips, throat, and gut turned to a raging inferno, as if they had swallowed a burning torch. It wasn't long before the men were writhing on the deck in agony and Josh and Levi were free to release their own crewmen. When William found them at dawn, the Brits lay bound in the hold and Captain Clement and his crew were back in control, steering their original course to the north. As Moll had predicted, the two young men had outwitted the British and saved the ship and its crew with nary a shot fired nor a drop of blood shed.

The boys were bright and had quickly learned to read, once they'd mastered their new language. They had read of the thousands of American white and black seamen who'd been captured from privateering vessels by the British. Should the prisoners refuse to join the British Navy, the white men would likely suffer horrific conditions in captivity aboard British prison ships—those which had been abandoned and moored in New York, or some other British-controlled harbor. There they would likely die of starvation and disease and their bodies dumped in the harbor or the mud flats. The dark-skinned men, however, would face en-slavement aboard a British vessel or taken to be sold into slavery in the West Indies for a good profit to the British. The British troops aboard were still alive, even if they wished they weren't, so they were taken aboard the *Fanny* and the *Marion* where they could be closely watched. Maybe a few might even be swayed to join the patriot cause.

William was aware of the risk of death or imprisonment for himself and Fanny, as well as every other able-bodied seaman that sailed with them. He was also painfully aware of the British practice of enslaving black sailors and he had spent the night worrying about his two young wards—Josh and Levi. To William and Fanny, the boys had become family and he couldn't stand the thought of them suffering such a fate. They were all greatly relieved when they learned of their safety and were impressed with their story of how the two clever young men had ingeniously regained control of the vessel. It was then that both William and Fanny agreed to give them more important positions on the ship and to teach them the ropes of sailing and navigation. They were confident that someday Josh and Levi would be valuable sailors for their cause.

Once the three ships found their way back on course they set sail for Massachusetts shaking out every piece of canvas aboard. They knew it was best for them to quickly put miles between them and the Gulf Stream, where British cruisers patrolled Florida and Bahamian waters. They were aware that much of the British military was stationed in Florida and the Caribbean during the Revolution in order to protect their precious, government-run sugar plantations in the West Indies—then vital to the world's economy. The fact that east and west Florida separated the West Indies from the rebelling colonies made Florida a perfect strategic staging-ground for the British to launch attacks on the Americans.

Florida was also an important base to launch attacks on French privateering vessels in the Florida Straits and the Caribbean and served as a gateway to protect Georgia from the Spanish. The British had acquired Florida from the Spanish under the Treaty of Paris in 1763 as spoils from the French and Indian War. East Florida's settlement was struggling when the British acquired the colony and the first British governor, General James Grant, set up good trade relations with the native population and established a new governmental structure. The new British stronghold quickly became a safe haven for loyalist refugees from the north as well as African Americans who fled to the British territory to fight for their cause in return for the promise of freedom. The native population also sided with the British due to their fear of the insatiable need by the Americans for more and more land.

The greatest asset to Governor Grant's newly acquired colony was the Spanish Fort Matanzas Castillo de San Marcos, which still remains at the mouth of the inlet leading to the Spanish city of St. Augustine—it served as the bastion for the British on the eastern coast of Florida. British cruisers patrolling from the colony's eastern shores wreaked havoc on American privateering ships sailing to acquire provisions in the West Indies and accounted for many of the captures of American vessels. In fact, in early 1776 East Floridians drafted an address to the king stating they were, "...*deeply deploring and disavowing the present unhappy and unnatural Rebellion, which prevails through most of Your Majesty's other Colonies on this Continent.*" They also promised to avoid any "...*connection and Correspondence with, or Support of [the rebels]...we shall be always ready, and willing to the utmost of our weak abilities to manifest our Loyalty to Your Majesty's Person, and a due Submission to Your Majesty's Government, and the Legislature of Great Britain.*"

East Florida would grow to be a thorn in General Washington's side—he knew that its strategic location between the thirteen colonies and the Caribbean would be problematic to the burgeoning American Navy as well as to America's loyal privateers. He recognized early in the game the need to oust the British from East Florida and wrote many letters to the Continental Congress, as well as to his generals regarding an assault on the southernmost colony. Washington originally assigned Charles Lee to head the operation and he would also authorize three unsuccessful attacks on East Florida in 1776, as well as several more over the next four years in an attempt to destroy the enemy's stronghold. The power of the Royal Navy against the fledgling American Navy gave the British the ability to thwart the Americans' advances. The support of the Indigenous tribes of Florida aided the British in the future battles of Amelia Island, New Smyrna, Thomas Creek, and Alligator Creek Bridge.

⚓

When the three ships neared the coast of Massachusetts, their lookouts were vigilant for British cruisers since their holds were full of valuable war supplies and provisions. As nightfall approached, they fell off to wait until dawn. All lanterns were doused onboard the three ships so as not to alert passing British cruisers. If all was clear come morning, they would use the early light to slip in through the rocks protecting Salem Sound, and into Beverly Harbor. Since the fighting had moved down the coastline to New York, the Massachusetts coastline had become a little less concentrated with British vessels. Also, with the issuance of letters of marque, there were many American privateers cruising the waters to protect those privateering and naval vessels entering Beverly Harbor. When morning broke the only sail cruising the coast was a friendly one—Fanny's and William's fathers' fishing vessel, *Love of the Sea*. Fanny smiled and sent up the Taunton flag to signal to Captains Herbert and Clement that all was well and it was safe to proceed. Henry Campbell in turn, ran up his Taunton in answer to hers. The *Love of the Sea* escorted the *Fanny* through the cut and the *Marion* and the *Mary of Lynn* followed safely into port, their bellies laden with much-needed provisions for the American Army. The *Fanny* made her way to the wharf first as the other two set their anchors and deployed tenders to row ashore.

As Moll had predicted, their first voyage had been a successful one and was profitable for their new West Indies Trading Company. She had even been right when she predicted the saving of her namesake ship by Josh and Levi. Moll had seen the ships' return in the clouds and in her premonitions and she was at the wharf days prior to their arrival. She made haste to communicate with Elbridge Gerry in Boston regarding disbursement and storage of the cargo intended for Washington's men. Gerry was quick to make arrangements to convey them to their destinations. Moll also sent word to the Sons of Liberty letting them know that they would soon have weapons to hide and deliver.

Fanny was careful to greet her father at the wharf as First Mate Connors, since she was still concealing her real identity to the men aboard the ship. After all there would be future missions to employ her guise as the Scottish seaman. To Fanny's relief, her father and Mr. Lovell played along nicely with the ruse. No one was happier than Agnes and Sarah to learn that Fanny and William had returned unharmed so it was a festive homecoming.

Samuel was thrilled with the cargo manifests of the three ships. The haul would be a rich first trip for the West Indies Shipping Company, not to mention a boon for Washington's army. Fanny was excited to tell Moll all about their adventures once she'd changed back to feminine attire, and traded her masculine Scottish brogue for Fanny's east coast accent. Once again before she had reached Moll's threshold, the door swung open and Moll threw her arms around Fanny,

"Welcome home my child, I have truly missed you and Maid Marion," she said, chuckling. "It's been quite busy around these parts in your absence, with the new wharf at Beverly Harbor and all of the American privateers prowling about these waters now that Washington and the war have moved south to New York. There have already been many successful deliveries of captured cargo since the letters of marque were disbursed. Mark my word, Fanny. It will be the private merchantmen that will help to win this war."

Moll was almost like a giddy schoolgirl, most unlike her usual calm demeanor. "I'm sorry, child, I'm not letting you get a word in edgewise. Come in, I have so much news to tell you."

She took Fanny by the hand and pulled her inside.

"And I you, Moll. We have had such a successful voyage and as you predicted your namesake was captured and Josh and Levi saved the ship and all men aboard with their clever plot to take back the ship."

"I knew those two young men would prove to be an asset to your crew. They will grow to be successful captains each in his own right someday."

"Yes…and William and I plan to see to that."

For hours, Moll and Fanny shared stories of all that happened on their latest mission and Moll brought Fanny up to date on the war—most importantly, the signing of the new Declaration of Independence.

Before Fanny left to go home for dinner, she and Moll made plans to travel to Beverly in the morning to help determine how to store and disperse the valuable cargo that awaited at Glover's Wharf. Both knew that the sooner they could get the arms and munitions into the hands of Washington's Army the better. They also made plans to distribute food stores and produce to the widows and orphans created by the war. Moll had always been generous with those who had less, even if her own household might go without, and she wasn't about to let a war deter her from her Godly mission of helping the needy.

Dinner that night was a lively affair now that the Lovells and the Campbells were reunited. Agnes and Sarah had prepared a fine feast of venison, potatoes, and peas, with a fruit-filled cake for dessert.

"How has the fishing been so far this season?" Fanny asked her father as she passed the peas.

The long-time fishing partners, friends, and active members of the Sons of Liberty, Henry Lovell and William Campbell, Sr., exchanged furtive looks.

"Fishing's been fine," Henry spoke first.

"I've lost count of the fish we've cleaned and salted," Sarah said. "Some nights my hands ache something terrible, but it's all for a good cause…feeding our army and those less fortunate."

"So many of our women and children have been left behind while their men are in danger," Agnes picked up the bowl of potatoes and passed it to her son-in-law. "I guess we should be grateful for the good living we make."

"But Henry and I have been up to a lot more than casting our nets." William, Sr. cut a bite-sized piece of venison.

"That's right," Henry agreed. "We've been running guns from Beverly back to Lynn so Moll could hide them, but then you children already knew that."

"Dangerous work." Agnes frowned, pointing her fork at Fanny. "But your father will not listen to me. It's bad enough that he and William go off to those Sons of Liberty meetings at all hours, but pretending to fish and risking their lives for gunrunning is very risky."

Henry leaned forward with a frown. "We are not pretending to fish. We just have a little extra business on the side."

"And if you get caught," Sarah said, blanching, "you both will be killed."

"Precisely why we won't get caught." William gave his wife a smile.

"I see where our children get their risk-taking nature from," Agnes said with a shudder. "May the saints protect us!"

"Oh, mother, we'll never gain our freedom from England if

we don't take risks," Fanny said. "William and I are proud of our fathers and you should be, too."

"So…you are only proud of your fathers?" Sarah pushed her plate away.

"Fanny didn't say that." William jumped in to support his wife.

"Well…I for one am proud of the ladies," Henry said, grinning. "They may not talk about it, but they have been helping Moll too."

"We all need to do whatever we can," Fanny said. "Our cause is what's important. Now is the time to take action…not sit back idly and wait for others to do it."

"I must admit, Fanny," Agnes confessed, "I now understand why you are off undertaking such risky business and let me say that I am so proud of you and my son-in-law."

Her mother's honesty brought a tear to Fanny's eye. "Thank you, mother." Fanny smiled, surprised at Agnes' honesty. "And as you always say…may the saints protect us all as we take on the Crown."

CHAPTER FOURTEEN

A Declaration

(APRIL 1 7 7 6 – LYNN, MASSACHUSETTS)

While sea battles raged to the south, Moll Pitcher received an invitation to visit Martha Washington at Cambridge. It seemed the general was making plans to travel to New York, knowing that the British would relocate their troops along the wide Hudson and East Rivers in order to better control their naval activities. There the Continental Army would once again meet the redcoats head-on. Lady Washington looked to the famous psychic of Lynn for reassurance that her husband would be, not only victorious, but safe.

Lady Washington's carriage arrived at Moll's cottage in Lynn early one spring morning. Moll left Ruth and Becky in charge of the younger children with strict orders not to bother their father at work unless there was a dire emergency involving blood. While the carriage rolled along, Moll had a lot on her mind that day as she closed her eyes and tried to gather her thoughts. She had visited Lady Washington twice over the last few months, passing along intelligence each time and trying to warn her about the mysterious traitor that she had dreamed of, but today was different. It would be their last meeting for a while since the Washingtons would soon be leaving for New York. Moll double-checked her bag making sure she had all the herbal remedies the general's wife might need while she was away—St. John's Wort to help with depression, elderberry to relieve headaches, and valerian to induce sleep.

As the carriage approached 105 Brattle Street in Cambridge, Moll gathered her things. She took a deep breath as the coachman opened the door and helped her step out. There was a certain sadness about the Vassal mansion that she hadn't noticed before. Preparations were underway for the general's departure with Martha soon to follow. Moll was taken to the elegant parlor where Lady Washington was giving instructions to one of the house servants.

"Make sure the general has his favorite boots," Martha ordered. "And pack his warmest coat in case he must stay in New York for the winter. We can't have the general falling ill."

"Yes, ma'am." The young girl nodded and gave Moll a sideways glance that revealed her uneasy feelings due to the arrival of the famed psychic of Lynn.

"And one more thing before you go," Martha continued, "stop in the kitchen and tell them that Moll Pitcher is here and that they should brew some tea for us. They can use the tea leaves I had sent up from Mount Vernon. The cook will know which ones."

The girl gave a quick curtsy before she sped past Moll without a word and left the room.

"Moll, you seem to intimidate the help." Martha grinned at her friend.

"Not on purpose." Moll smiled too. "I guess my reputation precedes me."

"Well, I for one am glad you are here!" Martha beamed. "Especially on such short notice."

"Of course." Moll smiled and held out her bag. "And I've brought you a few things I thought you might need for your journey."

"You are too kind." Martha took the bag and motioned for Moll to sit down. She opened the bag and examined the herbs. "Thank you. I can't tell you how much I appreciate your kindness."

"If you need more or if there is something else you might find useful, just let me know," Moll offered.

Martha reached for Moll's hand. "I am going to miss you. I will not have many lady friends at the Army camp."

"But you will have the general and that's what matters."

"Yes, of course," Martha agreed. "And the general is why I asked you here today. I am worried about him and where this whole war is going. We won back Boston, but there is so much more to be done and so many battles ahead—both on the field with the British and behind closed doors with the Continental Congress. I hope you can ease my mind."

"I will try my best," Moll said.

They began as always, with Moll detailing the intelligence she had gleaned from the many British soldiers and sailors who frequented her doorstep wanting to know about their fate in battle or at sea. She also spoke of the guns and ammunition she had hidden in the Lynn Woods—something she would continue doing as privateers received their letters of marque authorizing them to raid British ships. While she obviously could not have buried a cannon, there was still plenty of room in the old wolf pits to accommodate small arms and gunpowder.

By the time the tea was brought in, Moll was feeling more comfortable and ready to read Martha's tea leaves. Except for her suspicions about the officer-turned-traitor, Martha always took Moll's predictions quite seriously since she had, after all, forewarned them of the Battles at Lexington and Concord, after the British General Pitcairn had come to her asking if he would survive the conflict and become a hero. She had also reported her vivid visions about Breed's Hill, which proved more accurate than anyone liked. Moll had already predicted a fortuitous outcome of the war for America and that George Washington would one day serve as the first President of the United States.

When Martha finished her tea, she offered the cup to Moll who handled it as usual. While they waited for the cup to drain, Moll spoke up. "Lady Washington, has there been any word about the turncoat?"

"My dear, I have told you before," Lady Washington said. "We completely trust all our officers. They are all fine men. Each and every one is dedicated to the general and to our cause."

"Not everyone." Moll tried again. "I am telling you that there is a traitor among your men."

"But who could that possibly be?"

"I was not given a name, but I saw him clearly. He was much shorter than the general, and he had strange gray eyes."

"Gray eyes," Martha mused. "That sounds like General Arnold, but I can assure you, he is as trustworthy as John Glover."

"No," Moll insisted. "He is nothing like John Glover. He will betray us all and mark my words, his name will go down in history as a traitor of the worst kind. Lady Washington, if you don't believe me, I implore you to be wary and please warn the general to be extra cautious around him."

It was obvious to Moll that Mrs. Washington did not wish to continue the conversation so she simply turned the teacup right side up. She took a moment to quell her uneasy feelings as she studied the placement of the leaves.

"New York and Boston will become important harbors for most of the world, and America itself will become the wonder of the world. The time will come when honor, titles, and dignity shall be conferred on the descendants of the Fathers of the Revolution, giving birth to many heroes. Every foot of American land from east to west will be under the dominion of the Stars and Stripes, which will soon become our nation's colors. There will be no British dominion in America. And the women of this great nation shall rise up and take their proper place."

Martha smiled pleased with Moll's prophesies. I hope this means that women will finally be appreciated for their own merit and not their men's."

"On that I can promise you," Moll said with a wink. "It will take some time, but we will find our footing and as women, we will flourish."

"And my husband will prevail?"

"Mark my words." Moll peered into the cup, "The general

need not worry about his troops. Assure him that all positions will be filled when the time comes to fight the British in New York. He will not always be triumphant there, but he should not lose heart. America will win her independence."

"The general will be leaving for New York shortly," Martha said. "I have been very worried about this entire matter."

"Let me explain…there will be battles involved…bloody battles. But…the general will make his mark and a new nation will emerge under his leadership. I assure you that you need not worry about your husband's safety."

"Thank you for easing my mind." Martha sat back on the couch, relieved.

"There is one more thing," Moll began.

"What more could there be?"

"It's about Patsy."

"My daughter, Patsy?" Martha straightened.

"Yes." Moll reached for her friend's hand. "She came to me in a dream a few days ago. She wants you to know that she is fine and that you should stop worrying about her."

"I miss her so." Martha's eyes filled as she drew a lace handkerchief from her pocket.

"Of course you do."

"She was so young…only sixteen. We did everything we could for her."

"That's what she told me. She wanted you to know that it was her time and there was nothing you or the general could have done to change it. She wants you to stop blaming yourself."

"She'd been very ill." Martha dabbed at her eyes. "But that day when she left us, she seemed so much better and we were so hopeful that the worst was behind us. Then the very next minute she was gone…just that fast. We never even got to say goodbye."

"Patsy wants you to know that she is very sorry that it all happened so quickly, but she didn't suffer. She loves you very much and is very proud of all that you have done. She told me that you have always been an excellent mother and she cherishes her memories of you."

Martha closed her eyes and choked back a sob. "Thank you, Moll. You are a true friend."

But Moll didn't feel like a true friend at that moment. There was something else Patsy had told her that she chose not to share with Martha that day. Patsy said she was preparing a place for her brother, Jacky, Martha's only living child. After all her experience, Moll knew when it was best to keep such information to herself.

As for General Washington, he arrived in New York on April 13, 1776, where he quietly set up his headquarters at the former home of British Captain Archibald Kennedy located at Number One Broadway facing Bowling Green. That same day, he met with the New York Provincial Congress. When Martha arrived four days later, the Washingtons established their personal residence at what was once the Mortier Estate on Richmond Hill, but the general continued to conduct business from Number One Broadway, as well.

⚓

The individual colonies were also coming around to the realization that independence from England was essential. North Carolina passed the Halifax Resolves making them the first colony to formally declare its support of independence from the Crown. The adoption of these resolves encouraged other colonial delegates from the Continental Congress to do the same.

The tiny colony of Rhode Island officially renounced its allegiance to the king and Britain on May 4 when its General Assembly led its declaration for independence long before the remaining twelve colonies followed suit. One month later, the first Virginia Convention in Williamsburg also gave its representatives in the Continental Congress authority to introduce a resolution declaring independence from Great Britain. At long last, Europe began to recognize the newly formed nation. King Louis XVI of France pledged one million dollars in unofficial support of the American rebellion. Spain then followed suit, giving the colonies its backing. The Continental Congress also authorized each of the thirteen colonies to form its own provincial governments.

On June 7, 1776, Virginia statesman Richard Henry Lee proposed to the Continental Congress during their meeting in Philadelphia, "That these united colonies are and of right ought to be free and independent states."

Four days later, the Congress appointed a committee of five to draft a formal Declaration of Independence: John Adams (Massachusetts), Thomas Jefferson (Virginia), Benjamin Franklin (Pennsylvania), Roger Sherman (Connecticut), and Robert Livingston (New York). Although Thomas Jefferson was the delegate to actually draft the document, all five men had input. They worked in secret, risking their very lives, knowing that if caught by the British, they would be found guilty of treason to the Crown and most likely hanged.

The first draft denounced slavery, but this issue was struck from the final document despite the dire warnings of patriot Josiah Quincy II who visited the south hoping to encourage unity between the colonies. He was appalled at what he found and the very idea of slavery greatly disturbed him. He would not budge on his belief that allowing this type of human bondage could only result in 'resentment, wrath, and rage.' He insisted that 'Slavery may truly be said to be the peculiar curse of this land.' Quincy foresaw nothing but trouble if slavery continued. Because of the need to unite slave-holding southern colonies with their northern counterparts, however, the final version of the Declaration of Independence did not address this divisive issue.

General Washington would soon have other headaches as a

powerful fleet of British war ships carrying thousands of soldiers ominously convened in New York Harbor under the command of General William Howe and his brother Admiral Lord Richard Howe. They would soon be joined by the Hessian Army (England's German allies) and preparations for a decisive battle would commence.

⚓

While the Committee of Five toiled away at its task of formally declaring freedom, the British were busy blockading the Delaware Bay. Located between the colonies of New Jersey and Delaware along Cape May, the British hoped to keep war supplies from reaching the port of Philadelphia. Late in the afternoon of June 28, 1776, a British lookout spotted the brigantine *Nancy*, the privateer ship commanded by Captain Hugh Montgomery. The *Nancy* had a small crew with only six cannons and was just returning from the islands of St. Thomas and St. Croix in the Caribbean. In her hold, she carried almost four hundred barrels of gunpowder, as well as multiple firelocks, along with rum and sugar meant for the Continental Army. The British gave chase, but not before the *Nancy* signaled for help.

In response, three continental frigates, the *Lexington*, the *Reprisal* and the *Wasp* came to her rescue, anchoring near Cape May to wait for the morning light. The next day the *Lexington's* captain, John Barry, eyed the *Nancy* desperately sailing towards shore with British ships, including the *Kingfisher*, hot on her stern. Realizing how serious the situation was, Barry took charge and quickly met with *Wasp* captain William Hallock and *Reprisal* captain Lambert Wickes. Orders were given to the oarsmen from all three ships to take longboats led by Captain Barry and Lieutenant Richard Wickes (brother and third lieutenant to Captain Wickes) to aid the distressed ship. Since the *Nancy* could not sail into Delaware Bay, she headed instead to the nearby Inlet of Turtle Gut seeking safe harbor. By the time Barry and his men arrived, however, the *Nancy* had run aground—a sitting duck as the British opened fire.

Barry quickly enacted a plan to defend the *Nancy* and at the same time unload and store her cargo for safe keeping. He quickly split his crew into two distinct groups—one ordered to fire the cannons at the British brigs while the other removed the gunpowder and loaded it onto the longboats. The sailors then rowed back to shore, where locals helped them remove and safely store their cargo. Somehow the first group managed to keep the British at bay until most, but not all, of the gunpowder was retrieved for the Continental Army.

Captain Montgomery, as well as Captain Barry, knew that the *Nancy* was severely damaged, leaving them no choice but to abandon the ship. Before he did, however, Barry ordered gunpowder poured and wrapped into the *Nancy's* mainsail. The mainsail was then draped over the side of the brig, which created a long fuse that led to more gunpowder in her hold. As the crew vacated, they lit the makeshift fuse. One last sailor remained on the brig long enough to remove the American flag. Seeing the flag lowered, the *Kingfisher* assumed the *Nancy* had simply surrendered and orders were given for the British sailors to board her and seize her spoils. But, just as they did, the *Nancy* was blown sky-high in a thunderous explosion that was heard and felt for miles.

By early afternoon on June 29, 1776, the British vessels found themselves retreating while the Americans loaded their rescued cargo onto the *Wasp,* which then sailed to Philadelphia to deliver the goods to Washington's army. The British suffered several casualties, but only one American was killed—Lieutenant Wickes. Captain Wickes witnessed his brother's valiant death in the final moments of what came to be called the Battle of Turtle Gut Inlet—the American Navy's first victory in battle.

⚓

On July 2, twelve of the thirteen colonies declared that all political connections between them and England must be dissolved. Only New York abstained.

Two days later, the Declaration of Independence was formally adopted by the Continental Congress although it was not officially signed by members of the Continental Congress until August 2. Nevertheless, it was printed and distributed to the army, as well as to local assemblies throughout the colonies.

On July 8, 1776, the Liberty Bell could be heard ringing in Philadelphia as the Declaration of Independence was read publicly for the very first time. Local meetings were then held so that all Americans could hear the words penned by the founding fathers. Lynn, Massachusetts was no different. The Campbells, the Lovells, and the Pitchers were all present when these words were read out loud:

> "When, in the course of human events, it becomes necessary for one people to dissolve the political bands which have connected them with another, and to assume among the powers of the earth, the separate and equal station to which the laws of nature and of nature's God entitle them, a decent respect to the opinions of mankind requires that they should declare the causes which impel them to the separation.

> "We hold these truths to be self-evident, that all men are created equal, that they are endowed by their Creator with certain unalienable rights, that among these are life, liberty and the pursuit of happiness....

> "...We, therefore, the Representatives of the United States

of America, in General Congress, assembled, appealing to the Supreme Judge of the World for the rectitude of our intentions, do, in the name, and by authority of the good people of these colonies, solemnly publish and declare, that these united colonies are, and of right out to be free and independent states; that they are absolved from all allegiance to the British Crown, and that all political connection between them and the State of Great Britain, is and ought to be totally dissolved; and that as free and independent states, they have full power to levy war, conclude peace, contract alliances, establish commerce, and to do all other acts and things which independent states may of right do—and for the support of this declaration, with a firm reliance on the protection of Divine Providence, we mutually pledge to each other our lives, our fortunes, and our sacred honor."

CHAPTER FIFTEEN

Moll's Predictions

(JUNE **1 7 7 6** – MARBLEHEAD, MASSACHUSETTS)

*R*ight after the Declaration of Independence was read to the colonists, Colonel John Glover sat at his large oak desk in Marblehead trying to wrap up several business transactions that needed his immediate attention. Soon he and his men would leave for New York to join General Washington. The British were already gathering there, along with several Hessian troops and a mighty battle was expected to rage. With this upcoming battle weighing on him, Glover found himself a bit preoccupied with worry about his wife, Hannah, whose health continued to decline. Most importantly, he did not want to leave her with outstanding matters related to his many business dealings.

Glover was also worried about the five hundred men who made up the 14th Continental Regiment under his command. Composed mostly of experienced mariners who resided in Marblehead, members included Native Americans, along with African Americans, Spaniards, and Jews. These men were used to working together and treated each other as equals, making them the first integrated regiment in America. While others may have frowned upon the very idea, they were proud to serve together under a man they all respected and Colonel John Glover was proud to lead them.

An overwhelmed Glover was lost in thought concerning his duties to family, business, and country, when a light rap on the closed office door interrupted him.

"John?" Hannah's voice sounded a bit weak. "John? You have a visitor."

"I told you, I shouldn't be disturbed," he grumbled. "You know that I have a million things to take care of before I leave."

"But this is one visitor I think you will want to see, dear." She slowly opened the door and Glover realized that Hannah was not alone.

"Moll!" His frown turned into a wide smile as he stood up. "What are you doing here?"

"Do you think I'd let my oldest friend go off and join the general without a proper goodbye?" Moll grinned.

"But how did you get here?"

"I took a ride with a neighbor who had business in town," she explained. "He will be here for the day and I will meet him later at Black Joe's."

"Joe Froggers for the children?" Hannah grinned.

"Of course," Moll said. "I can't go back to Lynn empty-handed."

"How about some tea?" Hannah offered.

"That would be perfect!" Moll smiled as Hannah turned to leave.

"Moll!" Glover came from behind the desk and took both of her hands in his. "I never expected to see you today."

"Johnny, I had to come." Her face turned serious. "We need to talk and it's important. I've been having visions about you and your men.

"Well sit down and tell me what you have seen."

"Johnny," Moll began as she and Glover settled upon the two chairs opposite his desk, "a great battle is looming over New York. You and your men will soon be fighting alongside General Washington."

"Yes, Moll, of course, we all know that the British are gathering along the shores of New York. My men and I have been called to duty."

"Your duty will save the general on three separate occasions."

"I don't understand."

"I came here to tell you that you mustn't be afraid. You will be victorious and a hero, but each time things look dire, you will be the one to outwit the British."

"And how will I do that?"

"I don't have all the answers, but I do know that you will save the general three times before the year is out. I am here to tell you to do what you have to, don't second guess yourself. Above all…rely on your men. They are the bravest of the brave and they will not fail you."

"I will always do my duty," Glover said. "But I have never tried to be a hero."

"But you are a hero, Johnny." Moll took his hand. "And soon the rest of the world will know what I have always known."

"And what's that, Moll?"

"That you are the finest man to ever call Marblehead home."

"Moll, we have known each other a very long time." Glover patted her hand with a smile. "Perhaps you are just a little biased."

"Perhaps," she said. "But you and your men will save General Washington on three separate occasions."

"But my men are not like other soldiers," Glover said with a sigh. "They are a rough bunch of seamen who do not mingle well with the gentry…even General Washington has expressed his doubts about them."

"He will no longer have doubts about the men of Marblehead. He will be grateful to them and they will gain the respect of a nation."

"I hope you're right, Moll," Glover said. "But I am also worried about my Hannah. She isn't well as you can see."

"Hannah will be fine. She will greet you at the door when you return."

"She seems to be growing more and more frail."

"I have brought her several herbs to help her through the day and I'm sure the older children will look after the little ones."

"Thank you, Moll." Glover smiled. "You are such a good friend."

"And a good patriot!" Moll smiled, too. "And that's why I must also tell you to let the general know that any talks for peace with the British will be for naught."

"How do you see these things, Moll?" Glover sat back in amazement.

"I see what I see," she said with a shrug. "And that's all I can say about it."

"Is there anything else I should know?"

Moll thought for a moment before she spoke. "Whatever you do, don't make any rash decisions about remaining in the general's service once your term is up. He is a good man and he needs good men like you around him."

Hannah returned with the tea and the three friends sat together discussing the turbulent times in which they found themselves, before Moll headed to Black Joe's.

⚓

"Guess what that fool husband of mine did now?" Auntie Creese packed a generous bag of Joe Froggers for Moll as she sat at their bar waiting for Joe to make her a Sir Switchel.

"Now, Creese, stop that." Joe wiped a glass. "Moll don't want to hear your complaining."

She narrowed her eyes. "I'm not complaining, Joe, though the good Lord knows I have plenty to complain about."

"You might as well tell me what you've done, Joe," Moll said. "Or Auntie Creese will beat you to it."

"I joined Colonel Glover's regiment." He poured a sweet-smelling mixture into the glass. "And I am going to serve as the colonel's personal aide."

"Then I would say the colonel is one lucky man," Moll said.

"But that leaves me here all alone." Auntie Creese grumbled. "Cooking, cleaning, and serving the customers, not to mention taking care of the books."

"My term will be up at the end of the year," Joe assured her as he stirred Moll's drink. "I'll be back before you know it."

"Unless you go and get yourself killed." She glared at him. "And if you do…don't you dare bring your dead body back here."

"Auntie Creese!" Moll laughed out loud. "I assure you that the colonel will look after Joe and so will that French general when he gets here and Joe will return with plenty of stories to tell."

"There you have it, Creese." Joe grinned and handed Moll the glass. "Straight from Moll Pitcher's lips to God's ear."

"Hmmmph! It's not you I'm worried about, Joe." Creese set the bag of freshly baked Joe Froggers down in front of Moll. "I just hate the thought of renaming my famous cookies!"

As planned, Colonel Glover and his men left Beverly, Massachusetts on July 20, 1776. The very next day, Captain Biddle returned to Newport Harbor in Rhode Island on board the *Andrew Doria*. He wasted no time in hitching a ride on a fishing vessel down to Lynn, where he sought a meeting with Moll Pitcher. After his last ill-fated cruise, he wanted Moll's counsel on his upcoming mission patrolling the coastline from Connecticut to Virginia and then to Bermuda. Moll assured him that his luck would change and he would keep his prizes this time. Just as Moll said and much to Biddle's relief, he did go on to successfully capture numerous loyalists' and British ships while out on his next patrol.

⚓

With intelligence on the presence of General William Howe and his many Hessian troops in New York, General Washington ordered his men to construct forts and reinforce batteries. Although both sides were preparing for battle, on the same day that Glover started to march his men for New York carrying their belongings, as well as their armaments, Washington met with General Howe who had extended the patriots an olive branch. Upon offering a pardon to all the rebels if they agreed to surrender, Washington famously told him: "Those who have committed no fault want no pardon."

General Washington had already sent a protesting Martha to Philadelphia where he felt she would be safer by the time Glover's regiment arrived in New York on foot on August 9. Tensions had heightened as hundreds of British ships and thousands of redcoats and German soldiers gathered. Washington, with less than twenty thousand men, controlled New York City while Howe maintained Staten Island with over four hundred battleships and more than thirty thousand men. The Americans knew they were outnumbered, but before the actual battle began General Washington spoke to his men:

"The time is now near at hand which must probably determine whether Americans are to be freemen or slaves, whether they are to have any property they can call their own, whether their houses, and farms are to be pillaged and destroyed, and they consigned to a state of wretchedness from which no human efforts will probably deliver them. The fate of unborn millions will now depend, under God, on the courage and conduct of this Army. Our cruel and unrelenting enemy leaves us no choice but a brave resistance or the most abject submission; this is all that we can expect. We have therefore to resolve to conquer or die."

Washington then sent eleven thousand troops to Brooklyn, but mistakenly left one side of the area open to attack. In the early hours of August 27, the British sailed eighty-eight frigates from Staten Island to Brooklyn where two thousand troops disembarked. Five days later, the British launched three attacks. The first was easily stopped by the Americans, the second resulted in a bloody battle and while they were fighting, additional British troops snuck around the Americans' rear flank, surrounding them. Outnumbered and overwhelmed, the soldiers who could, retreated.

From his position atop Cobble Hill, General Washington watched in disbelief as his men were brutally assaulted. Before long it was clear that the Colonial Army would not defeat the British who suffered less than five hundred casualties, while the Americans counted more than two thousand. It was the bloodiest campaign since the Revolution began two years prior. Once the fighting was over, General Howe set up camp nearby in anticipation of Washington's surrender. This would mean the end of the American Revolution, making Howe a hero. Many of his officers urged him to continue the fight and finish off the colonists, but he refused. While his specific reasonings for this decision were not shared, it has been speculated that Howe wanted his men to rest.

Meanwhile, General Washington met Colonel Glover and his Marbleheaders on Long Island to plan an evacuation. Washington gave the order to have every able boat set sail to the East River by nightfall on August 29. Heavy rains pelted the men as they worked together gathering their goods, and that night just as the boats arrived, a heavy fog rolled in. The Marbleheaders, being men of the sea, took charge. Troops, horses, munitions, and other supplies had to be transported across the East River to the safety of New York. Black Joe tirelessly, despite the adverse weather conditions, delivered orders from Colonel Glover to his men, ensuring the evacuation ran as smoothly as possible.

For the next three hours, heavy winds forced the seamen to manually row each boat instead of hoisting their sails. At midnight, the wind died down and the water turned smooth, but the fog remained thick, offering a clandestine cover. The men finally were able to set their sails and continued ferrying men and supplies across the river for several more hours. The last man to leave the shores of Long Island was General Washington. During the thirteen-hour evacuation, not a single life was lost and, in the morning when the fog lifted, the British were shocked to find that the Colonial Army, as well as its armament, had completely disappeared. Thanks to Colonel Glover and his fearless men, the rebels would return to fight another day. Thus, John Glover had made his first heroic save as predicted by his good friend, Moll Pitcher.

⚓

During the course of the battle (later known as The Battle of Long Island), the British took several American prisoners including Major General John Sullivan, who was from New Hampshire and the son of Irish settlers. General Howe and his brother managed to convince Sullivan that a peace conference could very well end the fighting. Then they released him so he could deliver their proposal to the Continental Congress in Philadelphia, where they had just recently renamed the Union of States to the United States. The Congress had its doubts about the peace conference, but agreed to send three representatives to Staten Island—John Adams, Benjamin Franklin, and Edward Rutledge. The men were only given permission to ask questions and get answers. No decisions were to be made on the spot, which upset General Howe who had little authority in the matter himself. Nevertheless, he moved forward with the conference, which was held at the home of loyalist Christopher Billops on September 11, 1776.

The Billops' house was currently being used to lodge British troops and was unsuitable for a formal meeting. General Howe ordered one room to be cleaned and prepared to accommodate the peace talks where, after a hearty dinner, negotiations began. The Americans demanded that their independence be recognized. Howe refused, saying that he could only see the colonists as British subjects, nothing more. Adams took offense to this and told him, "Your lordship may consider me in what light you please…except that of a British subject."

Howe then turned to the other delegates and declared, "Mr. Adams appears to be a decided character."

As Moll had predicted to John Glover, further discussion went nowhere and after a few hours, the so-called peace talks ended without accomplishing a thing. The delegates returned to Philadelphia and completed a report detailing the events. Howe never did file a report of his own, but moved his troops to Manhattan, where they proceeded to occupy New York City.

⚓

Two days later, Colonel Glover was tasked with evacuating five hundred sick and wounded soldiers from New York City to the Jersey Shore where a makeshift hospital awaited them. Once the men reached safety, tents and light equipment were then loaded onto wagons and sent overland. Heavier items were sent up the river by boat. It took thirty-six hours of tireless effort by Glover's regiment after which they received orders to make the eight-mile march to Harlem. Before they even reached their destination, the exhausted men were told to go to Kingsbridge— seven miles past Harlem. After settling in at Kingsbridge, Colonel Glover received yet another order to return to Harlem.

General Howe had moved his troops up the East River landing at Manhattan's Kips Bay. Their approach caused panic among Washington's ranks and many of the men fled despite the general's orders to stay at their camp. As the men headed toward Kingsbridge, they met up with Glover and his regiment. Seeing these brave Marbleheaders marching toward battle without flinching gave the deserters pause. Inspired, many of them joined Glover's men in their march back to Harlem. Glover's troops had been on the road for two days without any rest. According to Glover: "We fell back about three miles towards Dobbs Ferry without food or drink, and camped for the night with nothing but the earth under us and nothing but the heavens over us."

On October 12, 1776, British forces landed at a peninsula known as Throggs Neck, located between Long Island Sound and the East River. Their intention was to surround the American troops at Harlem Heights. The lobsterbacks disembarked at Pell's Point and began their march toward Kingsbridge. A small group of American soldiers managed to hold them off for two days until Colonel Glover and his regiment arrived. Using a spyglass, Glover discovered that the British and Hessian troops were once again on the move. He then wrote a request to his superior, Major General Charles Lee, asking for orders. Glover summoned Black Joe to carry the message and wait for Lee's written response. Glover, however, knew that time was of the essence. He later wrote: "I did the best I could, and I disposed of my little party to the best of my judgment…I would have given a thousand worlds to have had General Lee, or some other experienced officer present to direct, or at least approve what I had done."

With four thousand British and Hessian troops combined against Glover's men who totaled less than eight hundred, the colonists were vastly outnumbered. Glover sent various groups to the left and to the right, ordering them to hide behind a stone wall for cover. With a group of forty men, Glover managed to stave off the British who retreated, but an hour later returned. As they marched within one hundred feet of the stone wall, the Americans attacked, taking them by surprise. Glover had ordered his men to fight as long as they could then fall back to the rear and let the next group continue the battle. The hostilities went on this way for most of the day with bullets and cannon fire being exchanged. Eventually Glover gave the orders to retreat and his men crossed over the Hutchinson Stream. General Howe made no attempt to follow. The colonists suffered eight men lost and thirteen wounded while the British counted three men lost with twenty wounded.

The battle itself was not significant, however Glover's quick action allowed General Washington to move his men from Harlem to White Plains out of immediate danger. Glover and his Marbleheaders had once again risen to the occasion. They not only saved the day, but also raised the morale of Washington's men who could now continue the fight. Glover's heroics at Pell's Point would be the second of his three saves predicted by Moll Pitcher.

General Lee sent his congratulations and thanks for a job well done. General Washington, a bit late, added his appreciation from his headquarters:

"The hurried situation of the General for the two last days, having prevented him from paying that attention to Col. Glover, and the officers and soldiers who were with him in the skirmish on Friday last, that their merit and good behaviour deserved—He flatters himself that his thanks, tho' delayed, will nevertheless be acceptable to them, as they are offered with great sincerity and cordiality—At the same time he hopes, that every other part of the Army will do their duty, with equal duty and zeal whenever called upon; and that neither dangers, difficulties, or hardships will discourage Soldiers, engaged in the Cause of Liberty, and contending for all that Freemen hold dear and valuable."

⚓

On the last day of October, King George III formally addressed the British Parliament for the first time since the Declaration of Independence was published. He was finally forced to admit that the war with the newly named United States was not going in his favor.

CHAPTER SIXTEEN

Privateers in the Windward Islands

(AUGUST 1 7 7 6 – THE WEST INDIES)

*B*ritish spies had discovered as early as the summer of 1775 that the French and Spanish were outfitting ships in the West Indies to look like American merchant ships, in order to avoid disclosing their direct aid to the Americans. The British were aware the French were helping the rebels from both Europe and the West Indies. Powder and arms were being sold and sent to the colonies from the French Antilles, especially from the island of Martinique in the Windward Islands. American ships arrived in Martinique carrying much needed produce, and as ordered by Congress—returned carrying supplies for the war—a profitable solution for both French and American traders. By early 1776, the French had not only commenced their support for trade with the Americans, they had also sent a convoy of military ships to the French West Indies for their own self-defense—their goal, to protect these new profitable trade routes.

Due to the heavy British presence in the West Indies, the Continental Congress convinced a young, ex-British Consul, William Bingham, then living in St. Pierre, Martinique in June of 1776, to serve as an ambassador of sorts for them on the island. His assignment—to secretly spread American propaganda amongst the islands. He was also assigned the critical task of enlisting new privateers to prey on British ships and to arrange for the acquisition of smuggled weapons and direct them to the American Army. The Continental Congress' offer to give him a portion of any and all British cargo captured, made it a profitable position for Bingham, and made him a successful liaison for the American cause. During his time in Martinique, he sent communications to delegates in Paris that the Americans needed support in the war effort. The French were planning to send a fleet to the Caribbean to protect their trade with the American colonies since the Americans provided critically needed produce for the islands in exchange for war supplies. In addition to the strategic arrangement, by sending communications from Martinique instead of America, it limited the ability of the British to intercept Congress' messages to Paris.

⚓

It was in early August of 1776 that Moll, William, Jack, and Samuel made a trip to Boston to meet directly with Elbridge Gerry. When Moll arrived at his building, she was expected and ushered directly to his office. Gerry had already risen from his desk and met her with a hug as she walked through the door.

"Moll, my dear friend, it's so good to see you."

"And I you, Elbridge."

"I haven't had a chance to thank you for all you've done for our cause," Gerry said with a smile.

"In fact, that's exactly why I'm here." She turned and ushered the three men into his office. "These are the captains and privateers I told you about. The ones with three ships. Captain William Lovell and Captain Jack Herbert, meet my dear friend Elbridge Gerry of our Continental Congress. And this is Samuel Breed, Operating Director of The West Indies Shipping Company."

The men shook hands all around making niceties.

"Please…" Elbridge ushered them to a large mahogany table opposite his desk. "Make yourselves comfortable, you've been traveling some distance from Lynn."

I brought you a gift," Moll said, handing Gerry a small package. "The last of the tea I had hidden in the wolf pits."

"Oh well! This calls for a celebration, real English tea is more precious than gold these days," he said, handing the tea to his aide. "Please Johnathan, would you be so kind as to brew us a pot?"

"Of course, sir," he replied as he took the precious gift to prepare afternoon tea.

"Elbridge, I read what John Adams wrote of you after your support of our new declaration at the debates. 'If every man here was a Gerry, the Liberties of America would be safe against the Gates of Earth and Hell.' You are a true American as I have always known you to be."

"Only defending what is right, Moll," he said with a chuckle. "Surely, Mr. Adams exaggerates for a dramatic effect."

"You have always been a modest man. But those of us who are close to you, know better."

Shortly after, as they continued to make conversation, the aide brought in the steaming tea and poured cups for the five of them.

Once the tea was half consumed and the aide had left the room, closing the door behind him Gerry turned to Moll. "I want to thank you for the generous supply of weaponry you secured for our army."

Moll replied, "Whatever I can do for the cause, Elbridge. And by the way…these are the three men responsible for much of that lucrative cargo obtained courtesy of the Royal Navy and for the recent shipment from the Virgin Islands for General Washington's Army. They are quite interested in further rendering their services as well their ships to the cause as privateers. The messenger you sent told me there was important cargo you wish to deliver to Martinique in the French West Indies."

"What, you do not intend to read my tea leaves before business, Moll?"

"When we are done with pressing issues we will see what is in store for our new country and our great general's army."

"Well then…we have printed somewhat exaggerated, if not purely fictitious, news about the war and wish it to be spread throughout the West Indies. Propaganda if you must. We wish it to fall into British hands to make them believe the war is wearing down our resources and our spirits. We want them to think the Americans are unable to sustain the rebellion much longer, in the hope that England will pull back its resources, giving General Washington time to rest and reprovision his men during the coming winter months."

"Do you think it will work?" asked William.

"I think it's a fine idea, as I've known the British to be rather gullible," Moll replied.

"If we can make them believe that the war is soon to be over," Gerry continued, "then we can buy a little time for ourselves. The Continental Congress has enlisted the help of William Bingham as the American Counsel of Martinique. He was previously the Secretary of the Committee of Secret Correspondence. His current job is to secure weaponry and most importantly to spread American propaganda in the islands. In addition, he is tasked with recruiting privateers to capture British ships."

"We would be happy to deliver your shipment to Bingham," responded William.

"As well as any other cargo needed in Martinique," added Samuel, the businessman of the three.

"Yes, they are desperate for our produce in the islands and it is the perfect time of year to find an abundance of crops," said Gerry.

"And we are also willing to purchase gunpowder and munitions on your behalf," said Jack.

"Excellent, excellent." Gerry beamed. "I have heavily leveraged my contacts in France and Spain. They are willing and anxious to do business with our burgeoning new country. In fact, they even have warships on their way to the Caribbean as we speak, to protect this new trade route. Although they are not willing as yet to do battle with the British on our behalf, they will certainly protect their own business interests. And this profitable trade route is one of them."

"So, what do you expect of us?" asked Jack.

"When you arrive in Martinique, sail into Fort Royal and raise the American flag. You will be escorted directly to Bingham's offices. I will draft a letter of introduction for you to present to Bingham upon your arrival. He'll see to it that you can purchase all the powder they can spare, as well as sugar and molasses. He will also arrange for you to obtain cargo for your ships at Pointe-à-Pitre, in Guadeloupe."

"How will this be paid for?" questioned Samuel.

"An exchange has already been arranged. You won't have to carry funds. You just have to handle cargo."

Samuel nodded, relieved that they would not be carrying large sums of notes or gold since such could attract pirates. "And how will our company be compensated for our service?"

"You will be paid in Continental Currency…half now and half when you return with the shipment."

"That's acceptable," Samuel said.

"In addition," continued Gerry, "should you have extra captains and crew for the journey down, it would be advantageous since the French have been preparing new privateering vessels to aid us in our marine support against the Royal Navy."

Samuel directed a subtle smile toward William and Jack at the thought of adding more ships to their little armada.

"When do we sail?" questioned William.

"As soon as we can get the produce to your wharf in Beverly."

"Seems we have accord." William grinned, extending his hand to Gerry.

"Wonderful." Gerry accepted the handshake. "You get your ships ready to sail in a fortnight and I will take care of the details." Then he turned to Moll and slid his nearly empty teacup closer to her.

Moll smiled and picked up the cup, rotating it the required number of times before turning it upside down on the saucer.

The three ships set sail for Martinique two weeks later. Once offshore, they set a course southeast at about 140° on their compass. It would take them within one hundred miles of the archipelago of Bermuda, which was held by the British and had been a Crown Colony since 1684, making it part of British America. Although it was just over six hundred miles to the east of North Carolina, it sat strategically in the Atlantic between Massachusetts and the Caribbean. The economy of the island had never really developed as a plantation-based island but focused instead on maritime trade due to its advantageous location in the Atlantic. It had become a base for the Royal Navy, privateers, and merchant ships and was quickly becoming an imperial fortress and Britain's most valuable naval base in the western hemisphere. They spent exorbitant funds on their maritime and military activities stationed there on the tiny twenty-square-mile grouping of islands.

Their little armada of three would have to be vigilant in their watch for British ships since the waters surrounding the islands were notoriously the most dangerous for American ships, but with at least two men aboard each ship on watch at all times, they should be able to spot any threatening sails on the horizon early enough to take evasive action. If they could catch a single British cruiser off guard however, maybe they could overtake the ship to add another to their armada and make this a very profitable expedition. But of course, they could not forget that threat of their own capture always loomed upon the horizon. The three ships did their best to hold the same course and speed at night since it was mandatory to extinguish all lanterns aboard, making it impossible for a British lookout to spot them on the water unless they sat as a dark silhouette against a full moon or starlit night sky. Luckily for their own safety, it was a new moon and the summer clouds barred much of the starlight, masking them from becoming prey to prowling British cruisers. Of course, the *Fanny* always took the lead being the fastest and most agile of the three ships, since she had been modified to be a fore-and-aft rigged brig. The *Mary of Lynn* came second with the *Marion* covering her stern. The sail to date had been an uneventful one, with light ten-knot summer winds from the southwest—putting them on a comfortable starboard beam reach. They were well past the island when suddenly the lookout on the rail gave the call of a gull, instantly capturing the attention of the crew and Fanny, who was serving as first mate and quartermaster that evening, while William got some much-needed shut-eye. Quickly, she turned over the wheel to the assistant helmsman and went to the rail to have a look for herself. Off to the southwest, heat lightning lit the sky briefly then the horizon turned to pitch black tar once again. Then, a second lightning strike served to highlight a ship on a port-reach with a reciprocal course to theirs—headed directly for them.

"There," whispered Jordan, the lookout, pointing just off their starboard beam not more than firing range away from the *Fanny*.

"A ship-rigged sloop...? questioned Fanny. "But is she British?"

"Hard to be sure," he replied. "But I'd bet my wages she is."

Fanny took the spyglass and studied the cruiser long and hard. The question is, do they see us or is it just plain luck that we find them blind, in our sites?" pondered Fanny. She thought a moment and then gave the order. "Wake the captain and be quick about it. We've only got one shot at this...she's in range of our Long Tom and we are still likely out of range of her metal. Prepare the Long Tom! Hopefully, they are none the wiser that we are even in her sites. Surely they cannot see in the dark that we are three ready to do battle."

With that, she made the call to go after the ship, giving the second whistle to alert the crew. Although they were downwind of the cruiser, Fanny did not want to take the chance of the crew onboard the approaching ship being alerted to the fact they were positioning their ship directly in the sites of the British guns. In less than two minutes, William was beside her peering through the spyglass and assessing the odds of capture for either party. "Where away is she?"

"Two points on the starboard bow. She appears to be a ship-rigged sloop, likely a British patrol boat," counselled Fanny.

"Ahh yes…she'd fit quite nicely in our fleet, don't you think," replied William matter-of-factly.

It took no time for William to set the gun in position to take the ship by surprise, carefully aiming to cripple her, but not totally disable her. After all, if she were to be a useful acquisition, she would have to still be able to sail. William aimed carefully to take down her mizzenmast and create enough chaos aboard to give them time to throw the British off-guard as they boarded the enemy sloop. The quiet night resounded with the blast from their Long Tom and the sky flamed brightly around *Fanny*, announcing their attack on the sloop. With a loud, cracking sound, William hit his mark and the splintering wood flew all around the deck of the enemy vessel. Slowly, the mizzenmast fell forward, crashing into the mainmast and tangling sails and lines, preventing the crew of the sloop from maneuvering to a defensive position. Fanny took back the helm upon William's orders and hardened up to the wind to ram the sloop just ahead of her port beam. Within minutes, the sailors of the *Fanny* had thrown grappling hooks and climbed over the rail onto the deck of the sloop, holding the surprised crew at gunpoint. William's perfect aim had created the desired effect onboard, allowing the crew of the *Fanny* to take charge of their new prize.

"Good shot, Captain Lovell," said Fanny admiringly. "Couldn't have placed that shot better myself."

"Well, Mr. Connors, good thinking on the capture."

The *Mary of Lynn* arrived just as the two stepped over the rail to inspect the damage and to determine the number of men and amount of cargo aboard. Within moments, the *Marion* arrived and turned into irons to sit alongside the *Fanny.*

"Good thing we brought that extra crew along," William shouted to Jack.

"Excellent planning I'd say…as well as shooting," returned Jack.

"Thank you, captain, and next time I'll give you first crack at it."

"Are we keeping score?"

"Only on how many British ships we take on this cruise," William said with a laugh.

Luckily, the sloop had been traveling solo and there were no other enemy ships to contend with—at least not at that moment. Within the time it took them to cut the mizzenmast away, the other two ships had deployed their tenders to ferry the extra crew they carried to their newest prize, ironically named the *Truelove.*

The British prisoners were split up between the four ships and shackled in the holds. The *Truelove* would be limping and the three ships would find it necessary to slow their pace in order to allow her to keep up, but the ship would prove to be a rich prize. Not only did she carry a hundred casks of gunpowder, but she also carried documents from Antigua regarding battle plans for the British Royal Navy to invade harbors along the eastern seaboard of America. With such information about the planned invasion, they would have to make a quick decision. Should they send one of the ships back to America immediately with the confiscated cargo? The logical choice was to send the damaged, yet still fast, *Truelove,* since her bowels held much-needed gunpowder for the Continental Army. So, a decision was made by William, Jack, Fanny, and Marion to expedite the ship back to Beverly to get their newest asset along with the documents and gunpowder into Moll's and Gerry's hands. They would know immediately how to disseminate the captured intelligence as well as the gunpowder.

Within a few hours the three ships were back on course to the Mona Passage, where they would slip into the Caribbean between the western tip of Puerto Rico and the Dominican Republic on the isle of Hispaniola, and then head directly to Martinique. Once they were past the Passage, they set their new course at 150° degrees southeast—approximately five hundred eighty miles to Fort Royal harbor in the Windward Islands of the Eastern Caribbean. Sailing at six nautical miles per hour in light winds, it would take the three ships nearly four days to reach their destination. It was midafternoon when the *Fanny* was first to arrive in the harbor, setting her anchor on the north side of the bay in front of the town dock. On the mainmast flew the national ensign—their newly designed American flag. As a show of respect for their host port, a smaller French (or courtesy flag) hung from the port yardarm.

"Oh, and don't forget our new house flag," Fanny reminded Finch as they went about furling sails. On their starboard yardarm the bosun ran up their new West Indies Shipping Company ensign—a white flag with a blue crest of the entrance to La Cabana Fortress in Cuba, where William, Jack, and Samuel were once held as prisoners—a symbol of their bond from the time spent together in hell and of their lasting brotherhood. Above were the gold initials of the West Indies Shipping Company—WISC.

It didn't take long for a tender to row out to meet the *Fanny* with an invitation for the captain and first mate to join William Bingham in his office for afternoon brandy. William personally helped hoist the first crate of the propaganda pamphlets into the tender as he and Fanny climbed down Jacob's ladder—the rope with wooden rungs on the port side of the ship. Within the hour, the *Marion* and the *Mary* had sailed into the harbor and set their anchors.

Upon entering Bingham's office, William presented the letter to Bingham with his left hand and shook his hand with his right. "Mr. Bingham, it's a pleasure. Inside is a letter of introduction sent by Mr. Gerry."

"Of course, my good friend Elbridge. Please…," he said, motioning to two large armchairs across from his desk. "Please relax, I will pour us a brandy."

Bingham took a moment to read the letter, then folded it, before stowing it in his vest pocket. "It seems you come highly recommended as a trustworthy company, Mr. Lovell and Mr. Connors."

William handed Bingham the printed document to peruse. "Gerry has manufactured these for distribution in the islands in hopes of spreading a little harmless misinformation."

Bingham handed his guests each a brandy. then took his own glass to his seat behind his desk, and began reading the announcement. It was obviously designed to sway the local British citizens in believing that they were close to winning the war.

"Please tell Mr. Gerry that he should be a journalist." Bingham chuckled as he browsed through the propaganda pamphlet. "Mon Dieu!" He howled with laughter, reading further. "General Washington's army is dwindling due to exhaustion, sickness, and desertion. They may not rise to fight another day. Talk has been heard they may soon give up the rebellion." He looked up. "This sounds so factual, the British are bound to believe it is true."

"That is the result we are hoping for," William exclaimed.

⚓

The *Mary of Lynn* now sat in the harbor at anchor and a tender was sent out to bring all officers ashore to join them in Bingham's office. Once everyone was seated around a grand Louis XIV table and chairs the seven men got down to business.

"Regarding our British prisoners? What do you suggest, sir?" asked William.

"We'll take them off your hands and put them in the Bastille for a while until we can convince them to join one of our privateer vessels, or yours, should they be willing. You'll find most men place loyalty to the flag that pays the highest wage."

"Yes, we've discovered that in the past," said Fanny.

"We also have twenty of the best available French and French West Indies sailors to add to your manifest of crew. They will be useful for your next British capture," Bingham said with a chuckle. "As well, we can give you a few British ships that lost their way, being refitted in Guadeloupe for your company to utilize for carrying cargo to the American Army."

"We can always use good sailors with local knowledge," replied Jack.

"As well as more ships for letters of marque," said William, raising his glass in a toast.

Bingham poured yet another round of brandy for his guests.

"We also carry three holds full of fresh produce, sir. Should you wish to have your boats start unloading, our men will be happy to aid in the transfer," Jack Herbert offered.

"Yes of course, we will start first thing in the morning. We do business at a different pace here in the West Indies."

"And about the north bound cargo?" asked William.

"Between the gunpowder and munitions, we can surely fill half your holds and our main trading port at Pointe-å-Pitre will fill the rest," insisted Bingham.

"Excellent!" exclaimed William, turning to Connors and Jack for approval.

"*On trinque*?" Bingham raised his snifter in the air and nodded approvingly at the Americans. "A toast to our new trade agreement…and our new friends."

All around the table glasses were raised to their new union, welcoming the French support, even if it was officially still unofficial.

CHAPTER SEVENTEEN

Hurricane of Guadeloupe

(SEPTEMBER 1 7 7 6 – THE WINDWARD ISLANDS)

*A*fter three days in Fort Royal, with their cargo transfer complete and the ships reprovisioned for the next leg of their sail, they weighed anchor on the three ships, unfurled their sails and set a course of 335° northwest towards Guadeloupe. It was an easy broad-reach, however the winds were unusually brisk for summer. After all, the steady trade winds of the Caribbean were still a few months away. William and Jack had calculated the one hundred-and-two-mile trip at approximately seventeen hours, so they left around dusk, projecting their arrival in Pointe-å-Pitre around midday the following afternoon. Although there were seasoned West Indies sailors aboard all three ships, there was no need to take any chances on navigating in the dark the cut between Dominica and Isles des Saintes—the tiny islands south of the Pointe-å-Pitre harbor—as well as through the cut between Les Saintes and Marie-Galante, the small island windward of Guadeloupe.

By the time they reached the cut south of Guadeloupe on September 5, the seas coming through the gap from the Atlantic were high. The fact that Marie-Galante somewhat protected the bay helped the three ships find safe anchorage in the outer harbor. However, William, Jack, and Fanny quickly realized how difficult the transfer of heavy cargo would be in that sea—so far out in the bay. Captains Lovell, Herbert, and Clermont rowed ashore with several men to make the arrangements for their purchases and transfer of cargo. They also brought with them the propaganda pamphlets to be distributed in the Leeward Islands to the north. Concerned about the increasing swell and the rising winds, arrangements were quickly made to load the ships first thing the next morning.

By midnight, Fanny checked the barometer in the captain's quarters—alarmed at how much the barometric pressure had dropped from normal sea level reading at around one thousand thirteen millibars, to nine hundred ninety, and it appeared to be rapidly falling south of that number. Quickly, she called a meeting of all officers.

"This storm must be a hurricane, based on how rapidly the pressure is dropping," Fanny insisted. "It is still hurricane season so best to not take any chances."

"We'll fare far better at sea than sitting here," William said.

"On that I agree," Jack concurred.

"We need to get out of this harbor now, while we still can," added Fanny.

"We're already getting three-to-four-foot swells. Our ground tackle will never hold us if this does indeed turn into a major hurricane." William voiced the obvious. "Otherwise, we'll be trapped with little chance of riding it out on anchor with huge swells pushing through between these islands."

"I agree, we wouldn't stand a chance in here," said Jack.

"The question is, what will be our safest course to sail out of the path of this storm?" asked Jack of their French navigator, Gustav Boudreau.

Boudreau studied the chart, mulling over his decision as if he were carefully savoring a fine French wine, then weighed in with his heavy French accent. "Tropical storms track north-northwest, never south. I am of the opinion we should head west-southwest away from its path as quickly as possible. Otherwise, it may chase us all the way to Cuba." He chuckled as he pointed at the chart.

They all studied the chart of the Caribbean, considering his advice.

"Seems we're all in agreement," William said. "We can come

back for the cargo after the storm. It's best we not have such a heavy load in our bellies, or it may very well drag us to the bottom of the sea."

So, with that, Lovell gave the order to reef all sails, prepare the ship for heavy weather, and weigh anchor immediately. They headed west-southwest on a course of 260° degrees, with the three ships setting slightly differing courses so as not to risk collisions in the dark while battling what was likely to become a major tropical hurricane. The rapidly falling barometer already read nine hundred sixty millibars by the time they sailed past the little island of Terre-de-Bas in Les Saintes and into the Caribbean. They would have to do their best to ride out the storm by running from it on bare-minimum canvas. Their hope was that the storm would track to the north, rather than directly across the Caribbean. Hatches were battened down and jacklines were rigged as lifelines for the men's safety from bow to stern to prevent anyone from being washed overboard. No one would be allowed above deck without a lifeline and only essential crew allowed on deck, period. Below decks, all gear and cargo were stowed and lashed down tight. A loose barrel of gunpowder might literally crush a man in a rough sea. They took every precaution to ensure the safety of the ship and the crew, but what they didn't know was that this was a storm destined to go down in history as one of the deadliest—to be forever known as the Pointe-à-Pitre Guadeloupe Hurricane of 1776.

The three captains and their mates made plans—if they were separated, they would rendezvous back in Pointe-à-Pitre harbor as soon as the storm had passed and the wind and swell had subsided. William and Jack had many years of experience sailing in serious storms, and even Fanny had experienced her own taste of excitement the year before while being pursued by the *Dolphin*, but they were uncertain about Clermont's skills when it came to navigating a tropical storm or hurricane. Luckily, much of the French and West Indian crew they had acquired in Martinique, were very well-seasoned seamen in the tropics. Thus, they split the men amongst the three ships to aid in navigating whatever Mother Nature had to throw at them. If Moll's prediction about the storm was indeed what they were facing, they would be prepared. After all, Moll's track record for proficiency was as accurate as the rapidly falling barometer.

Knowing that the storm would only grow worse during the night, William made the decision for he and Fanny to take the midnight watch and put Tom O'Hara and Gustav Boudreau on the helm first. It would get far too rough to put a lookout in the crow's nest, so a man was secured on deck to the forward mast for his safety. It would be a wet ride, but a necessary one. Of course, with the heavy cloud cover it was as black as tar on that angry sea, and only the whitecaps and froth distinguished the wave tops from the pitch-black sky. By eleven, they had blown out their after-mainsail and furled all but a small staysail on the foremast.

Down below, in the captain's quarters, William and Fanny were direly concerned with the welfare of their friends and crew on the *Marion* and the *Mary*. Until they returned to port, they had no way of knowing if the ships were safe, or if all aboard were still alive. It was too rough for the ships to have a lantern burning in the rigging so in more ways than one, they were totally in the dark. They watched as the barometer continued to fall until it had reached 920° degrees, and with it the feeling deep in the pit of their stomachs dropped—there was no doubt it was going to be a treacherous night. It was then that they knew this was surely to be, not only a hurricane, but a major one. Many of the seasoned sailors in their quarters were green at the gills, retching violently and the ship was beginning to take on a vile, foul smell. A few of the men actually wanted to throw themselves overboard to end their suffering, since there is nothing worse for a seaman than 'plague at sea'— their name for seasickness. Their mates even found it necessary to bind them to their bunks to keep them from actually fulfilling their threats to abandon ship in the middle of the Caribbean Sea.

At midnight, William, Fanny, and a replacement watch donned their lifeline harnesses and opened the hatch long enough to climb on deck to relieve the conning officer (officer controlling the ship), the quartermaster (the person steering), and the watch. They tied their lifeline to the port jackline and fought their way to the helm to relieve O'Hara and Gustave. Should a rogue-wave crash over the ship, they surely wouldn't stand a chance in this sea should they be washed overboard.

"It's been a wild ride, captain!" shouted O'Hara over the screech of the howling wind and the pounding of the ship as it launched from the wavetops into the next trough, running ahead of the counterclockwise winds.

"We'll take it now!" shouted William.

"It's been steady building," O'Hara called out, pointing at the anemometer. "It's been gusting upwards of ninety knots! Pretty sure we're a tornado ridin' on the back of a hurricane!" he screamed above the roar in his Irish brogue.

"The bottom has dropped out of the pressure so there's no doubt," shouted Fanny. "It's going to be a long night."

"Get below and try to get dry!" ordered William. "I've got the conn!"

"Gladly!" shouted Gustave, relieved.

The three men struggled to get the hatch open and lie below as William took over the helm. The watch then secured himself forward. It didn't take long before the anemometer was whirring so fast from the wind gusts that it was peaking at over one hundred knots.

"Oh my God!" shouted Fanny. "I hope the other ships are alright."

"I as well, but let's worry about our own skin about now! We need to bear up! Keep her beam away from the wind!" William screamed over the high-pitched wail of the wind through the rigging.

It was all William and Fanny could do to hold the ship on a broad-reach with the wind on the starboard quarter. At times, the gusts were so strong it would take both he and Fanny to hold the helm on course, fearing that if they lost control for even a moment she would round up and take the sea on her beam, potentially knocking her down. Hours went by as they struggled to maintain control of the vessel. Then suddenly, the worst of their fears hit them like a dam breaking, with a deluge sweeping over the deck—washing both William and Fanny from the helm to the port rail. Immediately, the unmanned ship rounded up to a beam reach as a hundred-knot gust hit them broadside knocking the ship down—her crossjack yard touching the sea.

As her port rail dipped beneath the waves, both William and Fanny were washed under, still tethered to their lifelines. Fanny surfaced first, sputtering for air in the violent waves and froth. Frantically, she looked around for William as the ship continued to round up into the wind with the sea washing over them. On deck, the watch unlashed himself from the foremast, leaving a lifeline attached and slid along the deck to reach the helm in an attempt to right the ship. With the wheel finally within reach, he pulled himself up the pedestal, fighting to turn her dead into the wind and force her into irons to halt her forward momentum.

Fanny surfaced, choking on seawater and hollered over the wind for William, but he was nowhere to be seen. "Moll, please help me!" she called out, desperately searching the water for him.

Back in Lynn, Moll paced in front of her hearth, sensing their jeopardy in the deadly storm. She wrapped a light shawl around her shoulders and headed quickly to the top of High Rock. Moll heard Fanny's desperate screams for William. "Remember Fanny, find your strength!" shouted Moll. "You saved William once and you can do it again!"

Back on board the ship, Fanny paused a moment as Moll's cries came through despite the howling wind. "I hear you loud and clear, Moll," screamed Fanny as she spotted William's lifeline pulled taut under water. Taking a deep breath she followed the line down into the dark angry ocean, inching her way to where she could feel the line tangled around the gunport. Underwater, William struggled, out of breath, to free himself, desperate to get to the surface and the oxygen that he needed before his lungs burst. Fighting to unwind the line from around the gunport, Fanny finally released him and pulled him to the surface. William gasped for air just as the ship righted itself—the rail magically rising from the water as if it were pulling them free from the depths of hell.

On deck, the watch had managed to wrestle the ship into the wind, holding her in irons as she all but stopped and started to drift aft with the sea. Several men, including Finch and O'Hara, threw open the hatch ascending onto the deck to see what had happened. The knockdown had caused chaos below decks with much of the cargo breaking loose and crushing and killing one of their crew under casks of gunpowder. The wind still howled and although the motion had calmed, the sea continued to crash over the bow like a tsunami, washing the decks as the men struggled to cling to the ship to stay onboard.

"HELP ME," screamed Fanny. "HELP ME! Get the captain onboard!

The crew spotted William and Fanny clutching the rail—too weak to pull themselves over. They raced to the port rail and heaved their captain and first mate onto the deck to safely. William collapsed and Fanny's first impulse was to hold him and tell him how much she loved him, but she stopped herself, realizing she would reveal her secret should she give in to her emotions.

Back at High Rock, Moll breathed a sigh of relief, knowing they would now be safe.

⚓

When the *Fanny* sailed through the cut between Isles de Saints and Marie Galante and into the bay at Pointe-à-Pitre, it appeared that they were the first of the three to return to Guadeloupe. The devastation displayed before them in the harbor was far worse than their imaginations could have ever fathomed.

Indeed, it seemed that they were the only vessel still afloat. It appeared that every ship who had remained at anchor had succumbed to the devastating effacement of the storm. Dozens of boats were tossed upon the shoreline and the bay was littered with masts rising from the water like dead trees after a flood. Along the shore, there was little standing as the waves ruthlessly continued to pound and deface what had solidly stood there only forty-eight hours before. As they navigated through the debris to set their anchor William stood on the bow, directing the ship through the underwater minefield of wreckage; he gave signals to Fanny as she steered his course. "Face her to the wind! Give her a wide berth and keep her aloft!" he shouted as he signaled the crew on the foredeck anchor watch set to release the chain on the windlass to drop the anchor.

"Aye, aye, sir!" Fanny answered, turning the ship into the light southwest wind to drop anchor.

When the crew finally made it ashore, they learned the death toll on the island numbered in the thousands, and the islanders were still working to rescue those further inland where heavy rains had created massive mudslides in the hills. Sympathetic to their disastrous loss, the crew of the *Fanny* set to work with the islanders on a rescue mission to search for missing survivors. They needed to stay busy and distract their worried minds from their own concerns for their friends and mates aboard the *Mary* and the *Marion*. Fanny and William did their best to avoid thinking of what might have become of Jack, Marion, Josh, and Levi, as well as all their crew onboard their two ships.

A sigh of relief was heard all around the next day when the

Mary of Lynn sailed into the harbor and set anchor abeam of the *Fanny*. Some of their rigging was damaged, however she appeared to have avoided any major impairments. William and Gustav immediately rowed their tender aside her midships to speak with Clermont on any sightings of the *Marion*. Unfortunately, they had hoped the same from William—no one had seen her. William had to share the terrible news of their crewman, John Toth, who'd been crushed in the knock down by several kegs of gunpowder that had torn loose from their lashings and crushed his skull. Once the storm had subsided, they had given him a proper burial at sea. They would be sure to compensate his family when they returned to port at Beverly.

Two more days passed, giving them all reason to believe that their friends and crew had suffered the worst. Quite possibly the *Marion* had not survived the storm. Another day passed and they had pretty much given up hope when, just as the sun was setting, the *Marion* limped into the bay with severely damaged spars and rigging. She had taken the course furthest north of the three and had suffered higher winds from the outer bands of the storm. Several of their crew members were injured by the falling spars, but none severely. Thank God, Jack, Marion, and the boys had survived the hurricane unscathed.

With the severe damage done to the *Marion*, a decision was made to make quick repair to *Mary* and fill her hold to capacity with cargo shifted from the *Marion*. Clermont would then return to Beverly with the first load of munitions for Washington's Army. The *Fanny* would escort the *Marion* back to Martinique to be repaired and refitted. Once there, Jack Herbert and his crew would take one of the privateer vessels the French had confiscated for the Americans' cause and the two ships would sail north to Sint Eustatius. William knew from his friends, Biddle and Robinson, that there they could acquire additional stores, provisions, and munitions before returning home.

CHAPTER EIGHTEEN

Visions, Spies, Salutes, and a Final Save

(FALL 1 7 7 6 – LYNN, MASSACHUSETTS)

*N*o one knew better than Moll Pitcher, the value that General Washington placed on his spy networks. Although they held their cover from the British, there were several spy rings, such as the Culper Spy Ring and Knowlton's Rangers, as well as many local groups like that of Moll Pitcher's. The intelligence they gathered continued to help the Colonial Army to gain information about British troop placement and strategy. It was dangerous work, but without his spies the general would have been at a grievous disadvantage.

Moll continued her undercover work with the Burchstead brothers, Fanny Campbell, and Marion Herbert, one the women had returned from the West Indies. Moll hid guns and ammunition retrieved by the privateers, and gained information from the British soldiers who called upon her for readings. Oftentimes, her visions also proved useful even when they were quite disturbing. While General Glover was fighting the good fight alongside his men of Marblehead, Moll Pitcher was having visions of another noble young man whom she could not specifically identify. Some days the things she saw gave her terrible headaches—enough for her husband to grow concerned.

"My girl, what are you seeing now?" Robert Pitcher asked his wife early one September morning before the children awoke. "You haven't been yourself for days."

"I'm not sure," Moll confessed as she poured them each a cup of tea—their early morning ritual before starting breakfast for the children. "I keep seeing a dark-haired young man." She took her seat across the table from Robert and lifted the cup to her lips.

"What concerns you so about this young man?"

"I keep seeing him surrounded by redcoats and then hanging from the gallows."

"Do you recognize him?"

"No, I don't believe we have ever met."

"Maybe you should write to Lady Washington and tell her about your worries."

"That's a good idea. I will do that today. I just hope I am not too late to save him."

Once Moll's morning chores were done, she sat down at her Queen Anne's table and penned the following:

My dearest Lady Washington,

I come to you today with a grave concern in my heart. There is a young man whom I believe is in serious danger. I don't know his name, but I can tell you that, according to my visions, which are very vivid, he has dark hair and a very youthful appearance. His work is treacherous and if he is not extremely careful, he will be apprehended by the British and hung. Do you know of such a young man? If you do, would it be possible to warn him of the danger he faces?

I apologize for bothering you, but I am not sure who else to turn to. I wish I had better information to give, but this is all I have seen and I have been worried sick about him.

Please write as soon as you can and let me know whether you can help me.

Your good friend always,
Moll Pitcher

Moll's letter reached Martha Washington in Philadelphia in early October and with a very heavy heart Martha responded one week later.

My dear friend Moll,

I fear your warning came too late. I believe the young man you saw in your visions was most likely Mr. Nathan Hale, a true patriot from Connecticut. He was arrested behind enemy lines a few weeks ago and taken to Long Island where he was charged as a spy and sentenced to death. I am sorry to report that he was hung as a spy in New York on September 22 according to recent correspondence from my husband. This is a tremendous loss for our side, but I am told that Mr. Hale faced death gallantly. His last words spoke of his regret for having but one life to give for his country. He was only twenty-one years old and leaves behind a grieving family. The general and I also grieve his loss. Please pray for his soul as that is all we can do for him now.

Sincerely,
Lady Washington

Moll was devastated by the tragic loss of this young man. She blamed herself for not doing more. As her grandfather had warned her, sometimes being able to see the future was more like a curse than a help. She had failed to save Nathan Hale and that weighed heavily on her mind. How many more young people would be lost before this rebellion finally ended?

⚓

William Lovell's friend, Captain Biddle, had been patrolling the Atlantic coastline aboard the brig *Andrew Doria* since they returned from the Battle of Nassau and their battle off Block Island. Under his command the ship had captured a number of

British loyalist ships. However, having been reassigned to command the *Randolph,* one of the four new frigates under construction in Philadelphia for the new Continental Navy, Biddle anchored his warship on September 17 in the harbor at Chester, Pennsylvania and turned over the command of the *Andrew Doria* to Captain Isaiah Robinson. Biddle had notified William of his pending reassignment and had previously suggested that the West Indies Shipping Company cruise down to Sint Eustatius, a Dutch Island in the Netherland Antilles, to purchase armament. Since their holds were still not fully loaded, William made the decision to sail from Martinique to Sint Eustatius with their newly acquired ship, the *Colleen,* and the *Fanny.* Their new ship had been named after Terrance Mooney's sainted mother, who'd had the most memorable funeral in Lynn, thanks to Bartholomew Channing. The two ships set sail the morning of November 13 on a course of 330° northwest to the tiny Dutch trading port in the Leeward Islands. They did not wish to risk the shallow waters of the Saba Banks, due west of Saba and Sint Eustatius, so they would be forced to sail within a near distance of the British Islands of St. Christopher and Nevis. Thus, they chose to do so under the cover of darkness. With such light winds, they calculated it would take just over thirty hours to reach their destination.

In September of 1776 Johannes de Graaff was assigned governor of the tiny island of Sint Eustatius, also known in the West Indies as the Golden Rock. He had previously served as the military commander of Saint Maarten, another Dutch colony in the Leeward Islands. The Dutch were generally known to be dedicated merchants and prone to do business with any and all flags that sailed into their harbors, and de Graff had quickly gained the reputation of someone willing to trade with the Americans. De Graff didn't see doing business with the patriots that were fighting for control of their homeland as dealing with smugglers as the British viewed it—he simply saw it as doing business.

The *Fanny*, being the fastest of the two vessels, arrived through the cut between the little volcanic island of Sint Eustatius to the north, and St. Christopher to the south, during the wee hours of the morning of November 16. Although Lovell had been told by his West Indian crewmen that the harbor of Statia, as they fondly referred to it, was a deep-water terminal, he chose to wait offshore until dawn to sail into anchor. As the sun rose from the east, the distinct outline of a brig could be seen coming through the cut from the Anegada Passage. William, who was familiar with the ship after sailing with Biddle, immediately recognized her as the *Andrew Doria*. Out of respect for Captain Robinson, William chose to lay in irons off the rocky coastline to allow her to be the first to choose her mooring.

The waters of the Caribbean were calm that day and the deep blue water ringed the jagged rocky island with little sand and surf surrounding it. On the island itself, a dormant volcano, or the quill, rose from the south end and the rest remained quite low with a light dusting of green vegetation stretching across its rocky soil. The lowest clouds drifting across the island were snagged momentarily by the quill, only to blow past without dropping any much-needed precipitation on the dry island. Fort Orange sat atop the cliff, overlooking the tiny town on the island's docks of Oranjestad Harbor. As the *Andrew Doria* tacked into the bay and dropped her sails, Robinson ordered the standard firing of the ship's cannon—a single merchant salute to the Dutch flag at Fort Orange. Overhead her mast flew the red-and-white-striped flag of the Continental Congress. Without hesitation, the fort answered the salute with the firing of their cannon of eleven shots in recognition of the new American flag. The rolling thunder of the cannon resonated over the little island and engulfed the quiet harbor, spewing small white puffs of smoke. It would become known as '*the salute of eleven guns.*'

Fanny and William smiled at one another onboard the *Fanny*, knowing that they had been lucky to witness not one, but two honorary salutes to the new American flag and the newly formed country—the United States. Aboard the *Andrew Doria*, Robinson carried a copy of the newly drafted Declaration of Independence. Little did the island officials know at the time how that small act of recognition of a new nation would lead to the future devastation of their prosperous, neutral island before the war would end.

After loading their holds to the brim with cargo and provisions from the island, the *Fanny* and the *Colleen* set sail back to Massachusetts on November 20. Their nearly two-week sail home was smooth and uneventful, arriving in early December with their profitable cargo.

⚓

Colonel Glover and his men spent most of November encamped in North Castle, New York before receiving orders to join General Washington in Pennsylvania at the west bank of the Delaware River near the New Jersey border. It was Washington's intent to conduct a surprise attack on Christmas Day on a group of German soldiers who had sided with the British and were now occupying Trenton, New Jersey. He hoped that the element of surprise would bring a successful victory and uplift his men's morale. So far, the winter had been extremely cold and treacherous. Many members of the Colonial Army were sick. They were not adequately clothed. Some even marched with rags wrapped around their feet as they had no shoes. Almost all were hungry. Their poor physical condition and accompanying mental fatigue left them discouraged with little hope of winning this wretched war. Such was the pitiable condition of Washington's army when Colonel Glover found them that frigid Christmas night.

Washington's original plan was to have three river crossings at three different points: one led by Colonel John Cadwalader with his eighteen hundred men who were to land near Burlington,

New Jersey; a second crossing directly at Trenton led by General James Ewing with his eight hundred soldiers; and lastly Washington himself, along with twenty-four hundred troops, which were to disembark about ten miles north of the target city. Cadwalader and Ewing never made it. Only Colonel Glover and his tough seafaring Marbleheaders were successful.

Glover assigned Black Joe to report directly to General Washington. It was his job to ensure not only the general's safety, but also to communicate any orders that were given. That night as the men were at the mercy of the wintry elements, it was Black Joe who called out encouragement to not only his fellow Marbleheaders, but also to the fatigued soldiers who were beginning to question what exactly the point was of all this misery.

The actual crossing began later than anticipated as the bitter temperatures continued to drop and the biting winds blew harder. The Marbleheaders used large dunham boats designed to carry coal and flat-bottomed ferries that had been secured by Washington. As the night progressed, the drizzle turned into freezing rain that mixed with blinding snow and wicked winds.

A few mariners from Marblehead, dressed in their marine clothes, manned each boat, taking forty troops at a crack and crossing the Delaware—time after time avoiding the dangerous ice floes as their stinging fingers pushed long poles in the shallow water and rowed with eighteen-foot oars over the deeper areas. Glover's brigade made trip after trip over the icy waters, with frosty breath and cheeks that burned from the extreme cold. They didn't stop until every man was set down on the New Jersey side along with their horses, supplies, and heavy artillery that included eighteen cannons.

When it was time for General Washington to cross, Black Joe made room in one of the dunham boats and sat at the general's knee, manning an oar of his own.

"We'll get you across, sir." Joe promised as the wind rocked the vessel. "If it's the last thing we do."

"You're a good man, Joe." The general smiled. "Colonel Glover is lucky to have you. You've spent this entire night of misery at my beck and call and never once complained about anything."

"We all could complain about something." Joe gave a weary smile. "But complaining don't get the job done, now does it?"

"Indeed it does not." Washington managed a smile. "You know, Joe, I think once this war is finally won, I would like to come to Marblehead and visit your establishment."

"That would be mighty fine." Joe grinned as he rowed. "And I will personally make you a Sir Switchel…on the house of course, and Creese, my wife, will load you up with some of her famous Joe Froggers. You can ask any man in our troop and they will all tell you that Creese's Joe Froggers are the spiciest, tastiest cookies you will ever eat."

"I look forward to it," Washington said as the sleet whipped around them while they made their way across the Delaware.

By three a.m., their mission was complete, but Washington now worried that they had lost their advantage of making a surprise attack. They had not. The ensuing battle was a rousing victory for the beleaguered colonists—twenty-two Germans were killed and eighty-three wounded. More than eight hundred were taken prisoner. In addition, much-needed supplies were obtained, including food, clothing, and artillery. Most importantly, the Colonial Army's spirits were lifted and they once again resolved to fight another day.

Sometime later, General Henry Knox reported directly to the Massachusetts Legislature:

"Sirs: I wish the members of this body knew the people of Marblehead as well as I do—I could wish that they had stood on the banks of the Delaware River in 1776 in that bitter night, when the commander-in-chief had drawn up his little army to cross it, and had seen the powerful current bearing onward the floating masses of ice, which threatened destruction to whosoever should venture upon its bosom. I wish that when this occurrence threatened to defeat the enterprise, they could have heard that distinguished warrior demand 'Who will lead us on?' and seen the men of Marblehead and Marblehead alone, stand forward to lead the army along the perilous path to unfading glories and honors in the achievements of Trenton. There, sir, went the fishermen of Marblehead alike at home upon land or water, alike ardent, patriotic and unflinching, whenever they unfurled the flag of the country."

CHAPTER NINETEEN

Glover's Second Thoughts

(JANUARY 1 7 7 7 – LYNN, MASSACHUSETTS)

The bitter cold of January had set in. The ground was frozen and a harsh chill permeated the air. The holidays, such as they were during this time of strife, were over and the children were all at school. Moll was busy mixing her potions for which she had several requests—potions for love, potions for conceiving, potions for memory loss, and other potions for curing the various ailments the locals seemed to suffer. Robert had just come inside carrying a bundle of kindling and logs, along with a letter addressed to his wife. The familiar handwriting made her smile as she took a seat nearer the fire while Robert fed the wood onto the flames. Clutching her worn shawl around her shoulders with one hand, she peered intently at the paper, hoping for good news about the trouble in New York, but the words she read made her tremble despite her proximity to the warm hearth.

"Moll, you can't possibly be cold." Robert hung his coat near the door. "I've kept that fire burning all afternoon and still I see you shaking."

Moll never once looked up.

"MOLL!" Robert stood over his wife. "Would you care to share what's troubling you so?"

"I must go to Marblehead at once." Moll folded the letter in half.

"But the roads are in terrible shape this time of year," Robert protested. "And it's freezing outside."

She handed the letter to her husband. "No matter. I need to talk to Johnny. He's made a terrible mistake."

Robert unfolded the paper and read out loud:

My Dearest Moll,

By the time you receive this letter, I should be back home in Marblehead or at least close to it. I did my best to serve General Washington and we safely crossed the Delaware into Trenton, New Jersey where we won a hard-fought battle with the Hessians. All of my good men from Marblehead served nobly and made me very proud to be their leader. As of January 1, however, our enlistment was up and I gave the general my resignation. Some of my men chose to stay under Colonel Lee, but it is imperative that I get home to take care of my beloved Hannah. I have been away much too long and her health is failing. I fear for her.

General Washington did not take this news well at all. He insisted that I think seriously about my decision, but trust me, Moll, I have taken everything into consideration and I must do what's best for my family.

Please pray for my safe return and for my dear wife and children. We cannot know what the future holds. We can only do our best as we see fit. And right now, I can think only of home.

Please feel free to call upon us at any time. Your presence is always a comfort and Hannah tells me that she enjoys your company.

I will close for now.

Your Good Friend,
John

Moll wasted no time in putting on her winter cloak and promptly marching next door to Jack and Marion Herbert's home, leaving her husband to wonder just what she was up to. The elderly Mrs. Herbert sat at the kitchen table wearing an old apron as she peeled imaginary potatoes into an empty white bowl with an imaginary knife.

"She thinks she's helping," Marion said, explaining her mother-in-law's odd behavior.

"Poor dear." Moll gently lay her hand on the elderly woman's sparse gray hair. Mrs. Herbert smiled, but remained silent.

"She rarely speaks now, but at least she seems happy," Marion said. "Sit down for a moment and tell me, Moll, what brings you here on such a cold day?"

"I am in need of a carriage." Moll took the chair next to Mrs. Herbert who put down her imaginary knife as if her job was done. "I must go to Marblehead to see Colonel Glover as soon as possible."

"I thought the colonel was with General Washington in New Jersey." Marion picked up the empty bowl and put it back on the shelf nearest the hearth.

"He was." Moll sighed as Marian returned with a second bowl, smaller in size than the first. "But I'm afraid he has up and resigned his post. It is imperative that he remains with the general. There are dark days ahead and his presence is needed with the troops."

"I can try and get word to Samuel," Marion offered, as she set the smaller bowl in front of Mrs. Herbert. "Since you did such a good job with the potatoes, mother, would you be a dear and shell these peas for dinner?"

Mrs. Herbert nodded and began silently working her fingers over the empty bowl.

"Do you think the Breeds might have a carriage available?" Moll asked.

"They might and you know they would do anything for you, Moll," Marion said. "After all, they remain forever grateful to you for Samuel's safe return."

And so it was before the month ended, Moll was on her way to Marblehead leaving Robert in charge of the children.

⚓

As the month of January drew to a close, the winter weather cleared for traveling and a warm sun greeted Moll when she arrived in Marblehead in the afternoon. She took the fair weather as a positive sign. Normally, she would have first stopped to see Auntie Creese, but today she was in a hurry to visit the Glover home. She carried with her a bundle of herbs and potions she had mixed specifically for Hannah.

Twelve-year-old Tabitha Glover answered Moll's knock. Her little brother, Jonathan, peeked from behind her.

"Come in, Mrs. Pitcher!" Tabitha, who favored her mother, was a lovely girl with long, dark curls. "I just got home from school so my mother is resting while I look after the little ones. She isn't well, you know."

"I know, child." Moll set down her bag and gave her cloak to Tabitha. "I have come to see her, but I must speak with your father first. Is he home?"

"Yes, ma'am. He's in his study," Tabitha answered and gave her little brother a push. "Go tell father that Moll Pitcher would like to see him." Jonathon ran off without a word.

Moll picked up her bag. "After I talk to your father, I would like to see your mother. I've brought some herbal remedies that might make her a little stronger."

"Oh, thank you, ma'am." Tabitha gave a quick curtsy.

"Be a good girl and put them in a safe place for now."

"Yes, ma'am. I will." Tabitha took the bag and cloak into the parlor just as her father emerged from his study with Jonathon in tow.

"I've been expecting you, Moll!" He beamed at the sight of his oldest and dearest friend.

"Johnny." Moll did not return his smile. "We have to talk. It's important."

"Run along, Jonathan!" Glover squatted down to meet his son at eye level. "Go find Tabitha and tell her to bring refreshments for Mrs. Pitcher and me in my office."

"Yes, father." The boy raced off, calling his sister's name.

"Shall we, Moll?" Glover offered his arm and they walked in silence.

"You received my letter." Glover settled behind his desk while Moll took the oversized chair across from him trying to gather her thoughts. "And I can see that you're upset with me."

"Johnny, you know I could never be upset with you," Moll began, "but I am worried about you."

"Oh, I remember a time you were upset with me." Glover idly picked up a pen from his desk. "Your mother was going to make an apple pie and I ate all the apples you picked."

"I guess I was upset with you that day." Moll couldn't help but let a grin escape.

"And if memory serves me, you hit me over the head with your empty basket and then you refused to talk to me."

"Until I found out how sick you were from eating all those apples," Moll said as she laughed. "Then I felt sorry for you."

"And you came around to check on me." Glover smiled and then turned serious. "Are you checking on me today, Moll?"

Before Moll could answer, Tabitha entered, carrying a tray with a tea service and a plate of Joe Froggers.

"My goodness, child!" Moll gasped. "Is that English tea? Wherever did you get it?"

Glover winked. "Let's just say that the Hessians were willing to share and we will leave it at that."

Moll sat quietly as Tabitha poured two cups of the steaming brew before leaving the room. She took a sip and smiled. "It's been a long time since I've tasted real English tea."

"But you didn't come all the way here just to share tea with me, did you?" Glover turned serious. "You've come to give me a scolding, haven't you?"

Moll set her cup down and leaned forward. "I don't want to scold you, Johnny, but how could you desert the general at a time like this?"

"I didn't desert," Glover replied. "I mustered out. It was all above board."

"But why? Why would you leave when this country needs you most?"

"Because my Hannah needs me. Moll, you haven't seen her. She is terribly thin and pale and she can't put two words together without coughing."

"I know you are worried about your wife," Moll said. "But some things are much bigger than two people. We have all been forced to make sacrifices for our freedom, our independence. The very fate of our nation is at risk and that, my friend, is greater than any one of us…you, Hannah, me. Your service is vital, and you must put your personal problems aside."

"I can't do that." Glover shook his head. "How could I live with myself if something happened to my wife while I was off serving my country?"

"Johnny." Moll tried again. "Whether you stay or go, Hannah's fate is sealed. You cannot save her, but you can help save this country and you must."

"Even if I wanted to go back," Glover said with a sigh, "my men are not well-liked by the others. They are looked down upon because they are sometimes crude and tawdry. They dress differently and many of them do not look like typical soldiers. We are poles apart from the rest of the Continental Army."

"But the men of Marblehead are heroes," Moll reminded him. "They have proven themselves time and time again. Can the others say as much?"

"I love every one of my men for their bravery and dedication. There are no finer men in any of Washington's army. I agree with you there, but I am afraid many others only see them as hard-boiled sailors not worth more than the fish they catch."

"Then there's nothing I can say to make you change your mind?"

"I'm afraid not, Moll." Glover shook his head. "I am through with my service and now I need to focus on my wife and children."

"You're wrong, but I'll say no more." Moll knew she had lost the battle for now. "But the general won't give up so easily and I would strongly advise you to take heed when he calls."

Several weeks after Moll's visit to Marblehead, the Continental Congress elevated John Glover from colonel to brigadier general based on General Washington's endorsement. Glover turned down the commission in a letter to General Washington dated April 1, 1777. Glover then wrote a letter of explanation to Moll and with his letter, he sent her a box of good English tea as a peace offering.

⚓

As the cold winter temperatures began to rise into more spring-like weather, Moll had her first of many terrible visions concerning a young girl murdered by a group of Native Americans. The first one came as she was preparing her garden for planting. She didn't know who the girl was or where the gruesome incident occurred, but the vision took her breath away and laid her flat on the newly dug soil. Moll made it to her knees, as a terrible headache besieged her. She took a deep breath and crawled back to the house, calling for her husband. Robert came from his small workroom and helped her to her feet.

"What is it, my girl?" He gently led her to a chair. "What have you seen this time?"

"Murder!" Moll gasped, trying to catch her breath. "They killed her and took the scalp right off her head!"

"Maybe you should lie down," Robert offered.

"If only I could warn her," Moll cried.

"Who is she?"

"I don't know," Moll said, trembling. "I only know she is young, and I fear for her."

"Try not to think about it anymore." Robert gently pulled her from the chair and walked toward the bedroom. Once inside, he helped her lie down and pulled the covers up around her.

"My grandfather said sometimes our abilities are a curse and I feel that this is one of those times."

"My girl, you cannot save everyone." Robert touched her cheek. "No matter how hard you try."

"And that is the whole trouble," she told him. "Why am I afflicted with such terrible visions if I can't do anything about them?"

"Moll, you know you do more good than not."

"But it's times like this that I feel so helpless."

"You rest now." Robert stood up. "You will feel better if you just close your eyes for a while."

"I won't feel better until these visions stop."

But they didn't stop. They continued periodically for the next few months, taking a toll on Moll each time.

⚓

Jack Herbert's mother passed away peacefully in her sleep in the middle of April 1777. Her death and burial occupied Moll for a time. Old Mrs. Herbert was laid to rest next to her husband in

Lynn's Western Burial Ground where many of the city's earliest residents were interred.

Moll continued communicating with the Sons of Liberty and hiding small arms in Lynn Woods whenever the privateers returned with their spoils. She gave readings for those who called upon her and sold herbs and potions for those seeking remedies. Robert worked hard, but still never seemed to bring in quite enough money for a family of six, so the extra income Moll earned was always welcome. Despite any hardship, both Robert and Moll were thankful for their children's good health, as many families in the area were not so fortunate, often burying more than one of their offspring. Those terrifying visions continued to distress her and the blinding headaches that resulted often made her sick enough to retch.

One such afternoon in May as a gentle rain fell, Moll was home alone resting by the hearth with a shawl around her shoulders. The need to be by herself was overwhelming that day so she had sent Robert to Boston for supplies while the children were in school. The air was damp and she had just had another vision of the young girl's murder when a carriage pulled up in front of her house. Soon after, someone knocked.

"I'll not be giving readings today." Moll called out, preferring not to open the door to a silly young girl looking for a new beau.

"I'm not here for a reading." The door opened a bit and a familiar face peeked in. "I'm here to see my old friend if she'll have me."

"Oh, Johnny!" Moll brightened. "Of course you can come in." She rushed to her feet and a wave of dizziness passed through her.

"Are you all right?" Glover quickly came inside to put a steady hand on her arm.

"Yes," she said, smiling. "I just wasn't expecting you."

"You mean the great psychic of Lynn didn't know I was coming?" he teased with a grin.

"I'm afraid the great psychic of Lynn has been preoccupied lately."

"Do you care to talk about it?"

"I will if you promise to sit down and have some good English tea with me."

"And wherever did you get some good English tea during these times?"

She gave a wink. "I can't say, but someone I know is very resourceful."

The two friends shared a warm brew and Moll told Glover about her frightening visions. "I can't control them," she concluded. "They just come and go and I can't think of a way to save this poor child."

"Maybe she isn't meant to be saved," Glover offered.

"Then why afflict me like this?" Moll blinked back tears.

"I don't know." Glover shook his head. "Life is full of mysteries and many things we don't understand."

"That doesn't make it any easier," Moll said with a sigh.

"Maybe this will help." Glover pulled a folded letter from his pocket and handed it to Moll. She read:

To Brigadier General John Glover
Headquarters Morris Town April 26, 1777

Sir

After the conversations, I had with you, before you left the army, last winter, I was not a little surprised at the contents of yours of the first instant. As I had not the least doubt but you would accept of the commission of Brigadier, if conferred upon you by Congress, I put your name down in the list of those, whom I thought proper for the command, and whom I wished to see preferred.

Diffidence in an officer is a good mark, because he will always endeavour to bring himself up to what he conceives to be the full line of his duty; but I think, I may tell you, without flattery, that I know of no man better qualified than you to conduct a brigade. You have activity and industry, and as you very well know the duty of a colonel, you know how to exact that duty from others.

I have with great concern observed the almost universal listlessness, that prevails throughout the continent; and I believe, that nothing has contributed to it more, than the resignation of officers, who stepped early forward and led the people into the great cause, in which we are too deeply embarked to look back, or to hope for any other terms, than those we can gain by the sword. Can any resistance be expected from the people when deserted by their leaders? Our enemies count upon the resignation of every officer of rank at this time, as a distrust of, and desertion from the cause, and rejoice accordingly. When you consider these matters I hope you will think no more of private inconveniences, but that you will, with all expedition, come forward, and take that command which has been assigned you. As I fully depend upon seeing you, I shall not mention anything, that has passed between us, upon this subject, to the Congress. I am Sir Your most humble servant.

George Washington

Moll looked up at her friend expectantly. "Please tell me you accepted the commission."

"I did." Glover nodded.

"Oh, Johnny." Moll beamed. "A brigadier general! I knew you wouldn't disappoint General Washington and forsake our country!"

"I'm afraid I may have disappointed Hannah," he said. "But I will be leaving soon."

"What can I do?" Moll asked.

"Oh, Moll." Glover smiled, touched at her concern. "Whatever did I do to deserve such a good friend?"

"You know there isn't anything I wouldn't do for you and Hannah," she said as she smiled back.

"Will you promise to send all the remedies she needs to keep her comfortable?"

"Of course," Moll assured him. "I will wrap up some things for you to take today and when she needs more, I'll see to it that she gets them if I have to deliver them myself."

"Thank you." Glover reached for her hand and the two sat in silence for a moment. "Moll, I'm afraid there are many things that have been left unsaid between us so before I go—"

"Let's not spoil the moment with words we might regret," Moll interrupted and clasped his hand in both of hers. "I know and you know and that is enough."

"You're right." He gently pressed her hand to his lips. "We mustn't dwell on what we can't have, but I find comfort in your presence and, even though I don't deserve it, your friendship."

"Your friendship brings me a joy, I wouldn't otherwise have," Moll said. "And that is the way it's always been and the way it will always be."

"Till death us do part?" he whispered.

"Yes, Johnny," Moll whispered back. "Till death us do part."

Not long after, Brigadier General John Glover left Marblehead for New York, where he took command of his brigade.

CHAPTER TWENTY

Turning Point

(JUNE 1 7 7 7 – LYNN MASSACHUSETTS)

During the spring of 1777, General Washington had all he could handle to keep his army intact. Men were deserting due to lack of pay, severe illness, and dwindling supplies. Individual recruitment from the colonies was at an all-time low. Morale was even worse. Strangely, it would take the murder of a young girl—a loyalist no less—and the appearance of a young Frenchman to turn the tide.

Nineteen-year-old Marie-Joseph Paul Yves Roch Gilbert du Motier de Lafayette, Marquis de Lafayette, left his native France and completed an eight-week voyage across the Atlantic, arriving in Georgetown, South Carolina on June 13, 1777. From there, he and several companions walked to Charlestown where they gathered supplies for their overland journey to Philadelphia—nearly seven hundred miles away.

Lafayette was born into a wealthy French family with a rich military history. He himself had become a commissioned officer at the young age of thirteen. With no wars to fight in France, Lafayette was intrigued by the rebellion in America. Seeking adventure and notoriety, he decided he would join Washington's army. To add fuel to his burning desire, there were still many hard feelings between the French and the English due to the Seven Years War, or the French and Indian War as it was known in the colonies, when France was forced to cede its New World holdings to the Crown.

While Lafayette and company were planning their trip to Philadelphia, the Continental Congress led by John Hancock was in session there. On June 14, 1777, they officially adopted the Stars and Stripes as the flag of America. The red, white, and blue colors each had its own meaning—red stood for valor, white for purity, and blue for loyalty. The alternating red and white stripes symbolized the fight for independence while the thirteen stars represented each individual colony. Some flags featured the stars in a circle to denote equality. This symbolic gesture was a way to unite the individual colonies which each flew its own separate flag—in some cases more than one.

Moll's visions of the young girl's murder were coming more often, leaving her in a severely weakened state each time. There were even days when she could hardly get out of bed. She still had no idea who this girl was or where the murder would take place. Only the gruesome details were revealed, but none of the particulars. Moll penned a letter of warning to General Glover and a second one to Lady Washington, but there was no reply from either. Then at the end of July, on the same day that the Marquis de Lafayette and his companions reached Philadelphia, the visions simply stopped. Moll's fear turned to grief. Whoever she was, Moll knew that this young girl had finally met her untimely and gruesomely violent end.

Twenty-five-year-old Jane McCrea was a loyalist and engaged to marry David Jones, a British officer. McCrea and several others were abducted by a group of Native Americans who were fighting alongside the British under the command of General Burgoyne, also known as 'Gentleman Johnny' for his philandering ways in New York. After she was killed, the natives scalped her and brought her hair to the British who had promised to pay them for each patriot scalp they presented. They collected their fee and later, when David Jones saw the scalps, he recognized his missing fiancée's hair. He was devastated to learn of her brutal demise.

When Burgoyne discovered the brutality that McCrea had faced in the massacre, he was furious. His first instinct was to arrest and prosecute the guilty parties, but he was advised against that by his subordinates. They convinced him that the natives would retaliate against his soldiers, so in the end Burgoyne chose not to pursue the girl's killers. Shortly after, it was reported by various colonial newspapers that the Native Americans in New York had abducted, murdered, and scalped a young woman without facing any consequences. McCrea's story was embellished with each retelling. One even claimed that she was murdered in her wedding gown. Dramatic drawings of her slaying circulated throughout the land and outrage amongst the colonists intensified, even though she was a loyalist, spurring them to join General Washington and avenge the young woman's untimely death. To the general's relief, the Colonial Army's number soon swelled with men now determined to not only fight against the callous British Army, but to win.

⚓

The same day that Jane McCrea was killed, the Marquis de Lafayette and his companions finally reached Philadelphia. After presenting a letter of recommendation from Benjamin Franklin to the Continental Congress, Lafayette was given a commission of major general, but there would be no pay and no men under his command. Later that evening, Lafayette made the acquaintance of General Washington who had come to Philadelphia believing that the British were about to invade the city. Impressed by Lafayette's youthful exuberance and commitment to the patriot cause, the general invited the young Frenchman to join him in touring their defenses along the Delaware River. The British had recently captured New York's Fort Ticonderoga and word had it that they were heading to Philadelphia with plans to invade the capital.

Back in Lynn, Moll Pitcher tended to her growing children and her ever-faithful husband. By now, Ruth was a comely fourteen-year-old and Becky was twelve. Lydia was the youngest girl at ten and John, who was spoiled by his older sisters, was just seven. Dark-haired Becky was closest to her mother and, when callers came for a reading, she always helped Moll by brewing and serving tea. She loved the blue-and-white teacups that held the steaming liquid and the way her mother read the tea leaves. Sometimes she watched as Moll read palms and she often wished to share her mother's unique and prolific gifts, but had not been blessed with visions or psychic gifts of her own.

"Count your blessings, child," Moll assured her one afternoon as they mixed potions together. "You do not want to see the things I see."

"I would if I could help people." Becky sighed as she filled several jars with an elderberry mixture that would ward off sickness when taken in the morning. It was one of Moll's most popular tonics.

"We can't always help." Moll shrugged as she crushed more elderberries in a large wooden bowl. "And that is when we feel powerless. It is not a feeling you want to have...believe me, dear."

"Like when the McCrea girl died?"

"Yes, but if you learn to make the potions," Moll said, "you will do more good than any vision would allow."

"What do you do when you have a vision like that?" Becky asked. "You know the kind that makes you feel powerless?"

"Why, you pray, my child," Moll told her. "You pray with all your heart."

Unknown to Becky, Moll had been praying as dreams were now haunting her—dreams of two great battles—one in Philadelphia and one in New York. She knew Philadelphia would be lost at least temporarily, but the patriots would one day soon and, after much bloodshed, claim victory in Saratoga, where General Glover would once again play an important role.

⚓

British General Howe and his men were now closing in on Philadelphia. General Washington, believing that his troops blocked all the crossing points along Brandywine Creek, felt sure that the Colonial Army held the upper hand. On the morning of September 11, 1777, the patriots engaged in battle near Chadds Ford, Pennsylvania thinking that they were fighting General Howe. In reality, they were up against a group of Hessians led by Wilhelm von Knyphausen, while General Howe and his men were crossing the Brandywine Creek further north. Undetected, General Howe's men attacked the colonists along their right flank. Outnumbered by the British, Washington had no choice but to retreat and the Continental Congress was forced to flee from Philadelphia.

Although General Lafayette had no troops to lead, he fought valiantly that day despite a leg that was seriously wounded by a musket ball. Bleeding profusely, he removed his general's sash to bind the gash. He then mounted a horse to continue the fight and help with the men's retreat. Word of his bravery soon spread throughout the colonies and the young Frenchman was hailed a hero. Washington then sent orders to General Glover telling him to release Black Joe from his command so that he could be assigned directly to General Lafayette. After all, a brave hero deserved only the best aide-de-camp.

General Glover had military business of his own. His troops were stationed at Van Schaick Island not far from Saratoga. The men were fairly healthy, but many lacked good shoes, decent clothes, and warm blankets. On September 18, 1777, the Colonial Army won back Fort Ticonderoga from the British. This inspired Glover's men and the other patriots to fight valiantly at an area known as Freeman's Farm the next day.

Freeman's Farm was located above the west bank of the Hudson River. Washington had sent a group of men who called themselves Morgan's Rifles for scouting purposes. Early on September 19, the men left camp to determine what Burgoyne was planning. A small skirmish ensued, but more America soldiers continued to join the fight. By that afternoon, a major battle was underway.

The Americans held off the British and Burgoyne decided to wait for reinforcements before initiating further attacks. Bodies were strewn across the battlefield and at night wolves howled as they rummaged through the corpses. It was apparent that the English troops were trapped with very few supplies. Burgoyne kept his men at Freeman's Farm for the next three weeks and in a letter to Brigadier General Henry Watson Powell, he wrote:

"I take the first opportunity to inform you we have had a smart and very honorable action and are now encamped in front of the field which must demonstrate our victory beyond the power of even an American news-writer to explain away."

Powell never received the letter as it was intercepted by the Americans. Nonetheless, the stage was now set for further conflicts. The Battle of Saratoga would soon be a deciding factor and a turning point for Washington's army.

While General Burgoyne and his men waited, the gathering American troops swelled in number. By October 7, Burgoyne had grown impatient and organized an attack, but the colonists were ready. General Glover and his Marblehead Regiment fought valiantly under General Benedict Arnold at Bemis Heights. Glover himself had three horses shot from under him and Arnold was severely wounded in the melee when his horse was shot dead from under him. When night came and darkness enveloped Freedman's Farm, Burgoyne ordered his men to begin their retreat.

They left behind their tents and a small group of British soldiers who remained to stoke several fires throughout the deserted camp, hoping that the Americans would not realize that they were gone. Before the night was over, rain began to pound down.

Burgoyne stopped the retreat, which concerned the soldiers who desperately wanted to get away from the colonists. He ordered an inventory of their cannons and claimed he wanted his troops to rest. When the weather finally permitted, they were once again on the move, but the cold, drenched soldiers only made it as far as Saratoga, a small village about eight miles away.

On October 10, the Colonial Army caught up to them. General Gates planned an attack on the beleaguered British. At daybreak, however, General Glover spotted an English soldier who claimed to be a deserter. Upon questioning the man, he admitted that Burgoyne was going to retreat further north. Glover advised: "If you are found attempting to deceive me, you shall be hung in half an hour…" Glover then had the deserter escorted directly to General Gates. After hearing the man's account, Gates decided not to attack, but instead ordered his men to block Burgoyne's retreat.

With more than one thousand men dead, very limited supplies, and knowing he was not just surrounded, but vastly outnumbered by the colonists, Burgoyne consulted with his officers, and they all agreed that a surrender was inevitable. He then sent a message to General Gates requesting a cease-fire while the terms of surrender were negotiated. The hostilities ended immediately. On October 17, General Burgoyne donned his finest uniform and met with General Gates. In a symbolic gesture of submission, Burgoyne offered his sword to Gates and the two adversaries shook hands. The two leaders exchanged a few words and then Gates returned the sword. The Continental Army took approximately five thousand prisoners—British, German, and Canadian soldiers as well as civilians. To save face, Burgoyne refused to refer to his actions as a 'surrender'— instead he called it a 'convention'.

The day after, the prisoners of war, now known as the Convention Army, were marched down to Stillwater where they were to be ferried over the Hudson River. There were not enough rafts to bring them all across the water so the British soldiers went first and the rest camped in the rain to await their turn. General Glover and his men were given orders to escort the English prisoners to Boston. They remained separated from the others and took different routes to Boston so as not to overtax the local citizenry and their limited provisions.

It took them two days to cross over the Green Mountains of Vermont and when they came to the Berkshires in northern Massachusetts, they were met with a heavy snowfall. Horses stumbled. Carts collapsed. Baggage was lost. Nonetheless, the group trudged on until it reached the city of Boston on the afternoon of October 23, where a thirteen-gun salute greeted them. The plan was to house Burgoyne and his men on Prospect Hill, while the remaining prisoners would stay on Winter Hill—both former barracks of the Colonial Army. The buildings were in need of repair and deemed unsatisfactory for officers—even British ones. Glover and his men then escorted the British elite to Cambridge where they were housed on Tory Row in mansions that had once been occupied by wealthy loyalists.

The prisoners needed wood for fire, food, and other supplies. The locals barely had enough to get by themselves and were not happy about having to provide for the enemy. One patriot, a lady living in the Vassal home where General Washington once headquartered, was known to say that she would not give up her home to Burgoyne, but if Washington asked, she would gladly vacate.

Under the terms of the convention that Burgoyne had negotiated, British ships would take the soldiers back to England with the understanding that they would no longer fight the Americans. The Continental Congress requested a list of the troops by individual name, but Burgoyne refused to comply. Therefore, Congress did not honor the terms of the Convention and the soldiers remained captive and were eventually sent to Virginia as prisoners.

When word of this decisive win reached Europe, King Louis the XVI of France finally arranged a formal alliance with the Americans. Sending money, troops, and supplies to the colonies was a good way for the French to avenge their past losses with the British. The rebellion in America now stood front and center as the fighting took on an international scope.

⚓

After Philadelphia fell to the British, the Continental Congress began meeting in the county courthouse in York, Pennsylvania, which put the Susquehanna River between them and their foe. Henry Laurens, a delegate from South Carolina, had just taken over the president's role from John Hancock. General Washington called upon Congress to proclaim a National Day of Thanksgiving to celebrate the Colonial Army's key victory at Saratoga.

Thanksgiving Proclamation 1777 By the Continental Congress
The First National Thanksgiving Proclamation

IN CONGRESS November 1, 1777 FORASMUCH as it is the indispensable Duty of all Men to adore the superintending Providence of Almighty God; to acknowledge with Gratitude their Obligation to him for Benefits received, and to implore such farther Blessings as they stand in Need of: And it having pleased him in his abundant Mercy, not only to continue to us the innumerable Bounties of his common Providence; but also to smile upon us in the Prosecution of a just and necessary War, for the Defense and Establishment of our unalienable Rights and Liberties; particularly in that he hath been pleased, in so great a Measure, to prosper the Means used for the Support of our Troops, and to crown our Arms with most signal success: It is therefore recommended to the legislative or executive Powers of these UNITED STATES to set apart THURSDAY, the eighteenth Day of December next, for SOLEMN THANKSGIVING and PRAISE: That at one Time and with one Voice, the good People may express the grateful Feelings of their Hearts, and consecrate themselves to the Service of their Divine Benefactor; and that, together with their sincere Acknowledgments and Offerings, they may join the penitent Confession of their manifold Sins, whereby they had forfeited every Favor; and their humble and earnest Supplication that it may please GOD through the Merits of JESUS CHRIST, mercifully to forgive and blot them out of Remembrance; That it may please him graciously to afford his Blessing on the Governments of these States respectively, and prosper the public Council of the whole: To inspire our Commanders, both by Land and Sea, and all under them, with that Wisdom and Fortitude which may render them fit Instruments, under the Providence of Almighty GOD, to secure for these United States, the greatest of all human Blessings, INDEPENDENCE and PEACE: That it may please him, to prosper the Trade and Manufactures of the People, and the Labor of the Husbandman, that our Land may yield its Increase: To take Schools and Seminaries of Education, so necessary for cultivating the Principles of true Liberty, Virtue and Piety, under his nurturing Hand; and to prosper the Means of Religion, for the promotion and enlargement of that Kingdom, which consisteth "in Righteousness, Peace and Joy in the Holy Ghost." And it is further recommended, That servile Labor, and such Recreation, as, though at other Times innocent, may be unbecoming the Purpose of this Appointment, be omitted on so solemn an Occasion.

Two weeks later, on November 15, after sixteen months of debate, the Continental Congress officially adopted the Articles of Confederation. The purpose of this document was to 'create a league of friendship and perpetual union' between the thirteen colonies. It outlined the responsibilities of a national government versus state government giving the colonies more authority to make decisions for themselves. It was flawed, but it was a start.

⚓

At the same time, after a long, successful record of captures under three captains starting with Manley, then Waters and finally John Skinner, the *Lee* was the only ship remaining of the original fleet after the *Lynch* struck her colors on May 19 of that year. William Lovell and Jack Herbert had sailed on the *Lee* with Manley during the Battle of Nassau in March of 1776. In midsummer of 1777 the *Lee* set out, with Skinner at the helm, to cruise the Atlantic coast starting from Boston. He managed to capture two more ships before finally taking the infamous cutter, the *Dolphin,* on October 1. The *Dolphin* had originally been the British cruiser belonging to Captain Ralph Burnett—Fanny's former nemesis. When the *Lee* returned to harbor at Marblehead with its prize, the *Dolphin,* word made it back to Fanny and William. Fanny was thrilled with the news of the ship's capture, although she wished that she could have been the one to take the vessel as her own prize. No matter who had made the capture however, it still pleased her to know that Burnett's ship now belonged to the American Navy. For a brief moment she wondered if he knew or cared of his ship's fate. And she also wondered what her life would have been like had she succumbed to Burnett's advances and proclamations of love and given up all hope that William was still alive.

Fanny rushed to tell Moll, arriving out of breath. When she got to her cottage, Moll was busy drying herbs in preparation for the winter ahead.

"If you've come to tell me about the *Dolphin,* I already know. I saw it in the clouds, and I was told by some fishermen when I went to the market today."

"I should have guessed you already knew, but I really came to thank you."

"Whatever for, child?" asked Moll as she bundled lavender.

"For not allowing me to believe in Burnett's insistence that William was likely dead and that I should marry him instead. If you hadn't helped me create the now-infamous Captain Bartholomew Channing, the story would have turned out quite differently."

"I saw your fate written in the stars from the time you were a little girl."

"If I had married Burnett, William would be dead," continued Fanny emotionally. On the brink of tears, she said, "But thanks to you I was able to rescue them from that horrible Cuban prison."

Moll gave Fanny a motherly hug, "But it was you, my child, who dared to save them."

Fanny wept in Moll's arms as Moll soothed her. "There, there, child, no need for tears, all is well…it is as it should be."

It seemed that in one night, by channeling Captain Channing and having the bravado to attempt to get the upper hand against Burnett, she had destroyed his career with a crew less than one-fifth the size of his own. Had word gotten out to his men and higher-ups that it had been a woman who had bested him, his reputation as a captain would have been destroyed for life. By limping back to England with his reputation relatively intact and the tale of being attacked by the infamous American Captain Bartholomew Channing, he had been able to retain some semblance of respect and decorum as a British Naval officer.

⚓

General Glover was ordered to remain at Cambridge—appointed to preside as president of the court-martial hearing of Colonel David Henley. Henley was accused of mistreating the British prisoners while they marched to Boston and Burgoyne had demanded justice. Henley was a well-respected officer but was known for his quick temper. Burgoyne had insisted on playing a role as prosecutor. This was unprecedented, but Burgoyne needed a way to save face. He felt by taking an active role in the court-martial, it would prove that he cared about his soldiers and would take away some of the shame that followed his surrender. His request was originally denied, but General Glover overrode that decision, and no one dared to challenge General Glover. The actual hearing wasn't scheduled until after the New Year, but the timing was perfect. General Glover would be able to celebrate the day of Thanksgiving with his family and friends in his Marblehead home.

Glover's homecoming was a true celebration and not just for his family, as he was a hailed a hero by his neighbors and townsfolk. The win at Saratoga and the frenzy that followed the killing of Jane McCrea had rallied public support for the war and Glover's return was a personal triumph for the people of Marblehead. He had put the tiny town on the map of history. The general was relieved to once again be with Hannah whose health had continued to decline. Even so, she exuberantly looked forward to a day of celebration with friends and family.

At Glover's request, Hannah herself sent invitations to the Campbells, the Lovells, the Herberts, and the Pitchers, asking them to join her family in honor of the holiday. They were a tight knit group who had served the new nation well, each in their own way and Glover wanted to thank them personally. Hannah was too ill to oversee the many preparations and activities, but her eldest daughter, Tabitha, who for the most part was now running the household, took charge of the festivities with help from Auntie Creese. With their men absent, Auntie Creese had often come by the Glover household to lend a hand whenever she could. Now the house had to be readied for receiving guests and a menu planned.

Beef was hard to come by since the war had begun and raisins were scarce, but venison and pork were plentiful along with fowl such as turkey. Pigeons and geese made tasty pasties that could be served to guests while vegetables were abundant since they could be grown in the garden. Wine was also scarce as it was reserved for medicinal purposes, but fine hard cider was plentiful. Pies made of apples and pumpkin were a crowd favorite along with an Indian pudding comprised of cornmeal and molasses. Rice apples baked in a type of bread pudding would round out dessert. Everyone prayed for fair weather so traveling wouldn't be hazardous for those coming to Marblehead.

Thanksgiving Day

DECEMBER 18, 1777 – MARBLEHEAD MASSACHUSETTS

It was a boisterous group that gathered in the Glovers' large dining room that December day. The weather had cooperated, and everyone had made it safely to Marblehead. Fanny and William, along with both of their parents—the Campbells and the Lovells—plus Jack and Marion and the entire Pitcher family enjoyed a rare day of celebration together. Auntie Creese, who delighted the children with dozens of freshly made Joe Froggers, was also there as an honored guest. Before the meal, General Glover stood for a toast:

"My dear friends and family." He raised his glass of cider. "Today is truly a day to be thankful. We have all felt the hardships that this war has brought upon us, but we know each and every one of us here is a true patriot. I, for one, am proud to be among you. General Washington has set this day aside for Thanksgiving and celebrating what we believe to be the turning point in this fight for our independence. Our work is far from over, but I want to thank you all for your heroic efforts, your unending kindness especially to my Hannah, and your loyalty to our cause. I cannot think of anyone I would rather be with today. May you all be blessed with full lives and happy times and may we soon find peace on our shores."

After dinner, as they waited for dessert to be served, Auntie Creese pulled out a letter. "I heard from Joe," she told everyone. "And I'd like to share his letter with you."

"I hope this means you've forgiven me for taking Joe away from you." General Glover smiled apologetically.

"Yes, I have forgiven you," Auntie Creese replied. "But that doesn't mean that I don't miss my Joe."

"Go on," Glover prompted her. "Let's hear what Joe has so say."

She took a deep breath and began:

My Dearest Creese,

I am writing this letter from Gloucester, New Jersey, where we just fought a hard-won battle with General Lafayette. Do not worry about me. I am fine, but I am afraid the lobsterbacks did not fare too well.

Please let General Glov know that things have worked out well for me and I hold no grudge against him nor should you.

At first, I was upset when he sent me to serve here, but I will say that General Lafayette is a real hero who knows how to lead men and I am proud to be associated with such a fine young man. He does not hold my dark skin against me nor do I hold his Frenchness against him.

I miss you and think of you every day and can't wait to come home again and serve Sir Switchels to our fine customers.

Love,
Joe

P.S. Can you please send some Joe Froggers to Valley Forge? I hear we will be heading there soon for our winter encampment and General Lafayette would like to try them.

Auntie Creese then folded the letter in half and placed it on the table in front of her. She picked up her napkin and dabbed at her eyes.

"Don't cry, Auntie Creese." Tabitha came from behind to put

an arm around her.

"Oh, I'm not crying for Joe, child. I'm crying because of all the baking I'm going to have to do," Auntie Creese said with a grin. "Even when he's gone, that man keeps me working hard."

"Whip up as many as you can," Glover laughingly said. "I will be joining the general there myself as soon as I finish up this Henley business and I can take them with me."

"I will load you up," Auntie Creese promised as the pies and rice apples arrived. "And I will send a note to Joe and let him know he is in trouble when he gets home."

After dessert, Glover asked Moll if she had any predictions for those around the table.

"As a matter of fact, I do," Moll said. "For the Lovells and the Campbells, I see many grandchildren in your future."

"Now that is good news," Agnes beamed.

"Auntie Creese, your cookies will live on long after you have gone," Moll said. "Joe Froggers will forever be a Marblehead staple!"

"I guess I will have to write that recipe down," Auntie Creese said with a sigh. "Because if they don't use the right amount of rum and salt water, no one will want them!"

"Marion and Jack, you might want to think about adding an addition to your little house so your children will have somewhere to sleep."

"And just when can we expect these children?" Jack's face paled.

"By my calculations," Moll winked as she replied, "sometime next year."

"I was not quite sure." Marion blushed. "But if Moll says so I guess there is a baby on the way."

The guests erupted in happy congratulations, while a shocked Jack kept silent—war was bad enough, but fatherhood was terrifying. Then Fanny spoke up. "Do you see an end to this war, Moll?"

"Of course it will end, but not right away. We will all have to be patient and not give up the fight."

"Not a chance of that," Glover said. "We have not come this far to give up now."

"Johnny, you will return to your family and be remembered as a great hero and a good man." Moll smiled, proud of her old friend.

"And what of our country?" he asked.

"I have seen a great eagle in the sky on more than one occasion," Moll answered. "He carries an olive branch in one talon and arrows in the other. He is strong and commanding as he soars over our land with his wings spread wide. This nation, our nation, will be like that eagle…majestic, powerful, and free."

THE END

Whatever Happened To . . .

Moll Pitcher
(b. 1738 - d. 1813)

Moll Pitcher, the great psychic of Lynn, was the inspiration for this book. In her time, she was known around the world for her paranormal abilities. Granddaughter of the Wizard of Marblehead, people came from all over the world to seek her counsel. She and her family lived modestly in Lynn, Massachusetts at the base of High Rock during turbulent times. Although, there is no real proof that Moll was an actual spy for General Washington, she was a patriot and a faithful supporter of the Rebel cause. She was a contemporary of Brigadier General John Glover as well as patriot Elbridge Gerry. She did readings for British officers and there is no reason to think that she did not pass along vital information she learned from them—after all spies did not leave a paper trail. We did take some liberties while writing this novel, but we feel that we accurately captured Moll's spirit and the historical events that took place during her lifetime. According to records, Moll died on April 9, 1813. Two of her children, Lydia and John, preceded her in death. She was buried in Lynn's Old Western Burial Ground and no marker was laid at the time. In 1887, a gravestone in her honor, simply bearing her name 'Mary Pitcher' with birth and death years inscribed, was installed. A play and a book were written about her posthumously, as well as a lengthy poem by John Greenleaf Whittier. Whittier's poem was not complimentary and in his later years, he regretted writing it.

Little is known about Moll's husband, Robert, but several entries concerning her death indicated that she was a widow when she died.

One more thing....During a research trip to Marblehead and Lynn, we discovered Moll's Queen Anne Table. Used by Moll when reading for her guests, it can be seen today at the Jeremiah Lee Mansion in Marblehead, Massachusetts.

The Pitcher Children

Robert and Moll had four children:

- Ruth b. 1763-d.1841; married Samuel Alley, Jr. 7/3/1786
- Rebecca b. 1765-d.1849; married John Inguls 8/28/1785
- Lydia b. 1767-d.1806; married Nathaniel Inguls, Jr. 5/27/1792
- John b.1768-d.1803; married Lydia Twison 1/20/1799

Brigadier General John Glover
(b. 1732 - d. 1797)

Marblehead's John Glover was a true hero of the Revolutionary War. He and his Marbleheaders saved the day for General Washington on three separate occasions as detailed in our book. He was also instrumental in the founding of the United States Navy in Beverly, Masschusetts. He and Moll Pitcher did know each other and it was Glover who introduced her to General Washington as 'the daughter of our regiment'. We cannot know the specifics of their relationship, but there was great respect between them and that is what we tried to convey. Glover remained in the Colonial Army joining Washington at Valley Forge for the 1777/1778 winter encampment once the court-martial of David Henley was over. Glover's wife, Hannah, died in 1778 and he married Frances Fosdick in 1781. He retired from the military the following year, but Glover continued his life of service including six terms as a town selectman, as well as a state delegate who helped ratify the U.S. Constitution in 1788. He also served two terms in the Massachusetts House of Representatives. Hepatitis claimed Glover on January 30, 1797 at the age of sixty-four and he was interred in Marblehead's Old Burial Hill behind the Wizard's house where Moll Pitcher was born. Every year on the anniversary of his death, reenactors of Glover's regiment pay homage to him by carrying lanterns in a procession to his tomb and give a solemn three-volley gun salute. His home in Marblehead was deemed a national historic site in 1972.

Elbridge Gerry
(b. 1744 - d. 1814)

A Declaration of Independence signer, Elbridge Gerry, remained in political life after the Revolutionary War. He served in the Second Continental Congress until 1780 when he resigned because he did not believe in political parties. In 1786, he married a wealthy girl, Anne Thompson, who was twenty years younger, and the couple had ten children together—nine of whom lived to adulthood. He believed in a clear delineation between the power of states and the federal government and as such, he was one of three delegates who opposed the U.S. Constitution, although he later came to support it after the Bill of Rights was included. President John Adams sent Gerry to France as part of a diplomatic delegation tasked with maintaining peace between the two countries who were once allies, but no longer on good terms. Their mission failed and upon returning to America, Gerry made several unsuccessful bids for the governorship of Massachusetts. Finally, in 1810, he won the gubernatorial election making him the state's eighth governor. While under his leadership, the state adopted electoral district boundaries, which created some oddly shaped territories including Essex County that was compared to a 'salamander'. The newspapers then coined a new term— gerrymandering. He went on to become James Madison's Vice President in 1813. On November 23, 1814, Gerry was felled by a heart attack while working in Washington, D.C. He died shortly after at the age of seventy. He is buried in the Congressional Cemetery in the nation's capital.

British General John Burgoyne
(aka 'Gentleman Johnny')
(b. 1722 - d. 1792)

After his defeat at Saratoga, General Burgoyne and his officers returned to England while his troops were held as prisoners of war. He arrived a widower as his wife, Lady Charlotte Stanley, who bore him a daughter, had died in 1776. Burgoyne received a cool reception from his country and requested a trial to clear his name, but that request was never granted. Instead, he was removed from his leadership role, as well as his position of governorship at Scotland's Fort William. He then allied himself with the Rockingham Whigs—one of Britain's political parties. When the Whigs came into power, they restored Burgoyne's rank and made him Commander and Chief over Ireland. He also took a mistress, Susan Caulfield, who was a popular singer at the time. She bore him four more children. When the Whigs fell out of power, he returned to private life. As such, Burgoyne was a successful playwright, who penned several popular dramas. His most successful play was a five-act comedy called 'The Heiress'. Gentleman Johnny died unexpectedly in 1792 at the age of seventy following a night at the Haymarket Theater where he appeared in good health. He is buried in Westminster Abbey.

British General Thomas Gage
(b. 1719 - d. 1787)

After General Gage's defeat at Bunker Hill, he was recalled to Great Britain and replaced by General William Howe as commander in Boston, but he did retain the governorship of Massachusetts. In England, Gage was greeted with a mixed reception and soon settled his family in London. His wife, Margaret Kimble Gage, was an American whose loyalties were divided. The mother of eleven was surrounded by suspicions that she delivered intelligence to the Rebels although nothing was ever proven against her. In 1782, Gage was given the command of the Seventeenth Light Dragoons, a cavalry troop, and later promoted to a full General. A few years later, his military career was winding down, but he continued to support the Loyalists who tried to recover their losses due to the Revolutionary War. Gage died from cancer in London in 1787 at the age of sixty-eight, and was buried in St. Peter's Churchyard located in West Firle, Lewes District, East Sussex, England. His wife outlived him by almost thirty-seven years when she passed away in 1834 at the age of ninety.

British General William Howe
(b. 1729 - d. 1814)

General Howe resigned from the British army in 1778. He and

his older brother, Richard, traveled back to England hoping to prove themselves blameless for failing to back up Burgoyne's troops in New York. Nothing was ever proven against either man, but they continued to face criticism from their fellow countrymen. William Howe did not see further action until Great Britain got involved in the French Revolutionary Wars in 1793 when he was promoted to full general. Two years later he became the governor of Berwick-Upon-Tweed, a town in Northumberland, England. After Richard's death in 1799, Howe inherited the title 5th Viscount Howe and was later appointed an official advisor to the king. In 1808, Howe was put in charge of England's Fort Plymouth in Devon. He died there in 1814 at the age of eighty-four after a long illness. He and his wife, Frances 'Fanny' Connelly, had no children, therefore, according to his obituary, his viscount title became 'extinct'. Howe is buried at Holly Road, Garden of Rest in Twickenham, England.

Joseph Brown
(aka 'Black Joe')
(b. 1749 - d. 1834)

We took some liberty with the character of Black Joe. He and his wife, Lucretia, were beloved citizens of Marblehead and we felt they should be included in our book. In reality, Black Joe did not arrive in Marblehead until after the Revolutionary War. He was born Joseph Brown in North Kingstown, Rhode Island. His father was a Native American and his mother was an enslaved member of the Beriah Brown household. Joe enlisted during the Revolutionary War in place of Beriah's son, Christopher, and served with a Rhode Island regiment for which he later received a pension. Beriah Brown promised Joe his freedom in return for his service, and honored that promise. Little is known about Black Joe until he appeared in Marblehead records in 1788 working as a laborer. In 1793, Black Joe became a property owner and on January 5, 1794, he married Lucretia Thomas at the 2nd Congregational Church. They moved to Joe's property on Gingerbread Hill and opened a tavern where they became Marblehead favorites known for their warmth and generosity. Black Joe is fondly remembered as a large man who played the fiddle, while Lucretia, called Auntie Creese by the locals, is famous for the beer she brewed, her rose water, wedding cakes, and Joe Frogger cookies. Black Joe died in 1834 at the age of eighty-four and was interred at Old Burial Hill not far from General Glover's tomb. Lucretia never remarried and died in 1857—twenty-three years after her husband.

Brigadier General Marie-Joseph Paul Yves Roch Gilbert du Motier de Lafayette
(aka Marquis de Lafayette)
(b. 1757 - d. 1834)

General Lafayette went on to distinguish himself in battle during the Revolutionary War. In 1778, he requested a leave of absence so he could to return to France. Once he arrived, he was put under house arrest for 8 days as he had disobeyed King Louis XVI by going to America in the first place. All was soon forgiven and Lafayette resumed his life of privilege. Now that the French were officially allies with the Americans, Lafayette was instrumental in gathering French troops to support the rebel cause. He returned to the United States in 1780, but not before his wife, Adrienne de Noailles, gave birth to their third child, George Washington de Lafayette. The general was given a hero's welcome at Boston Harbor, bringing word that the French King would soon send six-thousand troops and ammunition, as well as money. Lafayette once again distinguished himself in the line of duty. He returned to France and after the Treaty of Paris was signed, he traveled back to America where he visited John Glover and Elbridge Gerry in Marblehead. He was also an honored guest of George Washington at Mount Vernon. Upon his return to France, he became active in the French government advocating religious freedom and the elimination of slavery. He ordered the storming of the Bastille in July 1789 and sent the key to George Washington as a remembrance. The famous key can still be seen at Mount Vernon today.

While he tried his best to lobby for peace, the monarchy was eventually overthrown by radicals and Lafayette and his wife were imprisoned. Her mother, grandmother, and sister all fell victim to the guillotine. For safety reasons, he sent his fifteen-year-old son to America under the care of his dear friend George Washington who took the boy in. The Lafayettes were eventually freed and their son returned home. In 1824, U.S. President James Monroe invited Lafayette, now a widower, back to America. As the last surviving general of significance from the Revolutionary War, his return was triumphant. He was enthusiastically welcomed by one-hundred-eighty-two towns in all twenty-four states, including a visit to George Washington's grave at Mount Vernon. He also laid the cornerstone for the monument at Bunker Hill and met with Thomas Jefferson at Monticello, where the two men wept at the sight of each other. Lafayette also reminded Jefferson that they had fought for all men's freedom and that all enslaved people should be set free. Lafayette died on May 20, 1834 in his Paris apartment at the age of seventy-six. When word reached U.S. President Andrew Jackson, he declared an official state of mourning. Lafayette was buried in Paris's Picpus Cemetery with soil sent from Bunker Hill as he had requested. Every year on the Fourth of July, American and French representatives place a new American Flag on the general's grave.

John Adam Daygr
(b. 1736 - d. 1834)

John Adam Daygr came to Lynn, Massachusetts from Wales in 1750. He was a talented shoemaker who helped revolutionize the business. At the time, cordwainers worked independently and it took a long time for them to create even one pair of shoes. Daygr changed all that when he brought them all together, taught them new techniques, and organized their business. Working together, they were able to turn out more pairs of shoes with higher quality than they could make individually. The *Boston Gazette* even crowned Dagyr 'the celebrated shoemaker of Essex' and the small town of Lynn came to be known as New England's finest shoemaking city. Daygr married Susannah Newhall on August 18, 1761 and they had two daughters, Catherine and Sarah. Susannah died seven months after the birth of her second child. Dagyr then married Sarah Hawkes on July 29, 1765. They shared two sons, John Adam, Jr. and Joseph. Dagyr also served in the Continental Army during the Revolutionary War and fought in the Battle of Saratoga. He died a pauper, a resident of the Lynn Alm House on March 31, 1806 at the age of sixty-eight. He was interred at Lynn's Old Western Burial Ground. The Lynn Historical Society erected a marker in his honor in 1904.

Phillis Wheatley
(b. 1753 - d. 1784)

Phillis Wheatley was born in Africa in 1753. In 1761, when she was about eight years old, a local chief sold her to a slave trader. She was then transported to Boston by ship where the wealthy Wheatley family bought her and took her in, naming her Phillis after the ship she was on. The Wheatley children, Mary and Nathaniel, grew fond of Phillis and taught her to read and write. A quick study, she soon mastered Greek and Latin. At the age of fourteen and inspired by the classic poets, she composed her first poem. The Wheatleys were so impressed by the young girl's abilities, they encouraged her to continue writing poetry and allowed her to read her work in front of their friends. She completed a book of poetry, but very few women (let alone black women) were allowed to publish books. In 1773, Nathaniel took her to London where he thought she would have a better chance at having her work printed and distributed. She was well-received by the British upper crust and her first book of poetry was published in London. The Wheatleys gave Phillis her freedom late in 1773, but Mrs. Wheatley was ill and Phillis chose to leave British society and return to Boston to care for her. After Mrs. Wheatley died, Phillis composed a poem entitled 'To His Excellency, George Washington'. Genuinely touched by her words, the general personally invited Phyllis to Cambridge where the two met in March, 1776. Two years later, the poetess married a free black man, John Peters, who was never quite able to support his family. They had two children that died in infancy and Peters ended up in debtor's prison leaving Phillis to support an infant son by working as a scullery maid. Phyllis herself caught pneumonia and passed away on December 5, 1784 at the age of thirty-one and her infant son died shortly after. Phyllis Wheatley was buried in an unmarked grave in Copper's Hill Burial Ground in Boston.

Captain Nicholas Biddle
(b. 1750 - d. 1778)

Nicholas Biddle was born in Philadelphia in 1750 and began sailing at the age of thirteen. He was one of the original five captains initiated into the Continental Navy. Prior to that he had been in England's Royal Navy for three years after which he resigned in order to join an expedition to the Antarctic. In 1775, Biddle returned to the Colonies where he joined the Patriot cause. As a newly commissioned officer, he was put in charge of the *Andrew Doria*. He soon gained a reputation of bravery and daring as he successfully captured a number of vessels including several British transport ships. Biddle was then given command of a brand new thirty-two-gun frigate called the *Randolph*. On March 7, 1778, he was escorting a merchant fleet near Barbados when he encountered a much larger British ship, the *HMS Yarmouth*. Instead of taking flight, he met the *Yarmouth* head on so that the other ships could make their escape. During the brief battle, Biddle was wounded and while his men attended to him, the *Randolph* exploded killing three-hundred-five out of the three-hundred-nine men on board—twenty-seven-year-old Biddle included. One of the survivors gave this eyewitness testimony:

> "...early in the engagement Commodore Biddle was wounded, but ordering a chair was placed in it on the quarter-deck, and continued to direct the battle and encourage the crew. His tire was constant and well directed...Just then while a surgeon was examining his wound, the *Randolph* was blown up...."

Captain Biddle's body was never recovered and he is still considered 'lost at sea'.

Major General Henry Knox
(b. 1750 - d. 1806)

After Henry Knox's remarkable expedition bringing weaponry to Boston from New York's Fort Ticonderoga during the winter of 1775/1776, he became the Continental Army's chief artillery officer. As such, he not only joined General Washington in many major battles including the New York and New Jersey Campaign, but he also established artillery and officer training centers, as well as manufacturing workshops responsible for creating armaments. In 1782 just before his thirty-second birthday, he was promoted to Major General making him the Continental Army's youngest man to hold that rank. As the battles lessened, but before the war was officially over, General Washington put Knox in charge of the Army. Knox then formed The Society of the Cincinnati for the Revolutionary War officers, which remains the nation's oldest patriotic organization. In order to join, a member must be a descendent of one of Washington's military officers. After the revolt ended, Knox was appointed the country's second Secretary of War. In this position, he dealt primarily with Indian affairs and firmly believed that the Indian nations should be considered sovereign and allowed to govern themselves. Unfortunately, things did not always work out that way. Knox retired in 1795 and moved to Maine where he started a business. He died bankrupt in 1896 at the age of fifty-six after a chicken bone lodged in his throat causing an infection. He was interred on his estate with full military honors.

William Bingham
(b. 1752 - d. 1804)

William Bingham was a Pennsylvania delegate of the Continental Congress. In 1775, he was appointed the secretary for the Committee of Secret Correspondence. He then traveled to the island of Martinique where he ultimately made his great fortune. Working there as a successful merchant, he helped spread American propaganda throughout the area, drumming up support for the rebels. In addition, his privateering network captured British ships and provided the arms that they carried to the Continental Army.

By the time he returned to America in 1779, Bingham, who was not yet thirty years old, was considered one of the richest men in the country earning his fortune through privateering and trading. He then married sixteen-year-old Anna Willing and the couple had three children—two girls and a boy. In 1781, Bingham founded the first bank in the United States, the Pennsylvania Bank. He eventually purchased millions of acres in New York and Maine. Bingham also oversaw the creation of the Philadelphia and Lancaster Turnpike, which was the first long distance (sixty-two miles) paved road in the country (now known as Pennsylvania Route 462) linking the two Pennsylvania cities. He held many offices including Speaker of the Pennsylvania House and United States Senator. He also helped formalize the Louisiana Purchase in 1803. Now widowed, he soon sailed to Great Britain choosing to be nearer both of his married daughters who had already moved there. Bingham died in 1804 in Bath, England at the age of fifty-one and was buried in Bath Abbey. His estate was not completely settled until 1964 when it was dispersed among three-hundred-fifteen descendants.

Commodore Esak Hopkins
(b. 1718 - d. 1802)

In October of 1775, Esak Hopkins was given the rank of Brigadier General over Rhode Island's military. As such, he was able to strengthen the troops. Before the end of that year, he was appointed Commander and Chief of the newly-formed Continental Navy. He soon conducted the successful Raid on Nassua, which is considered the U.S. Navy's first amphibious landing. Upon his return to Rhode Island, Hopkins encountered the *HMS Glasgow*. The British ship inflicted heavy damage on Hopkins's small fleet before escaping. The Continental Congress formally admonished

Hopkins for the loss, which not only hurt his reputation, but also cost him the respect of his men. He was officially relieved of his duty on January 2, 1778 after being accused of mistreating his British prisoners. Hopkins then returned to Rhode Island where he served in the state's General Assembly. He died in 1802 on his Providence farm at the age of eighty-three and was buried in the North Burial Ground. His home is now listed on the National Register of Historic Places.

Things You Should Know. . .

Formal peace negotiations with Great Britain began in Paris, France, in 1782 with American representatives John Jay, Benjamin Franklin, Henry Laurens, and John Adams. David Hartley, a member of Parliament, and Richard Oswald, the British Peace Commissioner, represented the Crown. Aside from independence, England gave the United States a significant portion of the western territories for expansion and agreed to a peaceful withdrawal of their troops. In return, the Americans had to honor private debts and discontinue confiscating Loyalist properties. This settlement remained unofficial until Great Britain and France finalized their own peace treaty. Finally on September 3, 1783, the Treaty of Paris, based on their earlier agreement, was signed by all but Laurens and Oswald, formally recognizing American independence on a global scale. The hard-fought Revolutionary War was finally over!

Brigadier General John Glover's Marbleheaders are considered the first integrated army troop. Prior to the war, Blacks, Native Americans, Spaniards, and Jews lived and worked together as fisherman in Marblehead often relying on each other for their very survival at sea. As a result, they were used to joining forces, taking orders and fighting the elements. A rowdy and bold bunch of seafarers who weren't afraid of an old-fashioned brawl, they had great respect for each other as well as their leader. Many that served eventually mustered out and became privateers for the cause.

In 1789 when now President George Washington toured all thirteen states, Marblehead was not on his agenda, but he insisted on stopping there to honor not only General Glover, but also the Marbleheaders who served so valiantly. A grand celebration was planned with speeches and fireworks in the town square. He was warmly received at the Jeremiah Lee Mansion where he stayed the night. After his visit, he penned a letter 'To the Citizens of Marblehead' on November 2, 1879: It read in part:

Gentlemen,

The reception with which you have been pleased to honor my arrival in Marblehead, and the sentiments of approbation and attachment which you have expressed of my conduct, and to my person, are too flattering and grateful not to be acknowledged with sincere thanks, and answered with unfeigned wishes for your prosperity... .

Your attachment to the Constitution of the United States is worthy of men, who fought and bled for freedom, and who know its value...

G. Washington.

It has been estimated that, at the close of the war, there were four-hundred-forty-eight widows and nine-hundred-sixty-six fatherless children left in Marblehead.

⚓

The Declaration of Independence was not signed on July 4, 1776 as is commonly assumed. Historians believe the signatures were actually written on August 2, 1776. Signing the Declaration was very risky. The men who did so knew they would be hung as traitors if caught by the British. The British did capture five of the men, torturing and killing them. Others suffered in different ways. The homes of twelve signers were destroyed. Several died as a result of their service in the Revolutionary War while others lost their sons in the war. Many were forced into hiding. Some died bankrupt. A memorial dedicated to these daring men is located in Washington, D.C.'s Constitution Gardens on the National Mall. Below is a list of the 56 statesmen and the specific colony they represented:

From Connecticut:
    Samuel Huntington
    Roger Sherman
    William Williams
    Oliver Wolcott
From Delaware:
    Thomas McKean
    George Read
    Caesar Rodney
From Georgia:
    Button Gwinnett
    Lyman Hall
    George Walton

From Maryland:
  Charles of Carrollton Carroll
  Samuel Chase
  William Paca
  Thomas Stone
From Massachusetts
  John Adams
  Samuel Adams
  Elbridge Gerry
  John Hancock
  Robert Treat Paine
From New Hampshire:
  Josiah Bartlett
  Matthew Thornton
  William Whipple
From New Jersey:
  Abraham Clark
  John Hart
  Francis Hopkinson
  Richard Stockton
  John Witherspoon
From New York:
  William Floyd
  Francis Lewis
  Philip Livingston
  Lewis Morris
From North Carolina
  Joseph Hewes
  William Hooper
  John Penn
From Pennsylvania:
  George Clymer
  Benjamin Franklin

Robert Morris
John Morton
George Ross
Benjamin Rush
James Smith
George Taylor
James Wilson
From Rhode Island:
William Ellery
Stephen Hopkins
From South Carolina:
Thomas Heyward, Jr.
Thomas Lynch, Jr.
Arthur Middleton
Edward Rutledge
From Virginia:
Carter Braxton
Benjamin Harrison
Thomas Jefferson
Francis Lightfoot Lee
Richard Henry Lee
Thomas Nelson, Jr.
George Wythe

⚓

Three important documents shaped the United States of America. The Declaration of Independence that we celebrate on July 4 declared the Colonists' freedom from the Crown. In an attempt to unify the states, the Articles of Confederation was created on November 15, 1777, but not ratified until February 2, 1781. These articles gave little authority to the Federal Government, and instead empowered the individual states. This made for a weak Federal government and was impractical due to the lack of standardization. For example, each state had their own currency, taxation arrangements, and judicial system—sometimes more than one. States were also left to their own devices when it came to dealing with foreign affairs as well as threats both internal and external. A stronger Federal government and unified leadership were sorely needed.

This prompted the creation of the U.S. Constitution which was written on September 17, 1787 and ratified on June 21, 1788 and superseded the Articles of Confederation. The Constitution created three main branches of government: judicial, executive, and legislative further empowering the Federal government while leaving some authority with the individual states. Still in effect today, it remains the world's longest surviving written government charter,

⚓

Brigadier General John Glover oversaw the Court Martial of David Henley, which took place in Cambridge, Massachusetts beginning on January 20, 1778 and ending on February 25. Lieutenant Colonel David Henley was an American officer in charge of affairs at Cambridge when the British prisoners arrived from Saratoga. British General John Burgoyne, who surrendered at Saratoga, accused Henley of mistreating his men in an attempt to save face. Wanting to show his men that he cared deeply for them, Burgoyne requested that he be appointed prosecutor at the Court Martial—something that had never been done before. His request was denied by the judge advocate, William Tudor, but Glover overrode that decision and allowed Burgoyne to proceed. Henley was ultimately acquitted, which enraged Burgoyne. In return, Gentleman Johnny challenged Henley to a duel to occur in

Bermuda. Henley accepted the challenge, but the duel never took place. Henley went on to have a distinguished military career and died in Washington, D.C. in 1823.

⚓

In February 1781, the Dutch-owned Caribbean island of Sint Eustatius was captured by British forces. The small island had become a major trading center during the Revolutionary War due to the British blockade in the Atlantic that prevented goods from reaching the colonies directly. Once France officially entered the war in 1778, military supplies for the Colonial Army were shipped through Sint Eustatius, where American ships awaited them. The tiny island was also a point of communication between America and Europe. In December, 1780, London ordered the island be seized. On February 3, 1781, a large fleet of British ships under the command of Admiral George Bridges Rodney and Lieutenant-General Sir John Vaughan arrived at Sint Eustatius and urged Governor Johannes de Graaff to surrender. Outnumbered and outgunned, he agreed. The island was looted by the British as well as one-hundred-thirty merchantmen, a Dutch frigate and five American warships, not to mention a convoy captured off Sombreo where a brief battle was fought—all of which was confiscated by Rodney and Vaughn. Both signed an agreement stating that all goods taken thus belonged to the Crown with the two British officers expecting a large share of the captured spoils worth five-million pounds. Taking the time to personally oversee the inventory of such goods, Rodney and Vaughn were later accuse of neglecting their duties to capture a French fleet headed for the Chesapeake Bay in Virginia.

For the next ten months, the island remained under British rule as they banished or jailed the local merchants. Rodney arrested over one-hundred Jews and tore their clothes looking for valuables. He then deported about one-third of them. He even dug up the Jewish cemetery looking for loot. Non-military goods belonging to Englishmen were also seized and for the remainder of his life, Rodney fought lawsuits that were filed against him in England. French troops surprised the redcoats the following November and drove them out of Sint Eustatius after only a ten-month occupation. Three years later, they gave Sint Eustatius back to the Dutch. Business then resumed as the local merchants who could, returned. Rodney, despite, his self-serving interests was welcomed back in England as a hero. He died in 1792 at the age of seventy-four in Hanover Square. He was buried at the church of St. Mary the Virgin in Hampshire.

⚓

During the Revolutionary War, the fledgling U.S. Navy eventually boasted sixty-four ships, while the privateers outnumbered them with one-thousand-six-hundred-ninety-seven vessels. The privateers also claimed fourteen-thousand-eight-hundred-seventy-two guns compared with the Navy's one-thousand-two-hundred-forty-two. The small Navy captured one-hundred-ninety-six enemy ships compared to the privateers who seized two-thousand-two-hundred-eighty-three. Based on these statistics, the daring merchant marines played a major role in winning the Revolutionary War and their remarkable contributions should be recognized for their dedication and bravery.

⚓

History in general, has not been inclusive of women who served, aided, or played heroic roles in past American wars, such as the Revolutionary War and the Civil War. They have often been brushed off as hearsay or myth when, in fact, they secretly served or participated disguised as men. Sometimes, they covertly delivered army dispatches beneath their petticoats through enemy territory, or aided the cause as undercover spies. And spies of course, rarely advertise their secret hero services.

During the Revolutionary War alone, it has been surmised that as many as 20,000 women served or assisted the American troops, both during battle and on marches to new locations. Most were considered camp followers—wives who trailed their husbands due to loyalty, security, or economic circumstances. The areas that were occupied by the British soldiers caused many women, who had been left alone when their husbands joined the Army, to fear for their own safety. They followed their men seeking the protection of the Continental Army. Many others, however, actually disguised themselves as men and fought beside the soldiers. Those we know of, are the ones whose sex was ultimately discovered. These women were then honorably discharged—some even receiving pensions.

Women who were considered 'camp followers', provided such services as cooking, nursing, laundry, sewing, as well as bringing water to men in battle. They also scavenged for supplies, of which there was a dire shortage. Although General Washington felt these women put a strain on the supply chain for the Army, he also realized that they were 'necessary baggage', since their presence allowed the men to focus on actual battles, rather than their survival in daily camp life. Most officer's wives who joined their husbands, however, were present for moral support, rather than laborers and workers.

During battle, women often loaded and cooled the cannons for the soldiers, as well as gave medical aid to the wounded. Regardless of their duties, women who participated in war were always subject to the commands of the officers and could be expelled as easily as a soldier could be court-martialed.

As authors, we feel that any woman, brave enough to follow the troops and aid the cause, sacrificing their comfort and safety to support their men and their country, deserve recognition for their bravery, selflessness, and privations. Our series of SECRET HEROINE books is focused on the acknowledgement of these women as heroines—something that has been long overdue, and of which America should be proud.

Besides Moll Pitcher, the subject of this book, some of the women who played vital roles in the fight for America's freedom are:

- Molly Pitcher (aka Mary Ludwig Hayes) who fought beside her husband cooling cannons and providing water to the troops during the Battle of Monmouth.
- Deborah Sampson who served in the Continental Army as Private Robert Shurtleff for over a year before her gender was discovered.
- Prudence Patterson Hall, along with Lydia Darrgh who carried vital information past the British forces to the Americans.
- Martha Bratton who prevented the Loyalists from obtaining her husband's cache of gunpowder by blowing it up
- Rebecca Brewton Motte who allowed the Patriots to destroy her own home when it was seized by the British.
- Most importantly, 16-year-old, Sybil Ludington, who rode 40 miles through Putnam County, New York alerting the militiamen that the British troops were on their way to Danbury, Connecticut.

www.ingramcontent.com/pod-product-compliance
Lightning Source LLC
Chambersburg PA
CBHW021227310726
48971CB00006B/1721